CHATAINE'S GUARDIAN

ROBIN HARDY

NAVPRESS
BRINGING TRUTH TO LIFE
NavPress Publishing Group
P.O. Box 35001, Colorado Springs, Colorado 80935

The Navigators is an international Christian organization.
Jesus Christ gave His followers the Great Commission to go
and make disciples (Matthew 28:19). The aim of The
Navigators is to help fulfill that commission by multiplying
laborers for Christ in every nation.

NavPress is the publishing ministry of The Navigators. NavPress
publications are tools to help Christians grow. Although publications alone cannot make disciples or change lives, they can
help believers learn biblical discipleship, and apply what they
learn to their lives and ministries.

Cover illustration: Chuck Gillies
Interior map: Dennis Hill

The anecdotal illustrations in this book are fictitious. Any
resemblance to people living or dead is coincidental.

The psalm on pages 7-8 is taken from the *Revised Standard
Version Bible* (RSV), copyright © 1946, 1952, 1971, by the
Division of Christian Education of the National Council of the
Churches of Christ in the USA, used by permission, all rights
reserved. All other Scriptures quoted within the body of this
book are the author's own paraphrase.

Hardy, Robin, 1955-
    Chataine's guardian / Robin Hardy.
        p. cm. — (Annals of Lystra series : bk. 1)
    ISBN 0-89109-836-4
    I. Title. II. Series: Hardy, Robin, 1955– Annals of Lystra
series ; bk. 1.
PS3558.A62387C48   1994
813'.54—dc20   94-25936
                                                    CIP

Printed in the United States of America

FOR A FREE CATALOG OF
NAVPRESS BOOKS & BIBLE STUDIES,
CALL 1-800-366-7788 (USA)
or 1-416-499-4615 (CANADA)

Other books by Robin Hardy:

Stone of Help
Liberation of Lystra
(also published as *High Lord of Lystra*)
Streiker's Bride
Streiker the Killdeer
Padre

To Steve and Stephanie

He who dwells in the shelter of the Most High,
    who abides in the shadow of the Almighty,
will say to the LORD, "My refuge and my fortress;
    my God, in whom I trust."
For he will deliver you from the snare of the fowler
    and from the deadly pestilence;
he will cover you with his pinions,
    and under his wings you will find refuge;
    his faithfulness is a shield and buckler.
You will not fear the terror of the night,
    nor the arrow that flies by day,
nor the pestilence that stalks in darkness,
    nor the destruction that wastes at noonday.

A thousand may fall at your side,
    ten thousand at your right hand;
    but it will not come near you.
You will only look with your eyes
    and see the recompense of the wicked.

Because you have made the LORD your refuge,
    the Most High your habitation,
no evil shall befall you,
    no scourge come near your tent.

For he will give his angels charge of you
    to guard you in all your ways.
On their hands they will bear you up,
    lest you dash your foot against a stone.
You will tread on the lion and the adder,
    the young lion and the serpent you will trample
        under foot.

Because he cleaves to me in love, I will deliver him;
    I will protect him, because he knows my name.
When he calls to me, I will answer him;
    I will be with him in trouble,
    I will rescue him and honor him.
With long life I will satisfy him,
    and show him my salvation.

PSALM 91 (RSV)

I

I am Penuel. This is my account to you of what I have seen and done in accordance with your instructions regarding Deirdre of Lystra.

As you know, Deirdre was heir and Chataine to Surchatain Karel, ruler of Lystra. At that time the Continent was fractured into many small, independent states, each with its own lord, laws, and army. Before they were united under the great Ruler, each zealously defended its own borders and rule.

I will commence this narrative with the day during Deirdre's tenth year that her father, Karel, assigned a guardian, Roman, to ward her. . . .

❖

The nursemaid sighed as if to fortify herself and opened the door separating her room from the Chataine's sleeping room. She sighed again as she saw what she expected to see:

11

total disarray in the elegant room that had been perfect when she had put the Chataine to bed the night before. She bent to pick up a velvet overrobe and little brocade slippers. "I must speak to the guard about not letting her out of her room at night," she muttered. She gathered other items that obscured the thick-woven rug: dresses tried on and discarded; gold jewelry laid out in the semblance of a face; a platter with pastry crumbs on it, purloined from the kitchen.

Clearing this litter uncovered something else—a crude stick doll, like those the village children played with. "Ugh!" The nursemaid lifted it with two fingers and tossed it into the faintly glowing embers of the fireplace.

Turning to the windows in the far wall, she drew apart the heavy velvet draperies and opened the shutters. Early morning air and light filled the close chamber. "Chataine, dear, wake up," she said to the massive canopy bed. There was a child-sized lump under piles of downy quilts, but it did not move.

She crossed over to the bed and pulled back the quilts to look down on her charge. Slender little form and delicate little features; fair, creamy skin and thick wheat-colored tresses—who could be angry at such a child? Then the nursemaid saw her own missing necklace, her one piece of jewelry, wrapped around the little wrist. Sighing again in exasperation, she unwound it, urging, "Chataine, wake up."

"Go away, Nanna," the child mumbled, pulling up the quilts.

"You must get up now, dear," the nursemaid insisted, throwing the covers back.

Deirdre shrieked, "Nanna! What are you doing? I said leave me alone!" She yanked the quilts back over herself.

Nanna said, "Chataine, today is a special day. Your father has summoned you to an open audience this morning. I must get you dressed."

"An open audience?" repeated Deirdre, alarmed. "Why?"

Usually, whenever her father wanted to see her other than at table, he merely summoned her to his chambers. An open audience meant that he had something to tell her from his throne in the audience hall, and all of the court would be gathered to hear it. This was a scary prospect for a child of ten.

"Your father is assigning you to the care of a guardian today." As Nanna's round, wrinkled face seemed to go taut, Deirdre was quick to discern her disapproval.

"But Nanna, why? You are my guardian," the child pouted.

The nursemaid raised her eyebrows. "Your father has evidently decided you need more protection than an old woman can give."

"Nanna . . . does this mean I will never see you again?" Deirdre's eyes misted.

"No, dear, of course not. I will still be here to dress you and attend you. You will need the sol—uh, the guard only when you leave the palace grounds."

Deirdre caught the slip and wrinkled her nose in disgust. "Father is giving me over to a *soldier?*" Soldiers were different from the palace guards. The Cohort—the guards—were selected from the standing army or from the town at large to serve inside the palace as a special unit. They were picked on the basis of youth, a pleasing appearance and refined manner, and they dressed in much better clothes than the common soldiers. Appointment to the Cohort required no special skill in warfare or service. Rather, Deirdre's father often used it to repay favors owed to prominent townspeople. All Deirdre had observed of the soldiers, however, was that they were big and sweaty and usually covered with dust.

Nanna patted her hand reassuringly and sat on the bed. The shifting mattress tilted Deirdre into Nanna's plump side. "Your father has handpicked this one for you. I am sure he has selected the best to be found. He will take good care of you, dear. I know it."

Deirdre peered into Nanna's face to see if she believed

what she said, but the nurse had already turned briskly to the business at hand: "Now up and let me dress you, Chataine."

As Nanna helped her don lacy linen underclothes and a rose-colored dress with many folds, Deirdre's round blue eyes widened in apprehension. She envisioned her father handing her over to a great hairy brute and ordering, "Now teach her to mind!"

She began to whine. "I promise to be good, Nanna, if you'll let me stay with you."

"Poor dear," murmured Nanna, tying on the Chataine's little cap. "Don't worry. I will see to it that this—this soldier understands how to treat you." The nursemaid took her hand to lead her quickly down the cool stone corridor to the great stairway. Descending, Deirdre could see people crowding from the foyer into the audience hall. They parted like a furrow to let her pass.

The audience hall was a great, ornate room, with oaken paneling and bronze sconces. Costly needlework in brilliant colors hung centered in each oak panel. As they passed one needlework, Deirdre glanced at it and took comfort. It was a large tapestry depicting herself in the garden with a white horse and hound. It reassured her she was someone of position.

Leaving Nanna in the crowd, she advanced with trepidation up the deep purple runner to the black marble dais supporting a massive bronze throne. This was the Surchatain's judgment seat, from which he pronounced sentences and appointments.

Announcement of an open audience always drew a large crowd of courtiers, palace officials, and wealthy notables from the town of Westford, which was clustered around the palace. One never knew what to expect—the Surchatain at one time would single out a deserving person for praise and reward; more often, however, he pronounced judgments of death by hanging.

They waited. Deirdre took her position near the front,

shifting from one foot to the other. Then the murmur of the crowd hushed as the crimson-robed Counselor, Eudymon, entered and stood before the dais. Always straight, poised, and correct, the Counselor was the perfect statesman. His black hair, tinged with grey, was smoothed back to show a high, fine forehead. Deirdre did not like him. He was always thinking.

Eudymon announced: "The High Lord and reigning Superiority of the independent state of Lystra, the gracious and beneficent Surchatain Karel." In one wave the crowd dropped to their knees. The Surchatain entered in a swirling purple mantle, the symbol of highest authority, and sat on the bronze throne. The audience stood.

Karel at forty was slight of build but quick and tough. His movements were emphatic and his eyes habitually angry. Now those eyes went straight to his daughter. "Deirdre." She stepped up and bowed low before him, as instructed. He looked her over for a moment. "Deirdre, you are my Chataine and my only heir" (he paused and his lips tightened) "and I cannot risk losing you by accident or design in this perilous country. You are no longer a baby, and I cannot hope to keep you shut up safe in the palace forever. Therefore, I am assigning a guardian to you. He shall watch over you every moment that you are outside the grounds. *However*, he is not your servant; he answers to me alone. And this is he." Karel gestured through the crowd. A young man in common soldier's garb stepped up before the dais. "He is called Roman."

Deirdre looked. He was tall and solid, and wore the soldier's plain brown shortcoat, breeches, and high boots—except his clothes were clean. He looked middle-aged to her eyes, but actually had turned twenty-two a few months before. He had thick, straight black hair and brown skin. His face was, she thought, incredibly ugly—craggy and lined, with a broad nose and heavy brow. Deirdre was too young to realize that among the kitchen maids who cared about such

15

things, he was considered quite handsome. He stood silently, regarding her also.

Then Deirdre realized her father was addressing him: "Here is your charge. And here is your vow: Do you, Roman, swear to guard and protect Chataine Deirdre with your life whenever she is out of the palace, until she is married or until such time as you are relieved of your duty?"

"I do, High Lord." The voice that came out of that rough face was soft and very deep.

The Surchatain continued, "And do you swear to obey all my instructions and prohibitions to you regarding her?"

"Yes, High Lord."

"So be it. I have but a few last words of warning to you. If she is injured while in your care, you will be flogged. If she is injured severely, or kidnaped, or killed, you will be executed. And if there is any impropriety in your manner toward her—if you so much as touch her wrongly—you will be executed by torture. Do you understand?"

"I understand, High Lord," he said, blank-faced.

"Then this audience is ended." Karel rose to leave, and the spectators fell on their knees again. "Counselor, to my chambers." The two strode out without a glance behind.

The crowd melted away, some glancing curiously at the Chataine and the soldier. Deirdre stood evaluating Roman. He stood looking at her. "I want to go out and play," she said.

❖

The Chataine kicked her pony, urging him past Roman's mount. She could not possibly hope to outrun him, but at least she wanted to let him know who was in the lead. Then an inspiration struck her. "I want to go down and play with the village children." The villagers—the poorest element of Westford—lived in huts clustered on the branch of the river. Those children welcomed her in their games, while the town children inexplicably shunned her.

"No, Chataine; your father has expressly forbidden that."

"He need not know." She directed her pony toward the valley, but Roman cut her off on his charger. "I cannot let you do what your father has forbidden. You know that."

She eyed him petulantly, then shook her long hair. "If you do not let me go, I will tell him—I will tell him that I fell from my pony and hurt myself." She had heard her father's warning to him, and thought it might prove useful.

"If he believes you, he will have me flogged," Roman replied. "But I still won't allow you to play in the village, so it will have gained you nothing. Besides, I don't believe you are a liar."

She stared at him. Was he mocking her? But his face was unreadable. He glanced at her, then turned his horse toward the high crest of the hill on their right, up and away from the valley. He led up the long, winding path to the crest and she followed.

Looking down over the bluff, Deirdre reveled in the panorama spread before them. Her father's orchards and fields connected in a brilliant patchwork that met with the forest on one hand and the west fork of the river on the other. The Passage, many called it, for it was the only navigable river emptying on the Southern Coast. The Passage divided itself north of Westford and formed a lake on the eastern branch before trickling its way to the Sea through high rocky cliffs in eastern Lystra. The west fork was stronger, forming a large delta of rich farmland and natural ports. For that river, and the trade it spawned, Lystra was highly envied by her neighbors.

Surrounding a branch of the river Deirdre saw mushrooms—no, the thatched houses of the villagers. Smoke curled up in wisps from cooking fires, around which moved little people and animals. The forest was also beyond the village, stretching out to infinity. It strained her eyes to try to take it all in.

17

Roman pointed down to the village. "You see how many of the villagers use the fast water upstream for bathing and toileting. Then downstream, in the gentler waters, is where the children often play, and where they have of late been drawing water. It is no coincidence that many have become ill and died. We have repeatedly warned them about fouling their water, but many will not listen. It's simply not safe for you to play there."

Deirdre listened as he talked, watching him gesture. In all the times that she had been refused permission to go to the valley, this was the first time any explanation had been given. She had always assumed it was because the Chataine was too exalted to run with villagers. "Why hasn't anyone ever told me that?" she demanded. Roman only shrugged. She studied him thoughtfully.

❖

In his chambers, the Surchatain rubbed his hand through his woolly brown hair and dropped onto a velvet couch. Eudymon stood before the fire, watching him out of the corner of his eye. He seemed to be debating whether to speak or wait for the Surchatain to open. Finally, the Counselor offered, "You have made a wise decision in appointing her a guardian. That is sufficient action to take on the basis of a mere rumor."

"Rumors such as this are too dangerous to treat lightly," Karel answered. "If Corneus *has* hired an assassin, and if he succeeds in killing my heir, the whole province will be spoil for the highest bidder upon my death. And even though his country is small, Corneus is quite wealthy. A coup such as this would be child's play for him."

"True." Eudymon looked concerned. "And you cannot appoint another successor while Deirdre yet lives—which will be for many years," he added quickly at Karel's look.

The Surchatain nodded slowly and murmured, "But . . . have I done enough?" He did not seem to address the question to Eudymon.

"Perhaps you should remove her to safety for a while," the Counselor suggested.

"What place is safe, if not my own country?" Karel snorted.

Eudymon inclined his head. "Your law is well established here, High Lord. But I was thinking that perhaps she would find safety if taken in secret to live in the palace of her betrothed—whom you shall select, of course."

Karel slammed his fist upon a nearby table. "That is the catch! There is that insane, worthless law my late wife sealed into the books—that the Chataine will have the final say as to whom she marries! Regina made it law when I was in Ooster and the period of revocation passed before I was aware of it. I cannot rescind it now!" His fury at the years-old deception flamed anew. "Who knows what choice that child may make? Whoever it is may end my influence upon her!"

"Surchatain—if I may remind you, you are still Ruler. You will guide her choice, gently or otherwise."

Karel stopped and let his anger dissipate in that thought. "Yes . . . and that is years away. For now, Counselor, no one must think we pay any heed to this rumor."

"Certainly, High Lord." Eudymon inclined his head again. "And I trust that your selection will prove adequate as her guardian."

"I do not trust, Counselor. I will watch him with eagle eyes to see how he proves. You are dismissed."

❖

That evening, Roman joined the Surchatain's table for dinner. As Deirdre's guardian, he would enjoy the privilege of eating in the presence of the Surchatain every night thereafter. He sat next to the Counselor and across from Deirdre. She sat on her father's right hand, though there was an empty chair between them.

As the food was served and they ate, she watched Roman closely. He had good table manners for a soldier, though he used the wrong hand. He ate quietly, speaking very little. It occurred to Deirdre that he must be nervous eating at the Surchatain's table for the first time. But he picked up the right utensil for the right dish, and even used the finger bowl correctly. However, when the squid was served, he cocked an eyebrow at his plate and looked to the Counselor. Eudymon did not look up or speak, but properly sliced and ate his. Roman followed his lead.

Abruptly, Karel addressed his daughter: "Deirdre, what do you think of your new guardian?"

"I suppose he'll do," she said haughtily, not looking at Roman.

"You're not pleased with him?" probed her father.

"Not really," she sniffed.

"Good! Then he's just what you need. You have been manipulating your servants for too long. I'm glad to find someone who can control *you*." A ripple of laughter went around the table, and Deirdre blushed angrily. *We'll see*, she thought.

After the meal she intercepted Roman. "Take me out to Willowring Lake!" This was a great pleasure she had rarely been allowed in the past.

"Chataine, you know your father does not allow you out of the palace after nightfall."

"But with you to protect me, what could happen?"

"Any number of things."

"If you don't take me, I'll start screaming." She pursed her lips determinedly. This maneuver had worked well for her at other times with Nanna.

"As you wish. But first, Chataine, consider. If you scream,

the guards will come and take us to your father. He will ask what happened. You will have your say and so will I. After what he said tonight, whom do you think he will believe?" Roman posed. Deirdre looked away. He added, "I promise that I'll take you to the lake tomorrow."

She brightened. "Very well. You are dismissed." He bowed slightly and left her. She ascended the stone stairway to her chambers in deep concentration. He was going to be a challenge.

As Nanna helped her undress, Deirdre had a thought. "Where does Roman sleep?"

"In his room, Chataine."

"I know that," Deirdre said impatiently. "Where is his room?"

"That is none of your concern, dear."

"But where is it?" Once an inspiration had seized her, it would not let go.

"I think it's in the lower corridor by the kitchen. Several of the high-ranking soldiers have rooms there."

"I know the corridor. Which room is his?" She pressed the point because she knew Nanna would tell her. Nanna always did.

The nursemaid sighed. "It's the one next to the courtyard door. The one with a door that bolts." That bolts! That was unusual. Few beyond the Surchatain's family and palace officials were given that privilege. "Now listen, Deirdre, you must not go down there at any time. Your father has made it clear that you have no business in that area of the palace. Promise me you will not go down there!" Nanna's tone was so serious that Deirdre hastily promised. But as Nanna extinguished the light and closed the door, the Chataine was already plotting.

She lay awake for long minutes, waiting for the palace bustle to still. At last, when she sensed things were quieted, she got up and pulled on her overrobe.

She listened at the door to Nanna's adjoining room. All was quiet, so she tiptoed to the massive outer door of her receiving room and gingerly unbolted it, opening it only partway so as not to waken Nanna with loud creaks. Then she slipped into the dark corridor, stole past the slumbering guard, and stealthily descended the stairway. She made her way down passage after passage, flattening herself against walls or behind doors when she heard voices or footsteps. At last—there was his corridor. She had almost stepped into it when a noise froze her. It sounded like a low groan and came from the corridor ahead. She peeked around the corner.

What she saw intrigued her. It was Hana, one of the kitchen maids, wrapped up in the arms of a soldier. They were kissing in a way Deirdre had never seen. The soldier (who was it? she could not see) whispered in Hana's ear and she said, "No, no, not here. In the small clearing. I'll meet you there straightway." With one last kiss they parted.

The small clearing! Deirdre knew where that was. She located the courtyard door and hurried out. If she got there before they did, she could hide in the bushes and watch. For she felt sure the man was Roman.

She slipped out the rear gate, watching for the guard, and ran fifty paces to the forest's edge. It was a chilly night, but the Chataine wore a warm overrobe and shivered, rather, from excitement. How would she handle this? She envisioned confronting Roman with her knowledge, watching his stone face drop, and hearing him beg her not to tell her father. "Well, as you say," she would at last concede, "but from now on we'll do things my way!"

The imagined scenario disappeared as Deirdre halted in the forest. Now, where was the small clearing? Oh yes, over there. She hurried to a tree, but found it was not the landmark she expected. Well, now, where . . . ? She had been too preoccupied to mind where she was going. A chill ran through her as she spun around. She did not recognize any of these trees. She did not know where she was.

Fighting panic, she forced herself to stop and look around. Hesitantly, she started walking again—slowly, then faster, then—what was that? There arose in her mind the faint reminder that there were wolves in this forest.

She stopped to listen, but could hardly hear over the pounding of her heart. *I must get my bearings*, she thought, and looked up to search the stars. Standing very still and scanning the sky, she calmed. It was an endless April night— clear, but dark, with only a waning moon. The wind breathed gently through the trees like a soft voice calling her name: *Deirdre! Deirdre!*

Wait—it *was* a soft voice calling her name! And she recognized the voice. "Here, Roman, I'm here," she called just as softly. In utter relief she watched a dark figure emerge from the trees, and she ran to him before she remembered herself.

Silently he led her back to the palace, then to the receiving room of her chambers. Nanna, waiting there, exclaimed, "Oh! You're safe!" and hugged her tightly.

"You may go now," Deirdre informed her guardian, peeking out from Nanna's arms.

But Roman was not to be dismissed. He threw aside his cloak and asked, "What were you doing out there?" His voice was calm, but his eyes were angry.

She parried the question, thinking to trap him into admitting why *he* was out there: "How did you find me?"

"When your nurse found your bed empty, she came to me. For some reason, she believed you had come to my room." He stopped and eyed her questioningly, but she held her tongue, so he went on, "I found the courtyard door open, and your footprints in the mud leading out the rear gate. It was too dark to track you in the forest. I had to call for you." Why he regretted having to do that, he did not say.

But Deirdre turned to Nanna. "You found him in his room?"

"Yes, dear. I awakened him."

What a disappointment. It had not been Roman. Then she looked up and realized they were both waiting for an explanation. "I could not sleep, so I went out to walk."

Nanna started to protest, but Roman cut her off. "Chataine, I won't warn you again to stay inside the palace at night. And I'm not saying that in jest. I am telling you that your life has been threatened!" The seriousness of his voice made her start. She looked to Nanna for reassurance, but saw Nanna blanching, looking to *her*.

"Stay in your room at night, Chataine." Roman walked out, and Nanna gathered her in.

2

I, Penuel, continue my report concerning Deirdre, Chataine of Lystra. The morning after the Chataine ventured into the forest there was an extraordinary amount of gossip among the servants. Nanna seemed jumpy, and Deirdre had to pump her longer than usual for information. . . .

❖

"Nanna, what are all the servants talking about?"

"Why," the nursemaid laughed nervously, "how should I know?"

"You know everything, Nanna. What are they saying?"

"Nothing important, dear, that's certain," Nanna replied, brushing out Deirdre's long hair.

"But what are they talking about?" Deirdre demanded, turning to face her.

For a moment Nanna did not answer. Then she sat Deirdre down. "Darling, when you were in the woods last night, did you see or hear anything—strange?"

Deirdre held very still. "No. Why?"

"One of the servants was murdered last night. They found her body this morning in the small clearing." Nanna's voice was a whisper.

"Who was it?" asked Deirdre, her eyes wide.

"Hana, a kitchen maid." Nanna rushed on, "Chataine, you must not tell anyone you were out there last night. Let's forget it ever happened. Promise me!"

"I promise," the Chataine said in utter sincerity.

Deirdre did not concentrate much on her studies that morning, thinking of Hana. *Poor Hana. Why would some-one kill her? Roman said someone wanted to kill me*, she thought. But then her native skepticism surfaced. *He said that just to scare me into staying out of his way at night. He has other things to do then. Nanna says the soldiers are all busiest at night. . . .*

Her tutor was speaking to her, scolding her, but she paid little attention to him. She did not have to, as thoroughly as she had him cowed. "Chataine, you must do your sums," he pleaded.

"Rory, did you ever want to be a soldier?" she asked thoughtfully.

"Mercy, no," he frowned. "It's terribly dirty work, and a soldier's pay is miserable. They live in those horrid barracks—even the officers have only little cells, and they have to be running off to the border all the time."

"Roman doesn't seem to mind it. He seems proud of being a soldier," Deirdre observed.

"I suppose if that's all you can do, you have to be proud of it," he sniffed. "Do your sums, Chataine."

"Do you know him?" she asked, scratching meaningless doodles on the tablet before her.

"I met him once at the tavern in town, but he did not have any time for *me*—or anyone, it seemed. Boring fellow.

He just sat by himself in a corner while everyone else was having a good time," Rory said condescendingly.

"Why? Is he shy?" she asked, looking for weaknesses.

"Not really. He belongs to that amusing little sect who call themselves 'Followers of the Way.' They believe having fun is wicked, you know."

"Oh. What is the Way?" she asked.

Rory's close-set eyes squinted in derision. "That's their religion—like the worship of Mithra, though not nearly so interesting. They worship a fellow who was executed and—they say—came back to life."

"Did He?" Deirdre demanded.

"What?"

"Come back to life!"

"Of course not!" Rory snorted. "Anyone knows that's impossible. And they never could prove it. The whole thing is really so absurd." He lowered his voice and smirked, "We call them *Christians*."

"Oh!" Deirdre wrinkled her nose and giggled.

That afternoon when Roman took her on the promised excursion to the lake, she asked him, "Why do you believe having fun is wicked?"

"What?" His charger startled, being sensitive to its master's subtle commands. Deirdre's pony plodded along beside the great horse.

"Rory says you don't believe in having fun," she explained, kicking the poor pony harder. She did not like riding on such a small animal—it put her too far below him.

"Oh." He gave a short, ironic laugh. "Something as destructive as what Rory does is not fun."

"What do you do for fun?"

"Well . . ." he looked down at the path beneath them, guiding his horse around rocks with the light touch of one hand, "I eat and talk with my friends . . . hear their stories and tell mine . . . hunt and ride with them."

"How is that different from what Rory does?" Deirdre asked innocently.

"Chataine, I can't explain that to you now. But what it boils down to is that Rory and his kind have their fun using other people, even if it hurts them."

"Oh," she said. "Rory says that the soldiers are really bad about using the village women—"

"I try to avoid using anyone," he interrupted. "And does Rory ever teach you any history or mathematics?"

"No," she laughed, and he shook his head. She studied his painstakingly shaved face, not knowing what a burden it was for a soldier to shave daily, nor that it was required for his present position. But she decided she might like him after all.

Still, she had questions. "Roman, do you really worship a man who came back from the dead?"

He blinked. "Yes, you could say that."

"If He is alive, then where is He?" she wondered.

"In Paradise, with the Father."

"Where is Paradise?" she persisted.

"Beyond the skies, Chataine."

She squinted up at the bright blue expanse dotted with clouds. "How did He get up there?" she exclaimed.

He faltered, "Well—by the power of God."

"Who is God?" she asked.

He looked down at her, wary of being led into an argument for the fun of it. But he answered straightforwardly, "His Father, and your Father above. The Creator of the heavens and the world and everything in them." He paused. "The One who loves you unfailingly."

Deirdre pursed her lips, thinking she had caught him in an untruth. She did not even believe in God, so He certainly could not love her. Besides, no one loved her like that. Suddenly she recalled the two lovers she had seen last night.

She kicked her pony to keep it abreast of Roman's horse and asked, "Did you hear about Hana?"

He absorbed the abrupt change of subject and nodded. Then he glanced at her. "Did you see her last night?"

"No," she answered carefully. He scrutinized her face for a moment, but said nothing.

The path they were riding on ended at a grove of willow trees close to the lake. Roman dismounted and helped her off her pony. As they walked toward the grove, he began amiably, "I like to come here whenever I can. It is restful and—"

But Deirdre looked down at her feet and screamed. A snake slithered in the grass toward her. "Save me, Roman!"

"Chataine," he said, biting his lip, "it's only a grass snake. It won't harm you."

"Save me!" she insisted, fists stubbornly planted on her hips. Roman lowered his head at the arrogant command and picked up the snake, tossing it away from her. Totally helpless, she held up her arms for him to lift her and carry her back to the pony. She grinned triumphantly from the saddle.

But he had the last word. "Your father would not approve of your being amidst so many dangers. We have to return to the palace," he said, throwing a leg over his saddle. She protested in anguish, but he was firm.

❖

The following morning Deirdre made a halfhearted attempt at her lessons, then sneaked out when Rory's back was turned. Although she was not supposed to go near the kitchen, she wandered down there anyway, where she overheard the head cook discussing with her staff what they needed from the market. Deirdre popped in: "I want to go! Let me go to market with you!"

"Go ask your guardian, Chataine," the cook said, relieved not to have the burden of denying her request.

Deirdre ran to find Roman. Several times a week, the cook took her kitchen help to the market in town to buy whatever fruits and vegetables the Surchatain's fields did not supply, as well as fish, game, herbs for the physician's use, and other household goods.

"Roman!" She jumped around him when he appeared at her summons. "The cooks are going to market! I want to go!"

"No, Chataine. It would be too difficult to watch you safely in the crowds. You can buy anything you want from the merchants who come here."

"Oh, Roman, I never get out. And the crowds are just a bunch of old women." Her big eyes filled with tears. "Please, Roman?"

He weakened. "Will you stay right by my side and do as I tell you?"

"Yes, yes, I promise!"

He sighed. "Very well, Chataine. Your pony will be too slow, however—you'll ride in front of me on my horse." She jumped up and down and clapped her hands. They met the cooks at the gate and together drove to market—Roman and Deirdre leading on his bay, the cooks following in their wagon.

When they arrived at the cluster of stalls, Roman let her down off the horse and Deirdre shot like a true arrow through the crowds. "Chataine! Deirdre! Come back here!" He raced after her.

Several of the women around snickered at the sight of the soldier chasing the Chataine from cart to cart. He almost had her twice, but she slipped away from him, laughing, to run elsewhere. Finally, he seized her near the flower cart and hoisted her up under his arm.

She was too weak with laughter to struggle—until she saw that he was taking her back to the horse. "No! Put me down! I'll stay with you, Roman."

"That's what you said before." He plopped her in front of the saddle and swung up behind her.

"Roman, please, don't take me back. I want to see the market," she pleaded.

"You will when you learn to obey me, Chataine."

She pouted. "If you don't let me go, I'll—" He stopped her with a menacing look. "I don't like you, Roman! You're mean and ugly!" He did not respond, merely turning the bay's head with a tug on the reins.

They rode in sullen silence back to the palace, where he firmly deposited her with Nanna. "Come dear," she said soothingly, noting their grim faces, "now is a good time for me to teach you to sew."

"No," Deirdre pouted.

❖

At this time Surchatain Karel was meeting in his chambers with his Counselor. The Surchatain held a letter in his hand. "I wish to ignore this invitation," he stated. "Now, of all times, I do not wish to take Deirdre traveling, especially to see her uncle!"

Eudymon paused, selecting his argument. "You're right. She will not go. What care we if he is offended?"

Karel breathed out heavily. "I cannot risk offending him. He is too powerful."

"Then may I suggest, Surchatain, that this is the purpose for which you appointed her a guardian?"

Karel studied his Counselor for a moment, then opened his door and instructed the guard, "Summon Roman."

He appeared momentarily, bowing to Karel and Eudymon as he entered: "You summoned me, High Lord?"

"Yes, Roman . . . I am sure you are becoming familiar with Deirdre's willfulness, by now."

"She is a lively child," Roman shrugged.

"True." A look of mild exasperation crossed Karel's face. "I wished to forewarn you that we will be traveling soon— Deirdre, too—and that how well you control her could be crucial."

Roman paused, then replied, "I am not alone in protecting her, Surchatain. God is with me. He will enable me to guard her."

Karel regarded him skeptically. "For her sake—and for yours—I hope that is true. Dismissed."

The atmosphere at the evening meal was somber and restrained. Karel seemed preoccupied with troubling thoughts, and no one wished to transgress his mood with levity.

Deirdre watched Roman intently throughout the meal. He appeared unaffected by the Surchatain's darkness, eating calmly, without a word, as was his style. Occasionally he glanced up at her, and she grew puzzled to see amusement in his eyes.

At length Eudymon leaned toward Roman and whispered for her benefit, "The Chataine seems smitten with you tonight, Captain."

Roman raised his eyes to her again, and Deirdre quickly lowered her burning face. Then she glanced at her father and assumed an air of authority. "I wish to go riding to the lake tomorrow, Roman."

"I will be ready at your summons, Chataine," he answered cordially. She looked again toward her father, but apparently he had not heard.

As the dinner was finished and the dishes removed, the Surchatain roused himself and looked around the table. "You people are all stale and sleepy tonight. You need some entertainment to wake you." He turned to a guard standing nearby. "Summon Simien the magician!"

Deirdre clapped and laughed. Simien was one of her favorites—he could do so many amazing things. As the guests around the table applauded and pushed back their chairs, Simien entered with a flourish and bowed low before the Surchatain at the head of the table. Karel nodded for the magician to begin.

"Lords and ladies," exclaimed Simien, spreading his arms, "I am indeed lowly entertainment for such an esteemed assembly. Yet, as the Surchatain has so graciously given his attention, I will respond with what gifts I possess. Behold—" and he touched his forefingers together before him, then slowly drew them apart. As he did, a shimmering golden line traced the path of his fingers in the air. He snapped his wrists and dropped his hands, but the golden line still hung in space.

Some guests began to applaud, but he motioned for silence. Gingerly, he reached to the middle of the line and drew down on it. It opened like a tear in space, and he reached inside it with his free hand. The guests gasped in astonishment as his hand and forearm disappeared beyond the shining opening.

"What have we?" he murmured, as if feeling around. "Ah! Lights to enliven the table!" And he threw out a handful of lighted candles, which rested in the air above the table. Quickly, he thrust his arm in again. "More?" he murmured. "Yes!" he shouted as he flung out a flask—which, like the candles, hung suspended in the air. "Wine for your enjoyment!" The flask turned and out spilled a deep red wine. It poured and poured without ending, creating a river that ran down the middle of the table. Roman, unimpressed, sat back out of the stream's way.

"And lastly, for your pleasure—song!" The magician ripped the tear open wide and out flew a throng of skylarks in full song. They flew straight to the table and lighted on the candelabras. "Are you pleased?" he queried, and his audience clapped loudly, voicing amazement. Simien bowed dramatically, then with a snap of his fingers the illusions—the candles, the wine, and the birds—disappeared. The guests gasped and clapped louder.

"Now permit me to demonstrate, High Lord, that your guests have amazing powers of entertainment as well. Behold—" he gestured to one woman, who suddenly stood and began to sing with all the strength she possessed. She was quite off-key, and the rest of the table roared in laughter.

"And look!" Simien cried, pointing to a man. While the woman sat abruptly, red-faced, the man took up with a remarkable imitation of a rooster. He crowed and strutted and even tried to peck the table. Deirdre laughed until the tears ran down her face, then glanced across at Roman. He was not laughing, nor even smiling. Neither was the Counselor beside him.

Deirdre suddenly left her seat to whisper in the magician's ear. The rooster man sat, bemused. Simien smiled slyly as Deirdre took her seat, and he announced, "Lords and ladies, we have a special request from the Chataine for entertainment. Witness—" and he wheeled and pointed straight at Roman. Those at the table waited breathlessly, but Roman did not move. He simply returned Simien's glare.

The magician frowned. "Up, soldier, and dance!"

"No," Roman refused. Simien faltered, and Deirdre gaped in astonishment at Roman. The guests looked around in silence.

"I see your magic has limits, Simien," Karel said severely, though he appeared pleased. "You are dismissed."

The magician bowed stiffly and fled.

As Karel dismissed the guests, Deirdre turned to Roman. "How were you able to resist his command?" she demanded.

"I obey a higher command. Good evening, Chataine." He bowed and left her.

She was dumbly pondering what he meant when Nanna approached. "Chataine."

"What?" It irritated her to be interrupted when wrestling with mysteries.

"Your tutor tells me you have not been attending to your studies," Nanna began severely, and Deirdre made an ugly face. "Now you know how important this is to your father! You will go directly upstairs and prepare for tomorrow's lesson, or I will have to tell the Surchatain you need a new tutor. A harder one. Like Roman!"

Deirdre glanced at her darkly, but stiffened her lip and marched ahead of Nanna to her chambers. The nursemaid stood over her while she sat at a table and began scratching out sums on a soft wax tablet. Nanna watched her a moment, then nodded and turned toward her room. "I will come back shortly to check your progress," she promised before closing the door.

$8 + 8 = 16$, $8 + 9 = 17$, $9 + 9 =$ Deirdre scratched the numbers deeply into the wax, then finished with a row of angry Xs. Everyone ordered her about as if she were a peasant child! She could never do anything she wanted, only what they said. Do your lessons! Do not go down to the village! Stay with Roman! Stay away from the kitchen!—Her mind halted on that one, and she let the stylus fall. What was so interesting in the kitchen that she should stay away from there?

She peeked out the door of her receiving room. The guard who was supposed to be on duty was nowhere to be seen. At once she was out into the corridor, working her way down to the kitchen area.

She paused then—what if she encountered the soldier she had seen with Hana? What if he was the murderer and had seen Deirdre watching them? Her heart took to pounding as she considered the dangers she might meet in the kitchen. Forcing herself to go on made her feel very brave. At least it was not as late tonight as it had been when she slipped out before. Those passing her in the corridors nodded or bowed courteously, but showed no suspicion. Why should they? This was her palace; she had every right to be in its corridors. She lifted her chin and proceeded with authority.

Nearing the kitchen, she slowed timidly as she heard clatters, voices, and laughter. Large double doors stood open from the kitchen into this corridor, and she could not approach without being seen. Her confidence evaporated at this point; everyone knew she was not supposed to be down here.

But then she saw a hiding place! She scooted along the wall to one of the doors and pulled it away from the wall enough to slip behind it, then eased it back in place. Here, in the triangle formed by the open door against the wall, she was concealed from both the kitchen and corridor, and could peep through the crack between door and casing to watch the activity in the kitchen.

The first thing she saw was that the actual kitchen and cooking area comprised a small part of this large room. The greater part by far was filled with tables and benches to serve as a dining hall for the soldiers and servants.

There was much eating and laughing going on. Deirdre felt somewhat envious watching through the slit. Dinner for them was a festivity—no worrying about offending so exalted a person as the Surchatain, no qualms as to whether one was proper or not.

Deirdre twisted her neck to see farther through the slit, and caught a glimpse of Roman near one of the far tables. He was standing, arms folded across his chest, talking with a group of soldiers who were eating. One of them asked him something, and he began an extended answer. As he talked, the soldiers around stopped eating one by one to listen.

The din grew quieter, and Deirdre could discern a word here and there to match his gestures— "crowed like a rooster . . . the Chataine . . . to me and said, 'Get up, soldier, and dance!'" He finished telling of the magician's failure in a low voice, and the soldiers guffawed. He broke off from the group with a wry smile, heading toward Deirdre's door, but was stopped repeatedly by one person or another wanting a word with him.

Meanwhile, the story he had told circulated around the

room until it was repeated to a group directly in front of Deirdre's peeping spot. At its conclusion, a very drunken soldier who slouched with his back to Deirdre burped coarsely and shouted, "Good fer you, Cap'n! Now shall ya stare down ol' High Lord Tightfist to give us poor scum a raise?"

The hall became still, and Roman turned to the fellow with a retort on his lips. At once, though, he swallowed it and said lightly, "Come now, Forster, keg up your drivel before it gets you hanged. You're a loyal soldier when you're sober— once in a fortnight."

A laugh went around the room, but Forster lunged up drunkenly and slammed his fist on the table. "Curse it, I mean it! I'm fed up with being spit poor whilst that—"

"Forster! Silence!" Roman commanded. The imperative sat the drunken man down. Roman's glare did not let up, however; and Deirdre saw with a gasp that it was not directed at the soldier but at the crack through which she peeked.

She backed out of the door and fled down the corridor. She ran a straight path to her chambers and bolted the door, then sat panting and gathered up the fallen stylus and tablet.

An instant later Nanna opened her door and looked into the chamber where Deirdre sat. "Well!" The nursemaid seemed surprised. "I'm so glad you obeyed me for once. That's enough work for tonight, dear. Come let me dress you for bed."

"Yes, Nanna." Deirdre humbly laid the instruments aside and followed her into the sleeping room.

❖

The following morning she studiously avoided the mere chance of encountering Roman. She summoned Rory to her chambers for her lessons rather than risk meeting Roman in the corridor on her way to the library. She worked so intently over her tablet as to amaze her tutor. When they were through, she opened the door to dismiss him and choked to see her somber guardian waiting for her in the corridor. "I am ready to take you to the lake as you requested, Chataine," he said without expression.

Rory was watching. She cleared her throat. "Yes, Roman, I will be out directly." She closed the door and selected a jacket from the tall mahogany wardrobe, wishing she could jump in it and hide forever. But he would just wait there until she came out.

Resolutely, she opened the door. He nodded to her. She followed him to the courtyard, where her little pony stood saddled beside his great horse.

They rode at a leisurely walk in absolute silence. Her full, bulky skirts were beautiful to look at but impractical to ride in, and more than once got dragged or trampled. Periodically, Roman reined in his horse to a stop to wait for her to catch up, as his charger outpaced her pony two strides to one. He had not bothered to do that when they rode before. "Are you well today, Chataine?"

She startled. "Yes—of course. I was only worried that you would be angry—" she caught herself in confusion. It was totally unlike her to blurt out the truth so.

"Why would I be angry?" He cocked his head at her.

She cast around for an answer to satisfy him and save herself: "Umm—well—taking me to the lake after what happened last night." Had he not seen her after all?

"Oh, you mean Simien?" He smiled in his wry way. "I'm not angry. I don't blame you for testing me."

"Oh, good." She was sincerely relieved. "It made a good story, though, didn't it?" she chattered, then caught her error at his abrupt look.

"Was that you, then, behind the door last night?" he demanded.

She forced out tears, pleading with him not to tell her father: "Roman, I'm sorry—"

But he laughed outright, shaking his head. "Thank you, dear God!" To her, he said, "I am so glad it was you, and not someone who would use it to bring the soldiers to grief. Chataine, I beg you—please don't tell Forster's foolish words to anyone."

Her mouth dropped open, but she recovered sufficiently to consider pressing her advantage—should she tell him now that it meant doing things her way? "I won't tell anyone, Roman," was what came out instead.

"I thank you, Chataine." He smiled openly at her in a way that made her feel strangely warm. "Now let's see what we can find of interest here." They were already at the willow grove. She slid off her pony and walked beside him toward the trees.

A flock of sheep scooted away from them; she noticed with mild interest a lamb which had gotten itself hopelessly entangled in underbrush. Roman noted it, too. He bent down beside it and patiently worked its little legs free. He held it just long enough to rub its soft fleece, then let it down to run bleating to its dam.

Motionless in thought, Deirdre watched him. She had never known a soldier to evidence such regard for things little or easily broken. Lambs caught in briar and drunken men sounding off their despair . . . little girls with big tempers. . . . He gestured to her to follow him through the grove to a part of the lake she had never seen before. She said, "Oh!" at the sight of an array of lovely flowers with heads bowing at the water's edge. Some were red, some white, some a mottled color. "How pretty! What are they?"

"Lilies. I was told they were planted for you to enjoy." Roman pushed his black hair off his forehead to take in the view across the lake.

"For me? Then why have I never seen them?" she demanded, affronted.

"Disloyal flowers that won't come to you! You have to

go find them," he laughed. Then he made her bend down among the lilies near the water. "Be still and watch."

She waited in bemusement. As a solitary insect buzzed close to the surface, suddenly a little stream of water shot up and knocked the insect down. A small fish snapped it up and disappeared. Deirdre gave a little cry. "What was that?"

"They call it an archer fish, because of the way it shoots its prey down. The lake seems full of them now, though at first there were only a few. Sailors brought them from beyond the Sea for you, at your birth."

"For me?" She sat back on her heels to look at him. "I have never seen them either."

He shrugged. "They were here." He raised his eyes and looked over the lake contemplatively. "Remind me to bring bread crumbs next time we come. We'll train the ducks to eat from our hands. There are swans too—but they are less willing to be trained." As he spoke, he nodded toward the birds dotting the far shore.

Deirdre squinted across the lake. "Are those mine also?"

"Of course," he said, then knitted his brows. "Deirdre, don't you realize that everything your father has is yours? All will someday be in your hands, for good or ill."

She could not find words to respond, so they were both silent for a time. Then her eye caught a floating bit of brown, and she walked over to investigate. "A boat!" she exclaimed. A little skiff bobbed near the shoreline. "Roman, take me out in the boat!" He hesitated, and she began her pleading. "Please, Roman, please!"

"You *must* sit still in it," he said sternly, dragging it up on shore. "If you tip us over and I have to return you to the palace dripping wet, I might as well go ahead and drown myself here." She snickered. He held the boat steady for her to clamber in, then he stepped in and took up the oars.

As he guided them leisurely out onto the lake Deirdre lay back, sighing in contentment. The sun was warm, reflecting in pieces on the gentle waves. The fragrance of the lilies found her; the quacks of the distant ducks reached her ears. She turned her face up to the wide blue sky and billowy clouds. "Don't you wish you could stay out here forever?" she murmured, closing her eyes.

He smiled slightly. "If you did, you would miss greater pleasures to come."

She opened her eyes a little. "I don't know that any will ever come to me."

"A child of ten, already so cynical about life?" he asked, raising a brow. He had a manner of arching one brow while flattening the other that she found intriguing. "Yet we have been promised, 'What no eye has seen, nor any ear heard, nor the heart of man imagined, is what God has prepared for those who love Him.'"

She squinted at him, trying to imitate his contortion of brows. "Do you have that?"

"Not yet. Not fully. But it is coming," he said softly.

Laying her head back again and closing her eyes, she sighed, "I like to dream, too."

After a few moments of restful gliding, she opened her eyes to lazily scan the lake. "Roman, take me to the far shore!" she suddenly demanded.

"No," he said.

"Why not?"

"There is nothing over there for you to see." He turned the boat back toward their launch point.

"Not already!" she complained.

"Your nursemaid will have seizures if I don't return you to the palace on time for your noon meal," he grunted. She snickered again, allowing him to tie the boat and help her out. The edges of her embroidered skirts were now sodden and dirty.

As they rode homeward, Roman stopped every now and then to allow her pony to catch up. "Curse it!" she muttered, kicking her poor pony hard.

"What?" he exclaimed, shocked.

"How can I ride with you on this little pony? He can't stay abreast of your horse! It's not fair!"

"Don't trouble yourself about it much," he said calmly. "Tomorrow I will teach you to ride a horse—*if* Nanna can find you some riding clothes."

"Truly, Roman?" she cried, and he nodded. "A big horse, like yours?" and he nodded again. "Oh joy, oh joy!" she sang. He glanced her way, repressing a smile.

That evening the Chataine badgered her nursemaid into supplying her, under protest, with an adequate riding dress. Deirdre rose before the next morning's sun and dressed herself, then ran into the corridor to pounce on the guard stationed there. . . .

❖

"Summon Roman to me at once. He is teaching me to ride today!"

The guard bowed gravely. "Yes, Chataine." She impatiently watched him move so slowly away, then settled in her receiving chamber to await Roman. A messenger came from Rory to request her presence in the library, but she told him she was ill.

Waiting for Roman, she played with the tough, unadorned fabric of the riding skirt. It was very wicked and daring, being so short that it showed her ankles. Of course, she wore heavy riding boots, but Nanna still disapproved, to Deirdre's delight.

Long moments later there was a knock, and she eagerly opened the door to see another soldier standing there. "Who are you? Where is Roman?" she asked sternly.

The soldier bowed. "Chataine, I am Captain Basner. I am very sorry that Roman is unavailable now. I have come to explain to you the schedule set by Commander Galapos for all the captains. In the mornings, when you should be attending your studies" (Deirdre glanced away) "Captain Roman is required to drill his outfit and maintain his gear. He is on the grounds now, demonstrating the use of the pugil sticks."

"Is he good at it?" she asked vaguely, to draw attention away from her embarrassment and disappointment.

The Captain inclined his head. "He is our champion, Chataine. You may observe his practice from that window, if you wish." He pointed down the corridor.

"No, I am not interest in that," she yawned. "You are dismissed." She closed the door and listened for his retreating footsteps, then hurried over to the window he had indicated. Sure enough, below she saw Roman in the center of a ring with an opponent. They were about to begin. She looked on with interest.

The pugil sticks were five-foot poles of oak with thick round pads at each end. Each fighter gripped one horizontally with both hands, using it to strike and parry blows. Staying on one's feet required strength, agility, timing, and instant reflexes.

Roman and his opponent faced each other, wearing only the trousers of their uniforms. On a signal they began circling. The other struck first—a lightning bolt toward the head. Roman dodged it and struck him in the side with one end and the head with the other. He was obliged to wait a few seconds till his opponent had recovered enough to continue.

From then, they traded blows and blocks with such

ferocity that Deirdre closed her eyes at times, fearing to see Roman killed before he could teach her to ride. But on looking closer, she saw that he seldom was actually hit. He struck a blow, then bounded back, parrying a shot and striking again. Then he would speed up the pace and deliver a whole series of blows before the other man could strike back. It reminded Deirdre of the kitchen tom playing with mice he had caught.

Finally, Roman delivered a sharp uppercut that decked his opponent and the match was ended. Deirdre had almost joined in the cheers when she looked across the quadrangle and saw the Counselor in the window opposite her. He, too, was watching the match intently. When he caught her gaze, he withdrew from the window.

She looked again to Roman. Evidently her summons had reached him, for he was leaving the field. After wiping himself clean of sweat with a rag, he picked up his shirt and shortcoat and unfolded them as he walked. Then, curiously, he stopped in a walkway, hidden to all eyes but Deirdre's.

He glanced around to be certain he was not observed, and not seeing her in the window above, he took something out of his clothes and put it on. It was a gold medallion. She could not see it clearly from where she stood, but easily guessed it was not a piece any soldier could afford. He then donned his clothes, safely hiding it.

At that moment she heard voices around the alcove of the corridor—two guards who had been watching the match from a nearby window. "The Captain certainly can handle the sticks—eh?"

"Aye. I won't get in the ring with him. . . . Too bad he's gone as far as he'll go, now that they made him the Chataine's guardian."

The other tsked. "And I heard that Galapos was about to make him his Second. 'S no secret that the Captain's aspired to the position for ages—he worships the ground the

45

Commander walks on. So, who d'you suppose'll get the job now? Basner?"

Their voices faded as they walked away from her down the corridor. Deirdre reflected on what she had heard, then shook her head and ran down to the courtyard entrance to meet him. "Roman! You promised! Today I learn to ride!"

He almost smiled, regarding her skirt. "Come with me to the stables, Chataine. I have picked out a mare for you."

He left Deirdre waiting beside his horse, already saddled, while he entered the stables to bring out her horse. Her very own horse! Bobbing with excitement, she could hardly contain herself to wait for him to appear. At last he came out leading a dappled grey mare and carrying a small saddle.

Deirdre clapped and squealed, "She's beautiful!" As Roman draped the reins around a post, she stroked the mare's shiny mane and fretted, "Now, what shall I name her?" Roman smiled. Deirdre looked at his horse. "What is your horse's name?"

"He does not have a name," Roman answered a little disdainfully, throwing a thick square of wool on the mare's back. "He is just the bay hunter."

"Well, then you call him the Bay Hunter," Deirdre reasoned. "As my mare is grey, I will call her Lady Grey. Saddle her quickly so we can ride!"

"Come here and watch," he instructed, swinging the saddle up on the mare's back. "I want you to learn how to saddle her."

Deirdre impatiently protested, "Oh, the groom can do all that! I just want to learn to ride."

"Someday you may need to know how to do it yourself. If I am going to teach you to ride, I'm going to teach you right." So she settled down and tried to pay attention to everything he said and did.

When he was done, he lifted Deirdre onto the saddle.

How high she felt! He mounted the Bay Hunter, which was only a little larger, and took her reins to lead her through the rear gate. When they had gained the grassy fields, Roman let her have the reins, instructing, "Watch how I hold the reins, and imitate me."

Then at last she was riding with him out toward the hills. She was ecstatic. She could look him in the face now, when they rode, instead of up at him from the pony's low back. He kept up a constant stream of instruction to her—how to handle the reins, how to hold on with her legs, how to flow with the motion of the horse.

"The pony followed wherever he was led, but your mare has a mind of her own," he reminded her. "You must keep control at all times." Then, after watching her ride for a while, he allowed her to gallop beside him, and they raced across a flat stretch of land to the foot of the hills.

As they pulled up, he said, "You learn very quickly. You seem to have a natural affinity for riding."

Overflowing with the excitement of racing the wind, Deirdre recklessly stood in the saddle and threw her arms around his neck. "Thank you for teaching me!"

He laughed out, "Whoa!" and gently pushed her back into the saddle. With the movement, a tiny link of the gold chain was exposed under his shirt.

"Roman," she said, "where did you get that medallion you wear?"

For the first time ever she had caught him off guard. "How do you know about that?" he startled.

"I saw you put it on today, after your match." His face turned to stone, and he said nothing. "You could not have bought it. Did you steal it?" she prodded to draw a response.

"Of course not." He glanced at her darkly. "It was a . . . gift from . . . a friend."

"Who?" she pressed.

"It's time we headed back. Your father desires to have

you seated at the noon table." With that, he wheeled his horse around and left her to catch up.

Deirdre felt very important to eat with her father at noon. True, she usually had the evening meal with him, but many others were also present then. If he requested her company now, then surely he had important things to discuss with her. She imagined her father asking her opinion about whether soldiers should be paid more.

It came as a severe disappointment, then, to see that not only Roman but also the Counselor would share the table with them. After an extended conversation with the men about some boring dispute along the border, her father finally addressed her: "Well, Deirdre, I have heard that Roman is teaching you to ride. Have you learned yet?"

Her eyes gleamed. "Oh yes, Father! He says I have a natural divinity!" Abruptly, the three men laughed. She shut her mouth, confused.

"Well said," Karel smiled, "and good. In three days we are riding to Ooster in the province of Seir to visit your uncle—your mother's brother. He has not seen you since you were a baby, and has pressed us for a visit."

"Does he have children?" she asked. The prospect of meeting cousins her age was attractive.

"Yes. Two sons."

Was it only her imagination that her father sounded bitter? She said no more and kept her eyes on her plate. But happening once to glance up at Roman, she saw him looking at her kindly. After they were dismissed from the table, he drew her aside. "Chataine . . . we did not laugh maliciously at you. What you said was just amusing. Please don't be offended."

She shook her head listlessly. "I'm not. I always say the wrong thing around my father. It is a curse." Roman tried to look appropriately grave. She perked up and asked, "Do you know my uncle?"

"I know of him. He is a wealthy and respected man. He has brought order to a very unstable country."

"What about his sons? How old are they?" she asked eagerly.

Servants were glancing at them, so Roman began idly to walk out of the room while Deirdre persistently stuck to his side. He stopped in the corridor and gently pushed her back to a more seemly distance. Waiting for his answer, she never noticed. "His sons are six or seven years older than yourself," he said.

"Do you know their names?"

He reflected. "The oldest is Jason. The younger is Colin. Your uncle's name is Corneus."

❖

Soon provisions were gathered and preparations completed for the day's ride to Ooster. Nanna made a pest of herself in her anxiety. She packed and repacked the Chataine's bags, muttering to herself about the obvious lack of judgment shown by her exclusion on this trip. The traveling party consisted of Karel, Deirdre, Roman, and ten soldiers. Deirdre overheard an earnest discussion as to whether more soldiers were needed, but it was finally agreed that more would seem an affront to Corneus. He would expect to assume responsibility for the safety of his guests.

On the morning of departure, the Chataine and her bags arrived at the front gate. The Counselor, who stayed in the palace during the Surchatain's absences, was receiving final instructions from Karel. Roman helped Deirdre mount her horse, and the party set off.

At first, the ride was exhilarating for Deirdre. They began the trip at a fast, sustained gallop while the horses were fresh and the roads flat. The soldiers rode in protective formation around her: four before her, Roman to her left, another to her right. Her father, behind her, was flanked by two soldiers, and the remainder formed the rear guard. Deirdre visualized what would happen if this moving stronghold was ambushed by renegades. The soldiers would spring to the attack, with Roman shouting orders and brandishing his broadsword. Hoofs would fly and villains fall in pools of blood—all on account of her. And her father, of course. It was a splendid fight to protect them.

The reality of the ride, however, was something else altogether. Twenty minutes into the trip, Deirdre was ready to stop. An hour later she felt her teeth would be jarred from her head. At this point the road became bumpy and irregular, climbing hills and dropping into depressions. Even though the party slowed their pace and stopped time and again to rest their horses, Deirdre began to feel like a puppet bouncing on strings, ready to collapse when released. Still they traveled on over rough, hilly terrain—ground impassable for a carriage. The cool spring morning wore on and became a hot day. And Deirdre, unaccustomed to sustained travel on horseback, grew very sore and weary.

When Karel mercifully called a halt to rest and eat, Deirdre fell from her horse and hobbled about on unreliable legs. She took her portion of bread and moved off a few paces to eat standing up.

After sending two soldiers into the forest, Roman came over to stand beside her. "How are you holding up, Chataine? I fear we should have brought you a cushion."

"I'm fine," she bristled. "I just wanted to unbend my legs." She started to move off into the trees.

But Roman caught her arm. "Don't leave my side for an instant," he ordered.

"But . . . I have to . . . you know."

"I'll go with you."

"No!" The idea appalled her. "You don't dare! It will only take a minute!" Nanna would die if she heard of it.

"Chataine." He pulled her closer and whispered. "I believe we are being followed. I don't know who is among the trees with us, but I'm certain I spotted someone matching our pace. Now, would you rather me observe you, or someone else who is not so concerned for your welfare?"

She winced. "You can come." They found a suitable spot. She began to hike up the rough riding skirt and then stopped. "Turn your back."

His eyes scanned the forest around them uneasily. "Turn your back," she insisted. He complied. She needed only a moment.

Just as she let down her skirt, a massive pair of hairy arms from nowhere surrounded her. Roman wheeled an instant too late. Another man had sprung from the bushes and smashed him in the face with a bludgeon. As he fell, Deirdre glimpsed blood.

She tried to cry out, but a heavy hand covered the bottom half of her face. She heard shouts. The arms swept her up and carried her to a waiting horse. The hairy man threw her on it, then jumped up behind her and spurred the horse to a run.

The speed at which the party had been traveling was a trot compared to the run at which this horse carried her. Deirdre gritted her teeth, shut her eyes, and clutched the saddle in terror. She opened her eyes to see trees veering by wildly on her left and right, then shut them tight again.

A sudden plunge opened her eyes. They were running down the middle of a shallow stream; the spray soaked her dress clear up to the bodice. Miles later, her abductor directed the horse out onto a rocky bank that sloped steeper with every stride. When the horse began to stumble he stopped, put Deirdre off, and dismounted himself. Pushing her ahead of him, he led the horse up the slope. Deirdre's sodden skirt weighted her down like armor. Each time she fell, he jerked her up and pushed her all the harder ahead.

At length they reached a shallow cave in the face of a rocky cliff. Deirdre sat, gasping. Out stepped a silver-haired man in fine riding clothes. He studied her an instant, then handed the kidnaper a small bag of coins. As he weighed the payment in his palm, the hairy man advised, "You best be off quick. They'll be hot after me for sure."

"Did you come the way I told you?"

"Yes, lord, I did."

"Then by the time they track you to this point, I will be quite done. Where is your companion?"

"Well—uh—don't know. I didn't see him." The dim-witted abductor looked back uneasily.

"Fool! Go make certain he doesn't lead them straight here!" The aristocrat then took Deirdre's arm in a show of civility. "Come, my dear. We must be going."

As he led her toward his horse, she decided to faint rather than get on another animal. However, when she saw that he was simply going to throw her on it like saddlebags, she chose to wake up. He placed her in front of him on the saddle and pinned her with his elbows as they rode.

Deirdre could not long endure his cool reserve. "Where are you taking me?"

"We're almost there."

"Who are you?" He did not answer, and she twisted in his grasp to study him. He had a smooth, hard face and ice-blue eyes. He smiled, but it was not reassuring.

Without warning he reined in his mount. She looked around, unable to see why he had stopped. He dismounted and courteously lifted her down. Then he led her firmly past a few last scraggly trees. Twenty paces in front of them the ground seemed to cut into open sky. It was a cliff.

He took her to the edge. Below them was a deep, jagged gully lined with sharp rocks and brush at the bottom. If she fell down there, no one would ever find her . . . if she survived.

He shoved her. "No!" she cried, grabbing at him. She fell, but her stubborn little hands held. Dangling over the cliff, she had caught his shortcoat and brought him to his knees.

Surprised and irritated, he wrenched her hands free and she caught with a last effort on a brushy stump. The dead wood pulled readily from the rock, but she did not fall. She did not know why.

The man lifted his foot to dislodge her and—disappeared. In his stead appeared a bloody brown face, and strong arms lifted her back onto the cliff. She clung to Roman and would not let him go. He touched her hair. "Are you injured?" he asked. She could not answer. But when she raised her eyes and saw the ugly gash on his forehead, she began to sob.

❖

It was mid-afternoon before the party set off again. Roman's head had been cleaned and wrapped with makeshift bandages. He was a shade pale, but steady. Deirdre climbed up in front of him on his horse—she would ride nowhere else. The soldiers tied a body on Deirdre's mare, then they all pieced together what had happened.

After the initial attack, the soldiers came to Roman's aid and killed his assailant. Then Roman and two soldiers set out to follow the kidnaper. It was easy tracking him through the forest and stream, Roman said; at times they could glimpse him far ahead. But when he got on the rocky bank they had to search much harder.

Finally one of the soldiers spotted him coming down— alone. They caught him and, under pressure, he directed them to the cave. Roman sent the kidnaper back with the soldiers to face the wrath of the Surchatain. From there, Roman had followed the trail alone. He was almost on top of them when he heard her cry out at the cliff, and feared he was too late. But he saw her clinging yet to the rock, and sent a knife into the man's back to stay his foot.

"I thought I had killed him," Roman said matter-of-factly, "but after I had pulled you free of the cliff, I turned back and he was gone—with his horse."

The captured kidnaper was escorted back to the Surchatain's prison for later questioning. (All he could tell them, however, was that the gentleman had hired him and his partner in a tavern to abduct the Chataine. They were to be paid on delivering her to the cave, and no names were exchanged.) Deirdre described the silver-haired man as best she could, as Roman had not gotten a good look at him, but no one could guess who he was. At this point, she did not care. She felt safe tucked in close to Roman.

Their progress was slowed, somewhat, from then; Roman, his wound bleeding continually, suffered some light-headedness that required more frequent rests.

The air turned cool quickly as the sun dropped behind the mountains, and the travelers made yet another stop to dig out cloaks from their traveling bags. Deirdre found it more convenient, and more comfortable, to wrap herself in the roominess of Roman's cloak than don her own. Then in the growing darkness, the band tightened their formation and pushed ahead to Ooster.

It was late in the evening when they arrived at Corneus's gates. The Surchatain of Seir himself met them. . . .

✦

"Karel!" exclaimed Corneus, embracing Deirdre's father. "I was becoming concerned. I almost sent a regiment after you." Seeing Roman's blood-soaked bandages and the body on Deirdre's horse, he cried, "What on earth has happened?" Then he saw Deirdre as she unwrapped herself from Roman's cloak.

"Corneus, it is good to see you," Karel said wearily. "We encountered some ruffians on the road who delayed our trip a bit. It would be a great kindness to me if you would allow me to offer a reward to anyone who can tell me this fellow's name and village." He gestured toward the body.

"Certainly, Karel, certainly," Corneus assured him. He turned to a guard. "Have the body placed in the courtyard and post a notice offering—" he glanced inquiringly at Karel.

"One hundred royals," Karel answered.

"—one hundred royals from the Surchatain of Lystra to anyone who can identify this man." The guard bowed and the body was removed.

"Now, you all must be terribly fatigued from your journey—you, young man, need the physician!" Corneus declared, peering at Roman. "Summon him," was directed to a servant. "Come in, come in now—" Corneus herded them into the warm, plush dining hall paneled in walnut and hung with blue tapestries.

Roast duck and pottage, brown bread, red wine, cheese, nuts, pastry and honey came out of the kitchen in short order. Roman paused eating long enough to let the physician cleanse his head and bandage it to his satisfaction.

Meanwhile, Corneus did not press Karel for details of the incident, but talked merrily of trading profits and innovative ideas and consolidation of resources, or some such things. Finally he turned to Deirdre and said, "So this is Regina's daughter. You look so much like your mother, my dear. She had that same blonde hair."

"Thank you, Uncle," she replied properly.

"But you have not met my family!" he exclaimed. He sent a summons, and some time later a tall, regal woman appeared in the dining hall with two young men beside her. "Deirdre, this is your Aunt Bedelia."

Deirdre rose from the table to greet her, and Bedelia nodded coolly. "And this is Jason and this is Colin," continued Corneus as they bowed to her. She returned the gesture of respect while he winked to them, "This is your cousin Deirdre, boys."

"Do you want to go see the armory?" the younger Colin asked her.

Deirdre reflexively glanced at Roman, who looked spent and pale. "In the morning, Colin. I—I would like to retire now, Father."

The room given her was as fitting as her own, with many lacy pillows and quilts. The housemaid assigned her for their stay was motherly and attentive—much like Nanna. And, as Nanna certainly would, she objected strongly when she learned that Roman planned to sleep in the adjoining room. "It is not proper!" she scolded. "The Surchatain will be appalled!"

"He will understand. She is my charge," Roman said tiredly.

Deirdre lay in bed and tried to sleep, but vivid flashbacks to that afternoon kept her wide-eyed. She slipped off the bed and pressed her ear against the door to Roman's room. Was he asleep? Quietly, she opened the door.

Roman was on his knees in the center of the room. His head was bowed, his eyes shut, and his lips were moving. She watched him a moment, but he did not look up, so she closed the door quietly and buried herself in the downy bed.

In the morning, when he met her in the corridor to go downstairs for breakfast, she was alarmed to see his right eye swollen and somewhat blackened below the bandages. "Roman—you look terrible!"

"Thank you, Chataine," he said, one brow flattened.

"No—I mean—you look hurt worse today."

"Not at all. My head is clear this morning. I only look worse—as luck would have it," he ended on a mutter. But he walked slowly, pausing once or twice to steady himself on the stairway.

"Roman, are you sure you feel well?" she asked doubtfully.

"Yes," he said, and did not pause again.

They descended to the dining hall to find Karel and Corneus already being served. As Deirdre and Roman took their places, Jason and Colin entered to sit on either side of her. Jason had the thin, pinched face of his mother; Colin was dark-haired and stocky like his father. Jason took the lead: "You will be really glad you came here, Deirdre. Colin and I have a lot to show you. You are going to see how warriors train!"

"Do you have a lake?" she asked. "I would rather see a lake, with flowers around it."

Jason gave an incredulous sneer. "No, we don't have a lake. That's stupid."

"Father has a garden—" began Colin, but Jason interrupted him.

"That's nothing to see—just bushes and trees. Hurry and finish, Deirdre, so you can come watch." She looked across the table to Roman. He said nothing, but coolly assessed Jason.

As promised, the first event of the morning was a visit to the armory, which at least interested Roman, who smiled once or twice at the boys' quasi-knowledgeable descriptions of the weapons' uses. Then they sat outside in the courtyard to watch Jason and Colin spar with the pugil sticks.

Growing impatient at their many feints and misses, Deirdre exclaimed, "You should get Roman to teach you at it. He is a champion!"

"Really?" Jason smirked. Roman was only a shade larger than he. "Then let's have a match," Jason proposed. When Roman declined, Jason muttered, "Coward." Roman did not respond. So instead they watched the boys play a match of ground ball. Next they watched the boys at archery.

For Deirdre and Roman, sitting most of the morning as spectators at least gave them the opportunity to talk privately of the attempt on her life. "I don't understand why someone I don't even know would want to kill me," she whispered.

"Improve on that, guardian!" Jason shouted back at them after scoring close to the bull's-eye.

Roman, disinclined to exert himself, demurred with a wave. "You are your father's only heir," Roman said to her while keeping his eyes ahead. "Someone wishing to usurp his position would need you out of the way eventually."

"But who could have known we would be on the road then?" she asked. She also kept her eyes on the archery contest so they would not appear to be talking.

"There are spies all over, from every region. We have no way of knowing unless we can find your silver-haired gentleman." Roman scanned the grounds warily.

"Why didn't he kill me at the cave?" she whispered.

"To buy time, no doubt. Your father could not appoint a successor until you were proclaimed dead. That would be difficult to do if we couldn't find you. As long as you were missing, we would be obliged to search for you three years. Only then, if you still were not found, could he appoint another heir."

"You know much about law, for a soldier," she observed, looking at him.

He glanced down at her hand on the grass between them. "It was explained to me when I was informed of the appointment."

At that point they were distracted by a mild disturbance from the far end of the courtyard. It soon turned into a serious one when Corneus came storming from the palace. "Fool! How could you have allowed that to happen?"

"Surchatain—there was a mixup in the guards—"

"Excuses! You are relieved of your position! Now get soldiers out to find him!"

Roman and Deirdre got up and came over as Karel appeared in the courtyard. Corneus took on a humble tone: "Karel, a most embarrassing thing has happened." He cleared his throat. "My guards were negligent in their duties, and somehow, someone has stolen the body of the man you wanted identified. I can't imagine—"

"It is more than embarrassing, Corneus; it is critical," Karel seethed.

"So it is. And I have offered a reward of five hundred royals to anyone who can produce the body."

"The body alone does us no good!" burst Karel. "I want to know who hired him!"

Corneus's face altered slightly. "We will do what can be done, Karel." His voice suggested no anxiety on his part.

Karel braced his jaw and inclined his head ever so little. "I leave the matter in your capable hands, Corneus." Watching as his host returned to the palace, Karel uttered sidelong to Roman, "Be wary, guardian."

A bell sounded, signaling the noon meal, and the party assembled in the dining hall. Roman took his seat across from Deirdre. When her plate was set before her, he suddenly reached over and took it away. He tasted a little bit of everything on her plate, even drinking from her goblet, before he would let her have it.

Watching, Corneus bristled, "You offend me, guardian."

"That isn't necessary, Roman," Karel added insincerely.

"Apologies, my lords," Roman said unapologetically. But he waited a moment to see if there were any ill effect on himself before returning her plate to her. Deirdre watched him anxiously. He smiled at her and surrendered her plate.

As his food was served, she could hardly help but notice the attention a pretty serving girl paid to him. The girl smiled and leaned close to him, fretted over his bandaged head and even toyed with his shaggy black hair. Deirdre felt an unreasonable jealousy. She burned inwardly as she watched, but the others seemed to notice nothing amiss.

Toward the end of the meal, the girl put her hand on Roman's shoulder and whispered in his ear. He smiled and shook his head. She whispered again, then sauntered off. Roman watched her go and sighed very faintly. Then he saw the Chataine's cloudy face and lowered his eyes.

After the meal she cornered him beside the great fireplace and demanded, "What did she say to you?"

"You ask too many questions, Chataine," he brazenly replied.

"But what did she say?" persisted the blue-eyed bulldog.

He paused to see that no one else was close enough to hear. "She wanted me to come to her room tonight."

Deirdre's jealousy flared up. "Are you?"

"Of course not," he answered a little defensively. Then, turning thoughtful: "Besides, I don't believe her motives were the purest, if you'll pardon the word."

"What do you mean?"

Roman idly kicked a piece of charred wood back into the fireplace. "Well, I saw her yesterday when we arrived. She served us at dinner. She did not even give me a second glance then. This sudden interest is suspicious."

"Oh?" said Deirdre. She was still trying to recall her from yesterday. "I didn't notice her."

"I did."

❖

During the subsequent days of their visit, Roman was vigilant to the point of edginess in warding Deirdre. He locked her doors himself at night and, during the day, made sure that she was never out of arm's reach. So when Jason suggested to Deirdre a trip into Ooster to see the town, Roman immediately objected.

"If you can't protect her in a crowd, stay here," Jason taunted. "*I'll* be with her."

Roman leveled a cold stare at Jason and replied, "If the Chataine wishes to go, she may. But I am her guardian."

Deirdre raised pleading eyes. "I really want to go." Roman tightened his lips and she whispered, "I *promise* I'll stay with you!"

The four of them—Deirdre, Roman, Jason, and Colin—rode at a leisurely walk down the broad thoroughfare from the palace into the main part of town. "What a smooth road!" exclaimed Deirdre, admiring the paving stones.

"Father says nothing helps trade like good roads," Jason said proudly. "It's better than a river."

Deirdre nodded. "But how much you must pay the stone-masons to do it!"

"Nothing," laughed Jason. "The soldiers do it. Father says it gives the lazy brands something to do." He cut his eyes toward Roman, who turned him a deaf ear.

Jason then began to point out the best businesses and shops. Deirdre listened eagerly to his boasting about all the goods available and all the money that traded hands in that town. "Father says commerce is what builds an empire," he stated.

"And soldiers protect your commerce," Roman added casually.

"That's what I always say!" interjected Colin. Jason directed a threatening look toward his brother.

"Roman, look at that!" cried Deirdre. They stopped before a beautiful building of polished oak and glass. Stone steps led up to intricately carved double doors—which were bolted fast. "What business is that?" she inquired.

"That is the cathedral Father built for Mother. It is the most expensive building on the Continent. The floors and pillars inside are black marble, and the walls are covered with carved panels, which tell a story."

"Of what?" Deirdre asked.

"I don't know," Jason admitted.

"Then let's go in and see," said Roman, dismounting. "And while we're inside, we can pray."

"No," objected Jason. "We can't. The doors are bolted."

"When are they opened?" Roman folded his arms on his chest, squinting up at Jason. He had abandoned the bandage some days ago, exposing the ugly gash.

"When Mother gives her say," Jason answered impatiently.

"Then what use is this building to your people?"

"Fool!" Jason sputtered. "Can't you see how beautiful it is?"

Deirdre caught her breath at the insult and looked to Roman. But he remounted without a word. She got the definite impression he had made some kind of a point.

Jason continued them on their tour. He pointed out the bakery, blacksmith, woodwright, potter, and silversmith. At the tanner's, he urged them to dismount and examine the goods. "He sends much fine leather to the fair at Hycliff every year," Jason informed them.

"It's lovely," Deirdre agreed, glancing from the shiny leather to the plain brown shortcoat Roman wore.

As they remounted, Jason made no comment about a large house next door with scarlet curtains in its windows. "What business is that?" asked Deirdre.

"Ask Roman," smirked Jason. "He should know."

Deirdre turned inquiring eyes to her guardian. He inhaled. "It is a brothel, Deirdre."

"A brothel?" she frowned. Roman sat still, glancing malevolently at grinning Jason. Then she remembered something Rory had once described and her face took on color.

"Want to see the inside, Deirdre?" Jason teased.

Roman abruptly leaned over and took hold of her horse's bridle, turning Lady Grey in a tight half circle as he spurred toward the palace. "This is beneath you, Chataine. I will not permit it."

"Roman!" she protested angrily, but secretly she was glad.

Corneus, Karel, and an aloof Bedelia were standing near the front gates conversing as Roman and Deirdre came into view, galloping up the thoroughfare. Corneus watched them, then commented, "Your daughter's guardian is quite faithful, Karel—he never leaves her side. He does his job well."

"He should. His life depends on it," Karel responded.

"Deirdre, dear!" Corneus called out to her.

She and Roman gained the gates and dismounted. "Yes, Uncle?"

"You will be having your coming out here, Deirdre, when you are sixteen. Did you know that? It will be grand—young men from all over the Continent will be here. Won't that be exciting?"

"Yes, Uncle!"

"I can hardly wait, myself," Corneus said. Then he leaned closer to add, "And I hope you and Jason will get to be good friends—eh?" He winked.

Karel tapped him on the shoulder. "We'll talk about that, Corneus."

"Aunt Bedelia, will you be chaperoning?" Deirdre asked politely.

"I regret that I will not be here at that time," the Surchataine answered. "I plan to be visiting friends."

"Who?" Corneus frowned.

"I don't know yet." She turned haughtily to reenter the palace.

❖

The day of their departure, the party assembled in the court-yard before dawn. Corneus stood by, chatting and oversee-ing. "Karel, allow me to send an outfit back with you. Since we have not yet recovered the body of that ruffian, we don't know—there may yet be cohorts of his lying in wait for you."

"That's why we brought our own bodyguard, Corneus. No need to dispatch yours as well." Karel attempted to sound genial.

"As you wish," acceded Corneus. "Deirdre, I shall look forward to seeing you here again."

"Thank you, Uncle. I shall look forward to coming. Please tell Aunt Bedelia goodbye for us."

"I shall. Goodbye, my dear. Karel."

Deirdre's father lifted his hand in farewell, and the party rode out of the gates in formation, as they had come.

Deirdre was more prepared for the ride home. Roman had fitted a dainty little pillow to her saddle, which she accepted with no loss of pride. As they rode now, he demonstrated how to ride standing in the stirrups to relieve cramping in her legs. She was anxious to prove herself as capable as the men of enduring the long ride to Westford.

And she did well. The party achieved rapid travel until mid-afternoon, when a thunderstorm broke suddenly over the mountains and sent sheets of sleet and rain on the party. They stopped to don their cloaks, then resumed travel at a slower pace, for the horses were edgy and less surefooted.

The darker it grew, the more nervous Deirdre became. A lightning bolt crashed in the forest near them and Lady Grey, startled, broke into a run past the soldiers ahead of her. Deirdre hauled back on the reins and the mare tried to stop, but slipped and fell heavily on her side. Deirdre, thrown clear, bounced once or twice in the mud before coming to rest. As soon as her breath returned, she let out a wail.

But Roman was already on his knees beside her, wiping mud from her face. "Are you hurt? Are you hurt, Chataine?"

She stopped crying to feel herself. "No—I don't think I am," she said, surprised. Lady Grey staggered up, offended but unhurt.

Roman kept wiping her face. "Hold your head back," he murmured.

"What?" The rain was pounding around them. She pushed his arm away from her face in irritation. When she saw the blood on his fingers, she began to cry again.

"It's only a nosebleed, Deirdre. Don't cry," he pleaded.

"Roman! Is she injured?" Karel called from his horse.

Roman did not answer right away. He lifted Deirdre and carried her to his horse. "Do you want to ride with me?" he asked softly.

"Yes!" she said, grasping the saddle. "I'm not hurt, Father," she added over her shoulder. He nodded as Roman placed her in the saddle and sat behind her. Then Roman wrapped her up completely in his great cloak.

As they set off again, he leaned his head down to hers and murmured, "Thank you," for she had spared him a flogging. She grinned back at him and wiped her nose.

Hours later, they arrived at Westford a weary, bedraggled band. Keeping Deirdre covered under his cloak, Roman carried her, half asleep, into the palace where Nanna waited. "Oh, my poor baby, is she all worn out? Goodness, you're soaked! Get that filthy cloak off her, Roman—Aiiee!" the nursemaid screamed upon seeing the muddy, bloodied little girl. "Baby! What has happened to you?" She directed a murderous look at Roman, who glanced down the corridor as he hastily herded Chataine and nurse up the great stone stairway.

"My horse fell down with me!" Deirdre announced proudly.

"Oh! You—!" She glared at Roman, and he shrugged guiltily. "Come dear, let me get you all cleaned up," Nanna fretted, bustling her to her chambers.

Meanwhile, the Surchatain and his Counselor were conferring in Karel's chambers. Eudymon had heard from the soldiers who had brought back the kidnaper of the attempt on Deirdre's life. He posed, "Then the rumors must be true that Corneus is trying to kill her!"

"We don't know that it is Corneus," replied Karel. "We must interrogate this ruffian and see what he can tell us." After some discussion, they also agreed to send spies to Seir and the surrounding regions to try to locate an elegant, silver-haired man with a recent knife wound in his back. That resolved, they lapsed into troubled silence.

After a long moment of deliberation, the Counselor said, "Surchatain, I am loath to advise you on personal matters, but as it regards the throne. . . ." Karel looked up. "Will you not consider remarrying, High Lord, to provide yourself with at least one other heir—?"

"No," Karel said in an uncommonly soft voice. "Deirdre is Regina's daughter. It is the least I can do for her, to see that Deirdre succeeds me. It is the least I can do. . . ."

As he trailed off, the Counselor said, "A most commendable gesture, High Lord. Most commendable." Karel did not respond.

After another long pause, Eudymon stated, "Roman must be severely punished."

"Why?" Karel asked in some surprise.

"Deirdre would not have been taken but for his carelessness. He must be flogged." As Karel considered it, Eudymon pressed his point: "The fact that he recovered her unharmed, being injured himself, should merit no consideration. Nor should the fact that he alone seems able to control her. I shall order his flogging tonight," the Counselor declared, stepping toward the door.

"No. Roman shall in no way be punished. I have decided that," Karel said.

"Surchatain," Eudymon acknowledged, bowing.

"You are dismissed, Counselor."

Eudymon bowed again and stepped into the corridor, where he saw a soldier leaving the armory. "Roman!"

The soldier turned and bowed respectfully. "Counselor?" For a moment they eyed each other.

"You seem to have encountered a run of ill luck on this trip," Eudymon remarked.

Roman shrugged. "The Chataine is safely home."

"For that, I am most grateful. And how do you fare?" He regarded the broken scab on Roman's forehead.

"I will heal. I always do. I have been wounded much worse before," Roman said, his face granite.

Eudymon lowered his eyes. "We all take blows, at one

time or another. There is justice in life, but not much mercy," he said softly.

"Will that be all, Counselor?"

"Yes. Goodnight, Roman."

"Counselor." He bowed stiffly and walked away.

❖

Nanna bathed and dressed the Chataine for bed with many tearful hugs. When Nanna had heard of the attempted murder, she had fainted dead away. Now Deirdre began to recount to her every savory detail of the abduction. However, she changed it up just a little to save face. She did not want to tell Nanna she made Roman turn his back on her. So she said that he left her alone while *he* went to relieve himself.

Nanna burst out, "That worthless ———! Why the High Lord gave the likes of him charge over you I'll never know!"

Deirdre was mildly surprised. "Why, Nanna, I never heard you swear before."

"I'm not swearing. That's what he is—he's illegitimate." The woman was truly angry. "It's common knowledge that his mother was a harlot, and there's no saying who his father might be!"

The Chataine was intrigued. "Where is his mother?"

"She died of disease years ago. They put the boy in the Surchatain's army, as there was nothing else to be done with him." As her anger cooled, she saw that she had said too much. "Well, dear, that all means nothing now. I'm sure he does the best he can to ward you. Dear . . . please don't tell anyone what I told you. It's not important. Please promise me you will not repeat it to anyone."

"I promise," smiled the Chataine.

In the morning, Deirdre could hardly wait to spring her newfound knowledge on Roman. She dressed herself early and, ignoring her studies and his obligations, ran to summon him.

After having been gone for almost two weeks he had a backlog of matters awaiting his attention, but Deirdre insisted on coming first. She waited impatiently by the rear gate to see him bringing their horses from the stables, and he smiled when he saw her running eagerly to meet him. They mounted and rode west, out to the hills.

"Roman," she plunged right in, "I heard that you're a mistake and your mother was a harlot. Is that true?"

His face turned to stone. "You don't know when to stop, do you?" he said quietly.

"What?" She was suddenly uncomfortable.

"You're still trying to gain the upper hand on me—still putting me in my place."

He would say no more. As Deirdre studied him, the realization broke over her that she had just inflicted as brutal a wound as the kidnaper's bludgeon. But he was so strong and rocklike, she had not thought it possible to hurt him—until she saw him bleed.

They rode at a walk side by side. Deirdre tried to get him talking, but he answered politely and fell silent again. She began to feel remorse, then immediate self-justification: *I did not intend to hurt him.*

But as she looked at him another insight answered her as clearly as someone speaking: *Yes, you did. Did you really expect to say something so cruel and not hurt him?*

She startled. Her conscience had never been so assertive. Did just being with him make it so?

"Roman, I—I'm sorry I said that. I'm sorry I hurt you."

He nodded. She felt a sudden tightness in her throat.

At the table that evening she was especially deferential to him. He spoke to her kindly enough, but did not look up much.

"Roman," she said softly, so that no one else would

overhear, "have you ever said anything you wished you had not said?"

"Often." He looked at her now.

"I wish I had not said that."

"I know." He relaxed. "It's only that . . . is that what the palace thinks of me? Is that what they are all saying?"

"No!" she said. Some heads turned, so she lowered her voice to a whisper. "I heard it from only one person." She stopped, but the question remained in his eyes. "Nanna," she admitted.

"Your nursemaid should be a communications runner," he observed. But he smiled at her.

Days later, Deirdre was watching from her usual window as Roman practiced at archery on the grounds below. He was very good at that, as well. *That looks like fun—I must get him to teach me*, she thought. But for now she was bored and he was busy. She was supposed to be doing her lessons, but she didn't even know where Rory was. She sighed and turned from the window.

Then an inspiration struck. Eagerly, she wound her way down to the kitchen corridors. She approached the door to Roman's room and tried the handle. The door creaked open, so she peeked in.

Rory was right. It was a small, dreary room with no rugs or tapestries. There was only one book-sized window. Beneath it was a narrow bed.

She crossed the room and sat on the bed. Ouch—it was hard! Deirdre pulled back the blanket. What she had sat on was part of the frame which had thick, rugged cloth stretched taut over it. There was no mattress or pillow, only the thin blanket. She replaced it on the cot as it had been.

The only other piece of furniture in the room was a small stand with a washbowl. Beneath it, a pile of clothes lay neatly folded. She fingered them, and out fell a bronze medallion. She picked it up. It was a medal of valor. She had seen her father award them to soldiers who had acted with courage in battle. She was so intently studying it, she did not hear the door open.

"What are you looking for, Chataine?"

She whirled. "Oh—Roman—I came to see if—if we could go riding."

"You didn't summon me? You know where I am in the mornings." Wiping down his bare chest, he stood far back from the doorway until she had replaced the medal and come to the door.

"Well . . . I was really just curious to see your room," she confessed.

"This is it." He went in and looked back, waiting.

It's pitiful, she thought, but aloud she asked, "What did you get the medal for?"

"I'll tell you about it sometime. Now, I must wash and change. Chataine?" he hinted, a hand on the door.

"What? Oh, yes. . . ." And she stepped out into the corridor to wait.

"What are you looking for, Chataine?" a servant asked her respectfully.

"Nothing!" she snapped, and hastily moved off to wait at the rear gate.

When Roman finally arrived at the gate with the horses, she almost jumped on him. "Well?"

"Chataine?" One eyebrow went up as he handed her Lady Grey's reins to hold while he readjusted the saddle.

"What did you do to get the medal?" she asked, taking the reins.

"Oh, that. When I was a boy, I carried water to an outfit on the border," he said.

"Is that it?"

"Not exactly." He paused almost cruelly while repositioning the saddle on the mare. "They had been trapped between enemy lines without water for two days. With what

I smuggled in to them, they were revived and able to fight their way back to the outpost."

"How old were you then?"

"I'm not certain. Commander Galapos says about fourteen."

"You were in the army at fourteen?" she asked in admiration.

"I was the Commander's errand boy," he replied with a touch of pride.

She considered. "Roman, would you do that for me? Would you risk your life to save me?"

He looked at her almost in disbelief. "Haven't I already, Chataine?"

She remembered with sudden clarity the details of the recent attack and blushed at her forgetfulness. "Yes."

5

I, Penuel, continue this account. . . .

✛

Deirdre sat listlessly leafing through her books. This new tutor Father got for her certainly cut into her free time. History, geography, mathematics, law—she slammed the books shut and gazed out the window.

It had snowed again last night. The barren ground was hidden beneath a shimmering skin of white. She set her mind to planning how to persuade Roman to take her to the lake in the sleigh. Roman had promised—

Roman. It had been almost two years since he had become her guardian. Was that right? Yes, because in a few months she would turn twelve. It only seemed as if he had always been at her side.

She remembered the trip to her uncle's and shivered. None of the spies Father had sent out could locate the silver-haired man. But from the description they believed they had found who he was. His name was Stase. He was an assassin for hire. There had been not a trace of him since the attack, and some believed he must have died from his wound. But Roman would not chance it, so she had not been away from the palace environs since. And she was getting restless.

Deirdre said, "Pooh!" to the books, threw on a fur-lined cloak, and ran downstairs to summon Roman. The errand boy could not locate him, but one of the guards told her he was at the palace gate.

She found him heading up a group of soldiers who seemed to be waiting. "Roman! Let's go sleigh riding! Let's go to the lake!"

He glanced at her. "Chataine, please—we'll go later. Not now." Excitement seemed about to crack his usual cool reserve.

"Why not? What is happening?"

"There's an outfit coming in for leave from the border. Galapos is with them," he said, scanning the hills.

"Galapos?" She had heard of him often, but having never seen him, considered him something of a legend.

"Commander Galapos, the Field Commander. He is in charge of the army, under your father," Roman said.

So? she thought, but she let him wait.

Presently a shout sprang up from the soldiers as the outfit was spotted up the road. The wide gates swung full open, and a tired group of men entered to whistles and cheers.

She spotted Galapos immediately. He was right out in front—the biggest man Deirdre had ever seen. Roman ran forward to meet him. The Commander was shaking hands and receiving friendly slaps as he dismounted, but when he saw Roman his face changed. "Roman, my boy, how are you?" The two men embraced.

"Well, Galapos, quite well," he answered, then extended his

arm toward Deirdre. "Galapos, this is my charge, Chataine Deirdre."

"Eh? Yes, I heard you had been made her guardian. Come, sweetheart, let me look at you." He bent to study her. He was so big! He had flowing hair streaked with grey, a large moustache, and deep lines around his mouth and bright blue eyes.

"How do you do?" she said, lifting her hand.

"Oh! And how do you do?" he returned, with a wink up at Roman. He took her hand in his big bear paw and kissed it solemnly. "I hope I shall have your company at dinner tonight, Chataine. We have much to discuss."

"Oh?" she said, trying to sound mature.

"Yes. I am most anxious to know what trouble that lazy, ignorant, irresponsible fool is making," Galapos said gravely.

"Who?" she cried.

"Roman!" he burst, and all the soldiers standing around roared. *Roman won't like that*, she thought. But he was grinning broadly.

"Roman, may we go out in the sleigh now?" she asked politely, in spite of her impatience to get him away.

He tossed an aside to Galapos: "We'll talk later." The Commander nodded, eyes twinkling. "Wait here, Chataine, while I harness your mare to the sleigh," Roman instructed over his shoulder.

Deirdre smiled in satisfaction. Glancing self-consciously at the soldiers, she moved away from them to wait for him, but they paid no attention to her. Except Galapos. She pretended not to see when he turned her way and studied her reflectively for a moment.

When Roman at last appeared driving the sleigh, she scurried up beside him and began asking questions before she had sat down: "Who is that man? Why did he call you those names? Where—?"

He raised his hand in mock surrender. "Leave me some

air and I'll tell you everything." He first paused to cover her knees with the blanket from the floor of the sleigh.

Starting out of the gate, he resumed, "As I said, Galapos is Commander of the army. He's the one who took me off the streets and brought me here, years ago. He had no reason to do it but for the kindness in his heart. He made me his errand boy and personally taught me riding and archery and combat with all types of weapons. He treated me as his very own son. But when I was still a child, the Border Wars broke out and he had to assume command from Outpost One. I had hoped to join him, but . . . well, he has been away from the palace for most of these years. There is peace along the border now, so he has returned on leave." Roman guided the mare down the snowy path as he talked.

Deirdre leaned into his rough woolen cloak. "Why did you let him say such terrible things about you?"

"Because I know and everyone else knows that he doesn't believe those things about me at all. You saw he is fond of me. But he prefers to cover his tender heart with droll talk."

"Are you fond of me?" she asked.

"Of course, Chataine." He looked straight ahead as he said it.

"Well, I would order your flogging if you said such things to me," she declared.

He smiled grimly. "I would never speak to you so carelessly."

Satisfied, Deirdre listened to the jingling of the little silver bells on the mare's harness. Then she asked, "Did Galapos give you the gold medallion?"

"No," he said, concentrating on guiding the sleigh to a suitable spot near the shore of the frozen lake. "Here we are, as you requested." He dropped the reins and leaned back.

"I have a surprise for you!" she announced, digging a pair of skates out of hiding in the sleigh. "Wait till you see what I can do!" She drew up a foot to begin strapping on a skate.

He sat up. "Where did you get those? What do you think you're doing?!" His tone became threatening.

"Watch!" she said, stepping from the sleigh in her skates.

But he grasped her arm firmly. "You are not going out on the ice."

"But, Roman," she faltered, "I learned to skate. I wanted to show you what I learned."

He dropped her arm in surprise. "Who taught you to skate?"

"The merchant who was here the other day. I bought the skates from him to surprise you," she said anxiously. The look on his face was not pleasant surprise.

"Where did he teach you?" he demanded.

"Here, at the lake. We sneaked out for just a little while so he could teach me. I wanted to surprise you," she whimpered.

He abruptly lifted her up and sat her back down in the sleigh with a plop. "Deirdre, that was very foolish. You know you must never leave the palace without me. Have you forgotten the assassin? Anyone could be in his hire. If you don't value your own life, at least consider mine."

Her lip began to quiver. "I only wanted to show you what I could do."

He looked at her for a moment, then sighed, "So show me."

Elated, she stepped onto the ice and began gliding in shaky circles. He stood on the very edge of the shore to watch her. "See, Roman, see?" She waved as she skated in a straight line. He smiled and nodded.

Then she boldly built up speed and skimmed the ice in a whoosh toward him. Unable to stop properly, she crashed into him, laughing. "Did I do well, Roman?"

"You did well," he laughed, picking her up. "I'm proud of you."

"So am I!" And she set her skates on the ice again.

❖

That evening when Deirdre came down for dinner, she found to her surprise that Galapos had been given the seat between her father at the head of the table and herself to his right. She had always wondered about the empty chair there; now she knew.

She hesitated timidly at the doorway, but Roman saw her and stood. Galapos, turning, declared, "Chataine! You have come at last!" He rose and escorted her respectfully to her chair. "How gracious of you to insist I have this seat, sweetheart. But let's not tell the Surchatain." His voice dropped to a sly whisper. "We do not wish to arouse his suspicions." Deirdre giggled.

The Surchatain entered and they all stood until he was seated. Galapos picked up his goblet and said, "To the Surchatain!" The table did likewise. "We drink to your good health and long life, High Lord, as we profit from your good graces."

Karel smiled tightly as they drank their goblets down. Deirdre, remembering the drunken complaints she had overheard in the kitchen, wondered how much Galapos was paid. The Commander added, "And I thank you, Surchatain, for allowing the captains to share your table during my furlough. I must needs check up on these men by the minute!"

As the servants brought out white bread and roast lamb, an officer down the table demanded, "Tell us news from the outposts, Commander."

Galapos raised his bushy eyebrows and said, "Harumph. Nothing much. We have caught Loren and his band of merry men."

"Loren the outlaw?" Roman asked eagerly.

"Who terrorized half of Lystra?" added the officer.

"The same, Captain Dyek," Galapos confirmed.

"How did you do it?" asked Roman.

"Blind luck, actually," Galapos laughed. "He thought to rob two of my scouts I'd sent out dressed as merchants. He did not know they were armed and fronting for a unit following on horseback. It was a short fight." He stopped to bite into a shank. Deirdre watched him, spellbound.

Dyek exclaimed, "That demands a song!"

Galapos froze for an instant with upraised finger, eyes to the ceiling, composing. Then he sang,

> Sound a cheer for Loren!
> (May he rest in peace)
> Got his fill of robbin',
> Got himself deceased!

Those at the table—excepting the Surchatain and the Counselor—laughed riotously. Deirdre giggled and choked on a mouthful.

Galapos slapped her gently on the back to clear her airpipe and said, "Tell me now, sweetheart, about this villain"—nodding toward Roman—"and what despicable things he has done." Suddenly everyone was quiet, watching her, smiling.

"Well . . ." she began timidly, and her mind blanked out. What had he done that she resented most? "He makes me mind him!" she blurted, and the roar that followed made her hide her face. The Surchatain looked from Deirdre to Roman with an expression of interest and even the Counselor smiled.

"Such heartlessness," Galapos growled when he could catch his breath. He added mildly, "Then he's done no more than a nursemaid would."

"Actually, Commander, the Captain saved her life," Captain Basner said calmly, and the table stilled.

"Aye?" Galapos casually inquired, but his face took on a different cast.

"Spring before last, when we were traveling to Ooster.

On the road, he had suspected we were being followed and sent Kam and Marc into the forest at the noon rest to have a look. Before they had gotten around, though, a pair of renegades bludgeoned him and stole the Chataine." He paused, but Galapos was quiet.

"We caught one at the site, but the other got away with her and we had to give chase. Captain Roman insisted on the lead, though he was bleeding like a stuck pig. We chased the man a ways, lost him on the cliffs, then caught him coming back without the Chataine—but loaded down with silver. While we took the prisoner, the Captain chased a third kidnaper to the edge of a cliff where he was about to throw down the Chataine. The Captain knifed him and recovered her hanging from the edge of a rock.

"Back on the road to Ooster, though, we thought for sure we'd lose him. His head bled the whole blasted time. Those snatchers almost killed him after the fact," Basner related.

At that, Galapos made no comment and the table sat in silence. Deirdre gazed in dismay at Roman. She had never been aware he had come so close to dying.

Finally Roman himself blurted, "But they improved my face!" And he pulled back his hair to show the scar the bludgeon had left. Galapos laughed along with the others, but Deirdre felt his laughter was subdued.

In all the merriment, Deirdre could hardly help but notice the Counselor. He alone did not laugh, and had seemed only mildly interested in the Commander's tales. She thought he looked rather like a lone grownup at a children's gathering. It appeared that he did not much care for the Commander.

At one point a guard came to Karel's side and whispered in his ear. The Surchatain paused, then said, "Why not? Send him in." The guard bowed as Karel told his guests, "I am informed we have a traveling minstrel passing through offering entertainment. Let's hear his songs, then decide if he is worthy of a few royals." This plan was enthusiastically approved by all the guests.

Immediately a thin, pale man in ragged motley stepped up to the table and bowed low to the Surchatain. From the corner of her eye, Deirdre saw Roman give a little start. The minstrel said, "Surchatain, I have been given a song for you. I pray you to heed it." Then he strummed his guitar and began to sing in a minor key:

Hear a sad tale that I tell to be free
Of warring and honor and flights to the sea,
Of ills unforeseen,
Of fathomless dreams,
Of battles that ever were cast upon me.

I never had courage and never was bold
Till I saw my dreams in a woman unfold.
She became mine,
But perished in time,
And the grieving grew stronger that should have
    grown old.

The rage and the power I did not deny,
But gave them such sway that my spirit did die.
By slow degrees
It trickled from me,

And all that remains is this shell of my pride.
Fleeing forever the face of the sun,
I chose to run till my lifespan was done.
Who can I face?
Who will send grace?
Where is the mercy for what I have done?

Hear my lamenting and know it is true:
My warning will ever depend upon you.

Think you are wise?
With no one besides?
Know now that I myself thought once as you.

The last line had barely left his lips when Karel stood glowering and commanded: "Guard! Take him and—and—" the
guests were gaping at the extremity of his reaction. "Take
him to the whipping post—give him twenty lashes and send
him away," he ordered. "You are dismissed," Karel waved at
his guests. Deirdre promptly went up to her chambers. She
did not like to be underfoot when her father went sour this
way.

Roman and Galapos went to the Commander's quarters,
provided for him while he was on leave. "So . . ." Galapos began
slowly. "How goes it—warding the Chataine?"

"Well enough," Roman answered with downcast eyes.
"I've not yet suffered as the minstrel did for his song."

"Aye." Galapos raised his thick brows and coughed. "And
how long shall this appointment run?"

"Until she marries . . . four, maybe five more years. If God
sees fit to preserve my life that long."

"God!" Galapos uttered the Name in exasperation, turning
on Roman. "Where was He when you were almost clubbed to
death? When the Chataine was hanging over the cliff?"

Roman swallowed. "He preserved us then; He will do it
again."

"Roman, how long will you cling to this—this myth? This
wish? There is no God! Your own skill and strength delivered you, with a sweet helping of luck!"

"You're wrong, Galapos. I did what I could, yes, but God
intervened. I felt it." At Galapos's look, he rushed on: "I can't
explain it, but there have been times in my life when I have
felt God's power, when I knew with certainty His hand was
upon me."

"Next you will be telling me that God directed me to take

you in as my errand boy," Galapos said drily.

"Of course. You saved my life."

"I did, Roman! Not God!" His exasperation turned to anger. "I need a Second whose eyes are open, Roman. I'm sorry. You are dismissed." The Commander turned his back and Roman, stony-faced, withdrew.

✜

Deirdre's new tutor, Olin, liked to start unreasonably early every day, so the morning after Galapos's arrival she yawned through her lessons till Olin scolded her, "Don't you understand how valuable your lessons are? One day you will be Surchataine! You'll need to know all this, and much more. So few people ever have the chance to learn. Few can even read! Is that worth so little to you?" It was, but it gave her an idea. Here was something at last she could do for Roman.

Right after her lessons, she sent the errand boy to summon him. The boy was gone so long, she finally went downstairs to look for him herself. She met the boy, then, returning to tell her he had found Roman, alone, at the fenced pasture near the stables. He was inspecting a new bunch of wild horses captured that morning.

Deirdre hurried out to catch him, but was irked to see that Galapos had just joined him. "Roman, my boy, forgive me," Galapos was saying.

Roman turned to face him as Deirdre interrupted. "Roman, I want to talk to you!" she insisted, drawing him away.

"Chataine?" He looked annoyed for an instant, and she became suddenly tongue-tied.

"Roman—would you like—don't you think it would be a good idea if you knew how to read and write? I could teach you!"

"Thank you, Chataine . . . but I do read and write already,"

Roman answered, glancing back to the Commander.

She released his arm, surprised. None of the soldiers had any such learning. "What? Who taught you? Galapos?" He was watching them with a faint smile.

"No, the Counselor," Roman replied.

"The Counselor! Why?" asked Deirdre.

"As you said, Chataine, he thought it a good idea."

He turned back to the Commander, who nodded toward the horses and remarked, "A promising lot." Roman silently agreed.

Deirdre, meanwhile, slipped into a most sour mood. She slapped at the arms of her heavy brocaded jacket. Then she noticed a horse penned by himself, away from the others. She had started over to have a look at him when Roman caught her: "No! Chataine, don't go near that horse. He's untameable and dangerous. Come back here."

"I just want to look at him," she said crossly.

"No. He is very wild and easily provoked. Come stay right by my side."

She reluctantly obeyed, bristling at the sharpness in his voice. "What are they going to do with him?"

"He is to be destroyed." Roman made no effort to soften the statement.

Deirdre stared at the beautiful horse in dismay. He was so still and regal—surely they wouldn't kill him! Then she had a thought. She was an excellent rider for her age; everyone commented on how well she rode. She felt certain she could tame this horse. A vision came to her mind of the astonishment on everyone's face—especially Roman's—as she triumphantly pranced the horse around his pen. *Untameable? We'll see.*

Galapos had begun speaking to Roman again in a low voice, holding his attention. Her eyes narrowed in determination as she waited for just the right moment to slip away from his side. In an instant she was at the pen of the glistening stallion, talking to him softly.

He watched her with impossibly bright eyes. His sleek body was taut and trembling; his ears pricked high. The steam from his nostrils gave him the appearance of some mythical dragon. Deirdre slipped inside the fence and reached out to touch him. . . .

Someone shouted and the horse erupted. Rearing and screaming, he knocked her to the ground and reared again to trample her. Suddenly Roman was standing over her, bearing the crushing blows of hoofs on his chest and shoulder. Staggering, he grasped the legs and heaved with all his strength. It threw the horse off balance enough that it fell backward on the frozen ground.

Gasping, Roman scooped her up and tossed her to Galapos outside the pen. He had barely time to throw himself over before the horse had rammed itself into the railing, teeth bared and ears flattened.

Deirdre screamed, holding her bleeding hand. It had been gashed when she threw up her arms in defense of the flailing hoofs. Galapos shouted for the physician. Roman lay face down in the snow, wheezing. With an effort he sat up, clutching his ripped shortcoat in pain.

The physician appeared, and at his side was the Surchatain. He took one look at Deirdre and called for the guards. "Bring him!" he ordered, pointing to Roman. Two guards helped Roman to his feet, and he stumbled a few steps to face Karel. Livid, the Surchatain shoved a finger in his face and growled, "I warned you, soldier. To the whipping post!"

Deirdre leaped up, her pain forgotten. "No! Father, it was my fault! He told me not to—but I waited until he wasn't looking and I—don't beat him, Father! Please!" She was screaming now, but he ignored her. Roman was dragged off and everyone around followed.

The physician had to order guards to hold Deirdre still

until he could wrap her hand, then she broke away and ran for the courtyard. He followed close behind. There was already a large crowd around the whipping post. Deirdre pushed her way through till she could see Roman.

Stripped of his shirt and coat, he stood gripping the cold chains on the post. The deep marks of hoofs showed bright red on his chest and left shoulder. He seemed to be struggling to breathe. There was no sign of his medallion—then she saw that Galapos, next to her, held it clenched in his fist.

At that moment the Counselor pushed his way through the crowd. "What is happening here? Who—?" He stopped as if shot when he saw Roman on the post.

The physician pleaded, "Counselor, stop them until I can look at him. If he is badly injured, they may kill him!"

Eudymon shook his head helplessly. "Can I rescind an order of the Surchatain?"

"Twenty lashes," the Surchatain commanded. "Now."

A burly soldier stepped up with a metal-tipped whip and began the count. One . . . the whip cracked and Roman jerked. Deirdre screamed. Two . . . three . . . his face contorted at every blow, but he made no sound.

Seven . . . eight . . . nine . . . Deirdre pounded her head with her good hand. "Stop, stop!" she cried. "Roman, I swear from now on I'll obey you!"

Fourteen . . . fifteen . . . Usually anyone on the whipping post got heckled by the crowd, but this time there were no jeers or taunts. The soldiers stood at attention, all with faces as masked as Galapos's.

Eighteen . . . nineteen . . . Deirdre's eyes glazed as Roman's knees buckled beneath him.

Twenty. The last blow produced no reaction as Roman hung limp between the posts. The physician ran to him, fiercely beckoning two soldiers to release him. Deirdre snapped to and followed. The Surchatain turned away.

Roman was carried to the infirmary and laid face down on

a narrow bed as the physician directed. Other soldiers crowded in the doorway to look, but he allowed no one in but Deirdre and Galapos.

The physician wiped down Roman's wounds with wine and oil, then gingerly bandaged him. That done, he stood back and looked down on the semiconscious man with a grave face. "Isn't there more you can do?" Deirdre whispered brokenly.

"Nothing but watch him. I've felt no broken bones, but it remains to be seen how deeply he is injured," the physician replied heavily, turning to a washbasin beside the bed. Galapos nodded, then glanced up and caught sight of someone outside the infirmary. He left as if to relay the information.

Deirdre stayed by the bed, feeling her own arm throb. Lying face down, Roman breathed as if it were the greatest effort of his life. His face was grey, with sweat trickling down to his neck. She cried softly in remorse as she watched him, then took his hand gently. He opened his eyes a little.

She whispered, "Oh, Roman, I am so sorry. I swear I'll never question you or disobey you again. Please get better. Please, Roman." His lips moved and his eyes shut again.

The next few days they watched him closely. He did not seem to worsen, though he slept most of the time. He lay very still and drew in shallow, uneven breaths. The Chataine hounded the infirmary, wanting to do what she could for him, until the physician chased her away. The best thing for Roman, he said, was to be left alone.

Still, she sneaked back in whenever she was able; the burden on her conscience was too great to ignore. If he should die—why, she would have killed him. Envisioning herself being hanged for murder, she took grim satisfaction in the suffering she would endure.

Days later when she peeked in the infirmary, she saw him awake and sitting up. "Roman!" She ran to his bed and would have thrown her arms around him had he not caught her.

"Chataine—you were hurt," he whispered hoarsely, examining her hand.

"No." She pulled it back. "Not like you were. Roman, I am so, so sorry. Are you going to be well?"

"Certainly. But I'm weak. I can't go riding with you for a while. . . . Oh, what about the horse?"

"What?" she asked blankly.

He shifted, tugging at the bandages that were stuck to his back. "What happened to the horse? The stallion you were concerned about?"

"I don't know. I hope they killed it," she answered darkly.

❖

Deirdre spent most of the next several weeks in the infirmary, doing what she was allowed to succor him. She had been assigned a replacement guardian, but refused to go out at all. Galapos, also, kept appearing at his bedside. The Counselor came, and even the Surchatain. He seemed somewhat subdued on seeing Roman's condition, but said nothing remotely akin to an apology. He did not prohibit Deirdre from spending so much time ministering to him, however, even when her lessons lapsed.

After this incident, she began to think differently of her father. Before, she had always considered him unreachably wise, beyond her in judgment. But her child's sense of justice was offended that he had punished Roman so severely for her disobedience—after Roman had saved her by sacrificing himself, yet! She could have forgiven her father readily if he had only admitted the possibility of error. But such a confession never came.

The Counselor came often to see Roman, although he never stayed more than a moment. He had pressing business, of course. But Deirdre stayed. She relayed all the palace gossip to him ("I don't want to hear any of that," he would nobly insist, then eye her expectantly until she told him anyway); she brought him a book he had requested from the Surchatain's library; she played board games with him. She brought soap and water for him to bathe and shave, and helped change his bandages. She even brought his meals and took away the dishes.

After a fortnight, he was suddenly much stronger. He got up to begin stretching and loosening his stiff muscles. When Deirdre peeked into the infirmary one day and saw his bed empty, she went running in alarm to the physician. "It is well, all is well," he reassured her as she tried to tell him Roman was gone. "He only went to the service in the chapel. He'll be back soon."

Deirdre said nothing of it when Roman returned to the infirmary, but she thought it a little silly that a grown man—a soldier yet—made such a point to attend services. Her father allowed them because they had been requested, but he had disdainfully remarked that only old women bothered with such things. So why did Roman go? She wondered about it, but was not interested enough to investigate.

✥6✥

Spring came early that year, and the first scent of it made Roman restless to get out. And Deirdre was sick of the infirmary. Then the news came that this was the week of the Fair.

Twice a year, in the spring and the autumn, merchants from all over the Continent and beyond the Sea gathered in the port city of Hycliff to show off their finest merchandise. Since it was only a few hours' ride from Westford, the Surchatain gave Deirdre permission to go for one day and an allowance to spend. Roman readily agreed to go, and the physician gave him leave to ride. . . .

✤

Deirdre was up at dawn, ready to go. Roman was still rather weak and winced as he mounted the Bay Hunter. But, to her relief, he emphatically rejected any suggestion that he was unfit for the excursion. They rode out of the gates at a good stiff gallop.

By the time they arrived at Hycliff, the Fair had consumed the city. The merchants—hundreds of them—had raised their booths in the grassy fields just north of the city proper. The booths were open-sided structures with thatched roofs in which the sellers displayed their goods. Some of the booths were no larger than stalls; others were the size of Deirdre's sleeping room. It was truly said that anything that could be had for money could be found at the Fair.

Deirdre and Roman left their horses grazing under the eye of an errand boy and turned in hesitant wonder to the fields crowded with booths. Pausing at the edge of the com-motion, they watched as buyers haggled over prices, sellers called to passersby to stop and look, and merchants argued loudly over the placement of booths next to their own. It was a riotous scene.

Deirdre glanced excitedly up at Roman, and he grinned and pointed ahead. A minstrel was strumming his lute and singing straight at Deirdre: "Come join the Fair! Come join the fun! And buy! Buy! Buy!"

They stepped into the field. Deirdre quickly located booths of jewelry and expensive cloth goods. She fingered a pile of rich brown leather. "This would make a nice dress coat for you," she said, casting a sidelong look at the simple deerskin shortcoat he wore.

He glanced at the leather, saying, "It is kind of you to think of me, Chataine, but I don't need a dress coat. My uni-form suffices."

"Oh, but you do!" she insisted, comparing grains. "You must have it for festive occasions." He began a protest, but her mind was fixed. "Nanna keeps insisting I must learn to sew. I'll let her teach me so I can sew it for you." Roman shut his mouth and inclined his head.

She turned to the merchant at her elbow to ask, "How much of it do I need for a soldier's dress coat?" Roman looked away as if embarrassed.

"We sell it by the hide, Chataine," answered the merchant. "At six royals a hide—"

Roman looked back, coldly observing, "That is a high price for leather."

"But this is the finest, from islands across the Sea," the trader protested.

Roman ran his hand over a hide, noting the tanner's imprint. "This is from Ooster."

"And Ooster sends us fine leather also!" he agreed. "But since your pretty mistress wishes it so, I will give it to her for four royals a hide."

"Taken!" Deirdre exclaimed, paying him out of her father's purse. Leaving the booth, she asked Roman, "Don't you like it?"

"Yes, Chataine, of course—and I appreciate your generosity, only . . . it is so much to spend, and I'm not accustomed to such luxuries," he fumbled to explain.

"Nonsense," she said firmly, choosing to ignore that his discomfort was real. She began to look around for something he might really want, however.

They stopped to watch a puppet show, then ate their fill in booths of cheeses, sausages, and pies. Roman stopped to gaze at a booth of shining weapons, and Deirdre urged him to select something. "I noticed you broke your bowstring last time you practiced," she goaded him.

"That's true." He smiled a little shyly, then she watched with admiration as he expertly tested the strength and flexibility of several longbows before choosing one. It made her feel good to buy this for him.

Following that, they were off to examine booths of ornate saddlery, tapestries, metal wares, and tools. One booth they passed caught at her heart like an old friend. There, lining shelves and shelves, were dainty little dolls that winked and smiled. She longed to look, but—she glanced at Roman self-consciously—surely she was too old for dolls. But Roman pretended to be looking elsewhere. So she quickly went in and scanned the rows, then bought herself a new friend. Roman joined her outside the booth, and never once questioned her or mentioned it.

Even more intriguing than the booths were the crowds. Deirdre had never seen so many different kinds of people at once. Lords and ladies brushed shoulders with peasants, soldiers, merchants, seamen—Deirdre stared so much, some people stared back. She stayed close to Roman's side.

As they stepped from a booth of perfumes and spices, their attention was drawn by a loud, angry voice and derisive laughter attending it. The voice belonged to a sharp-eyed man dressed in a robe like a holy man. Catching sight of Roman's uniform, he pointed a bony finger at his face and demanded, "Repent, sinner, or burn forever in hell!"

Roman quietly replied, "I have repented. I am a follower of the Way." He gestured Deirdre forward and began to walk away.

Behind him, the man shouted, "Liar! You are a soldier—a murdering, blood-loving soldier!"

Roman stiffened, then turned around. "Yes, I am a soldier. But I am also a believer. I do not kill for lust—I do not murder. I do not extort money, nor rob. I perform my duty as it is required of me, and I follow our Lord in all that He commanded."

"No soldier can be a follower. It is a profession for the damned!"

Roman's face was flint and his eyes sparking. "Do you know the Scriptures?"

"Certainly!"

"When soldiers came to be baptized of John, he did not require them to leave off soldiering. And our Lord, when the centurion in a foreign army asked Him to speak a word and heal his servant, proclaimed the soldier's faith the greatest He had ever seen. Were these damned?" Roman demanded. A listening crowd had gathered by this time.

Roman's accuser countered, "You cite Scripture to cover your own blackness!"

"Are you God, to judge the heart?" Roman shot back.

"Well said!" someone commented. Inflamed, the holy man let fly a new barrage of declarations spiced with invectives. Roman saw the uselessness of continuing the argument and turned his back to walk away. At his side, Deirdre looked up at him in new respect.

But the holy man followed with his torrent of accusation. Roman turned once more and said, "Leave me alone."

"Ah ha! You cannot endure the holy fire of righteousness at your heels! You flee from the truth!" he shouted.

Roman rolled his eyes and took Deirdre's arm to walk away quickly. But still their harasser followed with his abuse. Not only was he souring their expedition, his diatribe against the Surchatain's soldiers was drawing a lot of attention. Roman looked around in sudden alarm. Too many people were looking at Deirdre, realizing who she was.

Roman turned and grabbed the holy man by his skinny neck. "You have pushed this blood-loving soldier beyond endurance. If you continue to molest me, I will satisfy my lust by wringing your righteous neck. Shouldn't you be off now?"

He released the man, who stood courageously facing his martyrdom. But when Roman convincingly drew his sword, the holy man chose to meet his Maker another day and scurried off, taking with him a fresh tale of persecution by wicked soldiers. Sword still drawn, Roman eyed the crowd with hard eyes and they quickly dispersed.

He paused a moment to regain his usual air and resheath his sword, then looked down at his charge. "Would you like to see the livestock now?" he inquired. She smiled and nodded.

It was late afternoon when Roman began to show his

fatigue. Deirdre was so tired that she could hardly hold on to everything she had bought (although Roman was carrying most of it). They trudged back to the remote field where their horses had been left grazing.

As they passed the last booth, she turned to him to comment about something, but stopped in mid-sentence as she saw a silver-haired man raising a knife at Roman's back. The expression on her face caused him to wheel, scattering merchandise, and he caught the man's hand as it plummeted. Roman threw Stase to the ground but was pulled down with him. "Run!" he rasped. "To the horses! *Now!*"

She could not. She was paralyzed as she watched them wrestle. The assassin gained the advantage and raised his dagger again for the kill. Roman stayed his hand for a moment, but weak and hurting, could not hold him off long. Deirdre screamed.

The dagger came down. Then it stopped in midair. Stase froze in a crouch, staring at Roman. When Stase slumped forward, she saw the shaft of an arrow protruding from his back.

Roman pushed the dead man away, and Deirdre rushed to his side. At that instant a robed figure came running from a booth toward them. It was the Counselor: "I heard you scream, Chataine—" he broke off as he saw the assassin sprawled on the ground. "What—is that Stase?"

"Yes—he tried to kill Roman. Counselor, we must get him back to the physician straightway. He may be hurt," Deirdre gasped, hands on her guardian. Roman, flat on his back, shook his head but still couldn't get his breath.

"Certainly. My carriage is here. We will return in it . . . your boy can ride your horses back." He paused. "You should not have killed him, Roman. Now we'll never know who hired him."

"I didn't," Roman panted.

"No? Who did?" the Counselor frowned.

Roman shook his head, struggling up. Deirdre answered, "I didn't see who it was."

"Really," Eudymon mused, then left to summon his carriage.

A merchant rushed past him to look over Roman and Deirdre and the dead assassin, giving a low whistle. "Good shot! Who'd have thought a fellow like that could handle a bow? You all right, sonny?"

"Who was it? Who shot him? Did you see?" grilled Deirdre.

"Sure, didn't he tell you?" The merchant looked surprised. "The High Lord's Counselor shot him. Saw them fighting, grabbed a bow, and let one fly. Perfect shot."

When the merchant returned to his booth, Roman cautioned her, "Deirdre, don't say anything to the Counselor about this. And don't tell anyone that he shot Stase." He began picking up her purchases from where they had landed here and there.

"But shouldn't Father know?" she asked.

"I'll speak to him," Roman replied. So, difficult as it was, she held her tongue.

The long, silent ride to the palace was somewhat strained. At every bump and jolt of the carriage, Deirdre looked anxiously at Roman. "I'm not hurt, Chataine. Only winded. Warding you is quite a challenge," he smiled. She returned a little smile to him, rubbing her hands nervously. The Counselor was quiet.

When they arrived at the palace Deirdre took charge of Roman, insisting, "You must see the physician."

"I'll go to the infirmary right away, Chataine. You must take all these things you bought and show them to your nursemaid." Deirdre thought that was a reasonable suggestion, so he called a boy to carry the goods for her.

"Nanna, look!" she called, bouncing into her chambers. The nursemaid came running as Deirdre laid out her treasures.

"Oh!" exclaimed Nanna. "How lovely!" She smiled and nodded, examining the doll, jewelry, trinkets, and cloth. But she picked up a corner of the leather with a questioning frown.

"That's for Roman," Deirdre said proudly. "I want to make him a shortcoat. You must teach me to sew now."

Nanna put the leather down slowly. "Chataine . . . that is so kind of you . . . but it is unseemly for you to make clothes for a soldier."

"Roman doesn't want it, and you don't want me to, but I want to!" Deirdre insisted, her face screwing up.

"Certainly, dear, certainly! I'll be happy to teach you!" Nanna hastily corrected herself.

Meanwhile, as he promised, Roman went to the infirmary and stuck his head in the door. The physician turned to him. "We have returned, and I am well," Roman said. The physician nodded.

Then Roman walked slowly to the Surchatain's chambers. He addressed the guard at the door: "I have a report for the Surchatain."

He was granted entrance. Karel pushed back from an ornate secretary and asked, "Yes, Roman, how did it go at the Fair?"

"Well enough, to a point, High Lord," Roman answered, bowing. Then he coughed. "We were attacked by the assassin as we returned to the horses."

Karel startled. "Deirdre?"

"She is unharmed. He attacked me. But, as we were fighting, someone shot him, and killed him."

"Yes?" Karel frowned. "Who?"

Roman bit his lip. "I didn't see who shot him. Nor did Deirdre. It could have been someone aiming at me."

"Indeed. So, we must assume that Stase's employer will have to hire someone else now. Blazes! We must find out who that is! Well, you are dismissed." Roman bowed and turned. "Er—Roman."

He looked back. "Surchatain?"

"Well done," Karel admitted. Roman bowed.

At dinner, Deirdre was pleased to find herself the center of attention as she recounted the incident to the guests at the table. She described how she had turned to see the assassin at Roman's back, and how they had struggled. "Then he brought up his knife, and poor Roman was so weakened— I thought he was good as dead," she sighed to a hushed audience. "Then from nowhere comes this arrow, and kills Stase!" A murmur went around the table and Roman sat watching her fixedly.

"A lucky arrow, to be sure," remarked Galapos, "but it could not have come from nowhere. Who shot it, sweetheart?"

"Well, that is the strangest thing!" she said, forgetting Roman's caution. "It was—" She caught Roman's intense gaze and paused. *He asked me not to tell,* she remembered. *But shouldn't I always tell the truth, Roman?* "It was—" *Why shouldn't I say the truth?*

Her conscience answered: *What do you wish to gain by saying all you know?*

"It was no one that we could see," she ended weakly. Galapos cocked an eyebrow at her. Roman breathed out and looked at his plate. The Counselor looked at Roman.

Oblivious to all this, Karel commented, "Yes, that is what Roman said," and proceeded to spear a chunk of venison. The guests sat quietly looking from face to face.

❖

Shortly after the Fair, Galapos gathered his men to return to the outpost on the border. New disturbances were continually arising, and the army required his coordination on the field.

Deirdre chanced upon Roman and Galapos conferring

one last time before his departure. They were standing alone on the palace steps, and neither saw her peeking out the great wooden doors which stood ajar. She could not prevent herself from eavesdropping. "Galapos"—Roman's voice was even lower than usual—"I wish more than anything to go with you and fight by your side, even just as your errand boy again."

Galapos shook his head slowly. "I have an errand boy. I do not need another." He paused. "I need a Second-in-command. I need a good fighter and a quick thinker. I need a man loyal to his Commander and his troops." Roman held his breath, and Galapos added grudgingly, "Christian or not, you're the best soldier under my command. When you have done with your babysitting, ride on out. The position will wait for you."

"Galapos—" Roman choked. He was actually beaming.

The Commander shook his head in mock disgust. "Don't go soft on me now, boy." His voice dropped to a whisper. "May your God ward you well until we ride together again." He departed.

Roman watched him go, his eyes frozen on the middle distance. Deirdre stood in shock. She had always assumed that he would rather be her guardian than anything else— that it was the greatest honor he could have. But now it was clear he would rather be with Galapos, off fighting in some bloody border skirmishes. Why? Didn't he have everything here? Wasn't he happy?

Then the inaudible voice of her conscience spoke again: *Why should he be happy? What has he received here but injury and abuse? And what have you yourself done for him but use him however it pleases you?*

That's not fair, she argued. *I cared for him in the infirmary.*

To console yourself for putting him there.

Roman turned up the steps and saw her. "Chataine—did you overhear—?"

100

"Roman," she rushed, struggling to control herself, "do you—are you happy taking care of me?"

"Happy, Chataine?" he asked as though the question had never occurred to him.

She struggled harder. "You would rather be with Galapos, wouldn't you?"

"I am a soldier under orders, Chataine. I have been given my assignment—my purpose—in guarding you. How useful could I be to Galapos if I deserted my assignment?"

It required seconds for her to understand what he meant. "But I thought you had volunteered to be my guardian. Didn't you want to be?"

He blinked and whispered, "No."

She let out a great sob and ran from the foyer. He called after her, but she ran harder, straight up the stairs to her chambers. She refused to stop even for Nanna, bolting her door and throwing herself on her downy bed to cry.

Ten minutes later she had stopped crying and started thinking. It was true. It was all true. Why should he care for her? What reason had she given him?

She got up from her bed and studied her reflection in the looking glass. Determination formed inside her. From this moment on he would have a reason. She would give him one. She would treat him with appreciation and respect, the way she saw him treat Galapos. Then perhaps he would feel the same about her as the Commander felt about him.

There was a knock on the outer door. Roman's voice said, "Chataine, please come out. I have been too harsh—"

She flung open the door and threw her arms around his middle. "I love you, Roman."

❖

Riding together that afternoon, she was so exuberant, he was smiling in response. When they dismounted to hike up a small hill, she took his hand in hers and swung it as they walked. Toying with his fingers, she marveled at how big and brown they were next to hers. And when they sat to rest at the top of the hill, she put her arms around his neck and kissed his cheek. She felt that here, in him, was her one true friend—someone to take care of her and stay with her regardless of how badly she acted at times. For the first time, she felt genuine gratitude toward him.

But he cautioned her gently, "I value your affection greatly, Chataine, but someone else seeing it might not understand. It would be best if you did not hold me or kiss me."

Deirdre's face burned as she released him. He didn't care for her—he was only doing his job, as he said. She would never be anything more to him than a chore. Tears filled her eyes and she jumped up to stumble to her horse.

As he helped her mount, he pleaded, "Chataine, I don't wish to make you cry, but you must understand that I could be put to death for such a small thing. We'll show our affection in other ways. Deirdre?" She nodded, sniffling.

And he made her see his affection in the way he was gentle and open with her. Even though she did not want to admit he might be right, by the time they arrived at the palace she was smiling at him again.

By dinner her high spirits had returned. She understood him better now—of course he cared. She could see that. They would always be friends. Roman, for his part, was marveling at the flexibility of her moods.

Her father spoke little until they had finished the beef pie. Then abruptly he said, "Roman, I heard a disturbing report today. It seems that you were seen embracing my daughter. Is this true?"

"Not entirely, High Lord," Roman replied calmly. "The Chataine put her arms around my neck and kissed me."

Before Karel could reply, Eudymon threw down his cloth and exclaimed, "High Lord, this is outrageous! This soldier must be punished!"

"I will decide that," the Surchatain said peevishly. "Deirdre, why did you do that?"

"I did it because I wanted to!" she flared. "He has taken care of me and saved my life, and I felt I owed him—something! Will you ever trust him? Or do you have spies watching us, too?"

"Enough!" Karel bellowed. After pausing to regain control, he said, "I merely wanted to give him the chance to deny it. You shall not be punished, Roman," with a glance at the Counselor. "And you, daughter—keep your hands to yourself!" Deirdre burned as a titter went around the table. Roman was not smiling.

She sat very still and straight until she was dismissed, then she went directly upstairs to her chambers, wishing she never had to come down again.

The next day she did not leave her rooms at all until Roman knocked on her door. "Chataine, come riding with me. It will be all right," he said from outside.

"No!" she shouted through the door. "I don't want anyone watching us."

"I have something to tell you about that. Open the door." When she did, he said, "It seems your father reprimanded the servant who gave him that report yesterday. I believe we'll not be watched as closely from now on—or at least not be reported to your father. We can still ride together."

She hesitated. "They were all laughing at me last night," she said glumly.

"And I am sure by today they have all forgotten why. Chataine," he said, "humiliation is a healthy draught if you drink it right down. It tends to keep your feet firmly on the ground." He added, lower, "That is a lesson I learned not long ago myself." She recalled his embarrassment over Nanna's gossip.

Relenting, she took his hand and began to walk with him

down the corridor, then remembered something. "Wait! Wait right here!" She rushed back into her rooms. When she came out again, she was carrying a bundle rolled up in her arms. Shyly, she held it out to him.

"What . . . ?" He unrolled it and then smiled broadly to see a nicely sewn leather shortcoat. He shed his old one to try it on. "It fits well," he noted, straightening his shoulders.

"Nanna helped me with it," she admitted. "Do you like it?"

"Very much," he smiled. "I thank you, Chataine." She grinned proudly and took his hand to swing it as they walked.

❖

A few days following, when she had finished her morning lessons, Deirdre wandered downstairs to look for something to do. Her first inclination was to find Roman, but little whispers were going around the palace about how much time she demanded of him. So she took her embroidery to the garden and began to work, but the sweet spring air, the scent of apple blossoms, and the sight of robins would not let her do that for long.

So she put the needlework aside and wandered back toward the kitchen. From within, she heard Roman's voice saying, "We'll need some bread . . . some fruit, too. We may be gone all day." A girl's voice answered him laughingly, and he said, "It will do us both good to get away from the palace for a few hours."

Deirdre wanted to feel jealous, but could only droop her head. He was not her slave. He had the right to be with other people and do other things once in a while.

As she started to go elsewhere he came out of the kitchen with his pack, a comely, black-haired serving girl behind him. They saw her and stopped in surprise. Seeing them standing together made Deirdre feel awkwardly out of place.

"Chataine, are you well this morning?" Roman asked in genuine concern. She nodded. "Good, because we are doing something different today. I think we have both seen enough of the fields and hills around Westford. I have secured permission to take you out farther today, to see more of your father's land."

"Me?" she exclaimed. "You are taking me?"

His brow furrowed in mild perplexity, and the serving girl glanced down. "Yes, you, if you wish to go. Do you want to go with me?"

"Yes, yes!" Deirdre cried.

"Well, come!" he gestured, then lifted his hand to wave goodbye to the girl.

He took Deirdre on a northeasterly route toward plains and gentle hills. They found a rough road that straightened to the east. Roman pointed out scurrying foxes and silken-antlered deer, and they laughed at magpies fighting over a berry bush. They passed the fuller's field and Deirdre wrinkled her nose at the odor. "Must they work so close to Westford?"

Roman laughed, "You had better be glad they do. They clean your clothes, and mine. We wouldn't be able to endure the smell of each other if they didn't do their smelly work."

"Chataines don't stink," she sniffed.

Roman laughed so hard he almost fell off the Bay Hunter. "Suppose we get an objective opinion on that. Let us ask Nanna, who changed your wraps when you were a baby," he proposed.

"Don't you dare!" she countermanded, then smiled a little sheepishly.

Farther out, they began to pass little cultivated fields. Peasant farmers paused in their planting to call greetings to Roman, and he always lifted his hand genially in response. Deirdre was amazed that he was so well known. "Does everyone love you?" she wondered aloud.

"No," he said. "Delmar, though, remembers when I spoke in defense of him against Lord Farquehart, who was trying to take his land. And Taine recalls when I helped him pull his prize cow out of a mud pit. Your actions come back to you. You reap what you sow." He said it with the confidence of having lived it.

They rode on, and talked, and ate from his pack, and Deirdre thought about how the light cast from just one person could color her world so intensely.

7

The spring of Deirdre's fourteenth year heralded major turning points in her life. She was disappointed not to be able to see the Fair that spring, as there were still concerns for her safety. But many of her favorite merchants brought their goods to the palace for a private showing. And as always, after her lessons, she and Roman rode out to explore the hills or the lake. Often, they brought crumbs for the birds, and Roman took her boating on the cool green water.

They returned many times to their favorite resting place on the edge of the lake under the willows. The lilies were in bloom now, drooping down to the water as if to drink. This quiet place was sheltered from the hot sun of summer as well as from curious eyes and ears. She and he could talk without fear of being overheard. Usually Roman would lie in the grass as she sat reading or sewing. Other times, when his head throbbed from the bludgeoning years before, he would prop his head on her knees and she would massage the pain down to a murmur.

They talked of many things. Once, when Roman had mentioned his mother in passing, she felt the itch of curiosity. . . .

❖

"Will you tell me more about your mother, Roman?" Deirdre asked delicately. He was sitting cross-legged; she was stretched out beside him. The riding skirts Nanna had been making for her as of late were simpler, straighter and split like trousers in order to withstand the rough treatment of an adolescent who rode horses and hiked for fun.

He shrugged, tossing a crumb to the ducks. "It's true that she was a prostitute at one time, but when she met my father she stopped seeing other men. She said he loved her too, but he never married her. Yet she was as faithful to him as if he had."

"Roman, I have always wondered . . . was he a believer?"

"No," he said emphatically.

"And Galapos is not, is he?"

"No."

"Then, how did you come to be one?" she asked, leaning on him with her elbows on his knees. He shifted back so that she was not quite so close.

His mind went back over the years. "You did not ask me if my mother was." Surprised, she began a rambling apology but he waved it off. "Of course not. Not a woman *like that*. But this is what happened: One afternoon some months before she died, I came home to find her crying on her knees. It frightened me—I thought she was hurt. But she looked up at me smiling so joyfully . . . she hugged me and said, 'Roman, all is well now. All is forgiven. God will take care of us.' I was really confused. I thought she was talking about the money my father was sending us to live on. But then I learned that a holy man had come and told her about God. She believed what he had to say. He used a different approach than the holy man we met at the Fair, by the way," he noted drily, and Deirdre grinned.

He continued, "That holy man came back to our hut often to teach my mother in the Way and pray with her. I always left when he came—I did not trust him. But then I would sneak back to listen to my mother's prayers. They were mostly about me. By the way, do you remember the minstrel who came to the palace, the man your father had flogged for his song?" She thought back, then nodded. "That was the holy man who had taught my mother. I'm sure of it."

"How strange! Did he teach you also, then?" she asked.

"No. I would have none of him. It wasn't until a year or so later, after I had come into the army. . . . I was cleaning Galapos's buckler and sword one day, listening to the soldiers talk about their battles. Blaine was telling everyone about another fellow who had taken a blow meant for him, when he was down and defenseless. It killed him, but by taking it he saved Blaine's life. So Blaine kept saying, 'He died for me. He died for me.' Those words—they pierced me to the bone. I remembered then something the holy man had told my mother. So I went and found Tychus, the holy man who holds services here, and asked him who had died for me. He told me the story of the Christ. I believed then, and was baptized."

He sat still, recollecting. She said, "What story is that?"

He looked at her in some surprise and said, "Many years ago, God sent His Son to earth as a man named Jesus, born of a virgin, to live among us and teach us about God. He performed many miracles, healing the sick and giving sight to the blind and even raising the dead. He taught us how to love God and love others, and called us to repentance—"

"What is that—'repentance'?"

"It means to admit that we have gone wrong, and to come back to God and obey Him. You repented to me, after I was whipped because of the horse," he reminded her. She winced and nodded. "Well, same thing, only it is God who forgives us. As I was saying, Jesus taught about God. But the religious leaders hated Him, for they were evil and He said so. Therefore, they condemned Him by trickery and executed Him by torture." Deirdre watched the hardness in his face. He knew what it was to be in pain.

"But it was only another part of the plan of God that His Son should die to pay the penalty for our crimes, to spare us. So on the third day God raised Him to life, never to die again. And someday all who believe in Him will join Him in Paradise," Roman said.

Deirdre regarded him as he gazed over the lake. It was a clearly incredible story, just as Rory had said. She did not wish to question Roman's intelligence for believing it, so she changed the subject: "Will you tell me . . . how your mother died?"

He blinked, then began slowly, "The winter following her conversion to Christ was very hard. Either the money my father sent was not enough or my mother was not very wise in spending it—she never turned away a beggar empty-handed—but we never had enough. I had no shoes—mother wrapped my feet in rags. I remember one time walking home with her when she looked down and started crying. I was leaving bloody footprints in the snow." He wiggled his toes in his boots.

"Well, she fell ill quite suddenly . . . in the morning I found her dead. I went to our neighbors. They came and buried her, then left me alone." He paused to keep his voice steady. "The next few weeks were hard, very hard. The money my father had been sending suddenly stopped coming. I didn't know where he was or how to reach him. I lived on what I could scavenge. . . . I pray you will never know the horrors of starvation, Chataine," he said in a gravelly voice. Her eyes began to water.

He inhaled. "So then, I went into town and stood at the

bakery window, and I determined to steal me some bread."

"They hang you for that!" Deirdre cried.

He shook his head. "What does that matter to a starving child? I cared only to die with a full stomach. But then a strange thing happened. Galapos came out of the bakery carrying a basket loaded with hot, fresh buns. He was swinging it so heedlessly that a bun fell out. He did not see it (so I thought), so I grabbed it up and ate it as I followed him. For someone who had just purchased such a quantity of bread, he was exceedingly careless with it. Another bun fell out of his basket, and another. I picked them up off the street where they fell and tucked them in my shirt. I kept after him all the way to the blacksmith's doing this.

"Then at the corner by the smith's he grabbed me as I picked up the last roll. He shook me hard: 'You little thief! If you are going to eat my bread, you are going to work for it!' That was when he took me into the army as his errand boy," Roman related.

"What luck!" she marveled. "What was the Commander doing at the bakery?"

"He had some swords on order at the smith's and had gone to get them himself. While he was waiting, he decided he was hungry, so he walked on down to the bakery. Inside, he saw me looking through the window and guessed what I was about to do. So he bought the buns and dropped them deliberately to lure me away from a hanging."

Deirdre sat pondering the union of fate and kindness that had favored Roman. "No wonder you love him so," she murmured. He nodded, faintly smiling.

❖

When they returned to the palace, Deirdre spotted the archers practicing on the grounds. "Roman!" she pulled on his arm, "teach me to use the bow!" It was the tomboy speaking again, whose abrupt appearance in place of the delicate Chataine dismayed Nanna to no end. The child had grown six inches overnight, creating a mild state of emergency with her wardrobe. Also, tiring of her waist-length hair, she had hacked it all off just above her shoulders with a purloined kitchen knife. Nanna had almost fainted on seeing chunks of golden hair scattered about the floor. Evening up the cut shortened it another few inches. Nanna tearfully gathered the strands and tied them with a ribbon, but Deirdre was quite pleased with the results.

Now, as Deirdre hung on his arm, Roman followed her gaze to the grounds and began to protest, "Chataine, that is not a fitting pastime for a young lady, and it is not so easy as it looks—"

She pouted, "You're ashamed to be seen teaching me."

"Certainly not!" he insisted, although he looked a little guilty. "Come then," he said, and led her to a weapons stall on the grounds.

He selected the lightest bow he could find and, taking his bow and quiver, escorted her to the target area. "Watch me first, Chataine; this is how it is done." He nocked an arrow to the bow, raised it to his face and released it smoothly. The arrow buried itself in the center of the target.

Deirdre picked up her bow eagerly. "Here—let me show you," he murmured, reaching around her to place her fingers and nock the arrow to her bow. Several soldiers turned to watch. "Now pull back, as hard as you can—hold tight!" She drew back with all her strength and the arrow fell limply to the ground. The soldiers snickered.

Ignoring them, Roman said, "You're not holding the bow correctly." He placed her fingers again. "Hold it higher," he instructed, pushing her arms up. She drew again, and the arrow covered half the distance to the target before falling. A few soldiers clapped encouragingly.

"This is hard!" she exclaimed.

"I told you it was. Have you had enough?" he asked.

"No!" she said. That elicited the full arched-brow–flattened-brow combination, and he moved the target up to where the arrow had fallen. He placed her hands on the bow again. She drew intently and released. The arrow hit the target before falling down. The soldiers cheered and clapped. "My arms are tired already!" she complained.

"It takes practice, day after day, to build up the strength in your arms. It's not something you can master at once," he observed.

"If I practice enough, will I get to be as good as you?"

He smiled. "Perhaps. If you practice." Determinedly, she nocked the arrow to the bow again.

❖

It was late in the spring when an unsettling request came to Karel. Tremaine, Surchatain of the neighboring state of Seleca, had a son he wanted Deirdre to meet. Would she come for a visit? Karel said she would.

On hearing of it, Roman was so upset that he protested to Surchatain Karel himself: "High Lord, it is much too dangerous. That is a two-day ride! If he wishes his son to meet her, have him come here. Your daughter's life is still in jeopardy."

But Karel was adamant. Tremaine was one of the most powerful rulers on the Continent. A marriage between the two families would end Karel's worries over the safety of his little country. He would certainly accommodate Tremaine at this time. "You are responsible for the Chataine's safety while traveling," he reminded Roman. "You were appointed to guard her on just these occasions—were you not?"

"Certainly, High Lord," Roman replied grimly.

"Then do so," Karel snapped.

"Surchatain." Roman bowed his head in acquiescence, then paused. "As I am responsible for her, I ask full freedom to arrange our travel as I think safest."

"Granted."

The Surchatain might have reconsidered had he known the guardian's plans. Roman had decided that he and Deirdre would leave quietly on horseback from the rear gate of the palace. No soldiers would accompany them to draw attention to them. They were to travel in disguise.

The morning of their departure, Roman brought some clothes up to Nanna. "Have her put these on."

Nanna stared in revulsion at the old peasant dress and shawl, stockings, and worn slippers he gave her. "Never!" she asserted.

"You put them on her, or I will," he said firmly. "And use this." He handed her a small pillow.

When dressed, Deirdre ran to the looking glass and laughed at her reflection. In the old clothes, with her hair hacked short, she could have been a real village girl. Nanna packed her good clothes in some old traveling bags, and Deirdre skipped downstairs to show herself off to Roman.

He, too, was in disguise. He wore the frayed breeches and open shirt of a peasant farmer, and an old wide-brimmed hat. They looked each other over. "Where is the pillow?" he asked.

"I don't know what it's for," she said, handing it to him.

He handed it back to her. "Tie it around your waist." Frowning, she began to obey. He bit his lip and stopped her. "Chataine . . . *underneath* your dress."

"Oh." She blushed at her own denseness. Going behind a curtain, she hiked up the thin cotton skirt and tied on the pillow as instructed. She emerged a pregnant peasant girl.

He regarded her, nodding, "We are husband and wife, traveling to Corona to find you a midwife." She giggled. He smiled, too, then his face clouded and he took her hands for a serious talk. She seemed to listen better when he held her hands.

"Chataine, I have great misgivings about this trip. I don't know if I can protect you adequately. You must promise that if we are attacked you will flee in the time I give you. You must not hang back for my sake, but ride home as hard as you can. Will you do that?"

"Roman . . . I couldn't leave you."

"Chataine, what good would it do for you to die? You will have made me a failure. Swear to me you'll ride."

She choked out, "I swear it."

"Then let's go."

Roman loaded up Lady Grey and the Bay Hunter, then they mounted and quietly rode out of the gate. They wound their way around to a well-traveled market road. Along the way, they met several fellow travelers who nodded or waved, and some smiled at Deirdre's big stomach.

She kept glancing at Roman. His disguise was certainly clever, but somehow unconvincing. He looked like no peasant she ever saw. What gave him away? Suddenly she knew. His attitude betrayed that his clothes were a lie. He rode too straight, too easily, and his eyes flashed keenness and purpose.

"Roman," she murmured, "you ride too straight for a peasant."

He cocked his head questioningly, then caught her meaning and slumped in the saddle a bit, pulling his hat down. But the alertness in his eyes still divulged itself from under the brim. She sighed. Some things just could not be hidden.

When they had passed the slow carts clogging the road, they spurred to an easy canter. Deirdre was grateful that this route was flatter and smoother than the road to Ooster—"Why didn't we take a carriage?" she asked suddenly.

Roman glanced at her. "They are too easy to waylay and too slow for escape. Besides, you don't need a carriage. You ride well enough to make the trip on horseback." Pleased, Deirdre proudly flicked the reins just as Roman did, knowing that he did not make empty compliments.

After several hours of unremarkable travel, they were slowed again by a cart blocking the road. It was driven by a fat, richly dressed merchant carrying cheap wares. "Well, hello there, fellow! And such a pretty little wife! Where be the two of you headed—eh?" He leaned out of his seat to address them.

"Corona," said Roman.

"Fine city, beautiful city, been there often myself. Why, they have the prettiest wh—" he coughed and glanced at Deirdre—"the finest wares of any city around. You going there for business?" He looked at their horses. "You got nothing to sell."

"We're going for a midwife," Roman replied, looking to maneuver around his cart.

"Oh, well, certainly! Say, you don't have to go all the way to Corona for one! I know a great little midwife who lives only a few miles from here. Just follow me and I'll take you to her."

"Thank you, but we are going to Corona," Roman answered him flatly.

"Well, sure you are, if you say so," agreed the man. Roman was directing his horse off the road to pass him when the merchant said, "Those are certainly fine-looking horses you got there. I'd give you a good sum for those horses."

"No," Roman refused. Deirdre thought he looked apprehensive.

"Well, as you say, certainly," the merchant responded brightly. Then, "Well, look, here's my turnoff! Good travel to you both!"

As soon as he was off the road Roman barked, "Ride!" and they spurred their horses to a run. At a fork in the road on the edge of the forest, he led her up one trail twenty strides. Then they circled back and hid in the trees.

"What—?" she began, but he gestured her down and pointed to the road. Seconds later she heard hoofs, then caught a glimpse of two armed riders thundering up the trail he and she had just been on. Then Roman and Deirdre quickly mounted again and galloped up the other fork. They ran the horses to a lather, until Roman felt it was safe to stop and rest.

"They won't chase us this far," he panted. "It's not worth that much to them."

"Who are they? What did they want?" She could hardly get the questions out fast enough.

"Renegade soldiers, of course. The merchant is in league with them. You don't think he could afford all those fine clothes by selling that junk in his cart, do you?" She was starting another question when he stopped her. "He's a lookout for them. He spots chickens—unarmed folk—determines their valuables, then alerts his friends. They split the profits." He wiped his mouth, scanning the forest.

"They wanted our horses?" she asked.

"Only thing of value we have."

They continued their travel until dusk, when they made camp in a tiny clearing in the forest. Roman would have preferred to spend the night in the outpost along the way, but that would have rendered their disguises useless. For safety's sake he did not build a fire, so Deirdre huddled close to him as they ate bread and dried beef from his pack.

Night in the forest was very black and cool. When she began shivering violently under her shawl, Roman unwrapped the blankets and made her a little bed beside him. As she continued to shiver, he put his arms around her. She snuggled up to him and dropped off to sleep.

She woke in the greyness of early dawn as he was building a small fire. They ate dry, crusty bread standing over the fire to shake off the chill of the morning fog. With the reassurance of daylight, Deirdre began to feel a great sense of adventure and cunning—regardless of what he said, she could not imagine any danger surpassing his abilities. She tied her pillow back in place as Roman saddled the horses, and they began the second day of their trip.

The cool of the morning carried into the day and the road was flat and fast. The ride would have been pleasant if it wasn't for Roman's constant wariness. He seemed particularly uneasy while they crossed the plain and rode through Falcon Pass, but relaxed somewhat once they were past the Fastnesses. They talked then, and he even sang a silly drinking song for her:

A man and his love had a terrible spat:
She scratched his face and he knocked her flat;
She spit at him and he threw her around;
She jumped from behind and he fell to the ground.
How sad to see such trouble as that
Between a man and his household cat.

Deirdre laughed. "I'll wager you learned that from Galapos."

"No," he admitted, "from my father."

"Shame on him for teaching a young child drinking songs!" she scolded.

"Oh, no," he laughed, "it wasn't until years later that—" He cut short, but Deirdre had caught his slip.

"Then you saw him again after your mother died?"

"Yes."

He gave her a warning look, so she only asked, "Did he give you the medallion?"

"Yes," he sighed. "Deirdre, please don't ask me any more about him." Momentarily satisfied by this new bit of information, she allowed him to ride unmolested.

❖

They entered Corona late that afternoon and blended into the city. Deirdre strained her neck staring down the narrow, dirty streets crowded with busy townspeople, bands of children, and sinister figures. The scene reminded her of the Fair, only so much more tawdry. They stopped at an inn to wash up and change into their good clothes, then slipped unobserved out a back way.

Shortly, they stood in front of the imposing gates of Tremaine's residence. A guard in a glittering tabard escorted them to the audience hall. Accustomed as she was to luxury, even Deirdre gaped at the splendor of this room.

At the far end stood an awesome golden throne resting on the backs of four golden lions, all facing outward. The throne was detailed in spiraling patterns of precious gems. The wide expanse of floor before it was completely covered in a brilliant mosaic of sapphire, jasper, obsidian, amber, amethyst, and more. Like a mural, it seemed to depict a story—she noted many bloody battle scenes and long rows of people in chains. There were beheadings and pictures of torture. Entranced, she followed the scenes until they ended in the center at a colossal representation of a man in a golden robe, holding a sword in one hand and the sun in the other.

"Supposedly, that is Tremaine," Roman said through her thoughts, nodding toward the mosaic. "The tenor of his rule is apparent."

Deirdre looked toward him, but her attention was distracted by the paneled walls, which extended up at shifting angles to golden chandeliers. Gazing up at the light from thousands of candles made Deirdre dizzy. Roman steadied her.

Moments later Tremaine himself appeared, wearing the golden mantle depicted in the mosaic. Tall and bearded, he walked in power, and Deirdre trembled as he approached them. He stopped and looked down on her with eyes of seizing intensity. "Chataine Deirdre, I am so pleased to greet you at last. You are welcome in the palace of Corona." He had a curiously dry voice, which made every word sound like an irony.

Roman squeezed her arm gently, and she came to life. "Thank you, Surchatain." She bowed unsteadily.

Tremaine turned his intimidating eyes to Roman. "And this?"

"This is my guardian, Roman." She began to breathe with some regularity now.

"Karel is a cautious man," Tremaine observed as Roman bowed.

"He deemed it necessary, High Lord," Roman answered.

"Come, then. Dinner awaits you." Tremaine turned in a swirl of gold and led them to a dining hall that mirrored the luxury of the audience hall—literally. For this hall was paneled with seamless sheets of glass on silver that reflected the entire room more truly than any looking glass Deirdre had ever seen. Staring into the endless reflection of mirror in mirror caused her vertigo to return, but Roman guided her to the chair Tremaine indicated near his own.

As they sat, the Surchatain introduced his son Rollet—a tall, proud eighteen-year-old. He looked Deirdre over, then nodded curtly to his father.

Tremaine then condescended to smile on her. "Deirdre, this is a long-awaited pleasure for me. Your father and I have been discussing your future since almost the day you were born."

"I know Father respects you very much," Deirdre said carefully—Rollet was irritating her with his cool, haughty stare—"but it is law in Lystra that I choose my own husband."

"Truly?" Tremaine looked genuinely surprised. "How interesting. I shall endeavor to make a good showing, then. You know, an alliance between us would greatly profit Lystra."

"There are other provinces which claim that also. My uncle Corneus wants me to marry his son Jason," Deirdre said aloofly. Her first line of defense in any threatening situation was to try to take control.

"Indeed?" Tremaine raised a finger toward a servant

120

behind him to order more herbed bread from the kitchen. Deirdre felt pressure from Roman's knee, and she turned to see a discreet, cautioning look in his eyes. She understood at once that she was talking too much.

When Tremaine turned back around Deirdre asked, "Surchatain, will you explain the pictures in the audience hall?"

He smiled. "That is the history of my conquest of this region and the expansion of its borders. When I assumed the throne, Seleca was smaller than Lystra, our northern border being the Fastnesses. But through a series of campaigns I extended our region to three times its former size. Yet, we are still landlocked, and the Passage is not wide enough for large vessels until well into Lystra. . . . So you see, we are serious about an alliance." He raised his eyes, and Deirdre was shaken by their intensity.

"What—do the sword and the sun mean?" she stammered.

He leaned back, smiling again, though he did not relieve her of his gaze. "The sword represents my power. The sun represents my domain. Both are invincible."

Servants brought in savory dishes of delicate roast dove, but Deirdre was too distracted to pay much mind to the food. Tremaine then turned to Roman. "So you are her guardian. That must be a shamefully pleasant task."

"At times, Surchatain," Roman answered.

"Or does it bore you—to wait at the door of fests while your charge dances?"

"She is only fourteen, High Lord. Her first fest is not for two years yet."

"Ah, yes, I had forgotten," Tremaine breathed, though obviously he had not. "You look mature for your age, Deirdre—like a Surchataine already. Don't you agree, Rollet?"

"She has promise," he conceded. "But her hair wants growing." Then, as bowls of creamy custard were set before them, Rollet suggested, "When you finish your dessert, I will take you to see the Sorcerer's Rooms, Deirdre."

She glanced in panic toward Roman, who said, "It would be rude of us to leave the High Lord, Chataine."

"Not you. Her," Rollet articulated.

"Forgive me, Chatain," Roman said without a tinge of remorse, "but I have been charged with her safekeeping at all times."

Rollet opened his mouth but Tremaine interposed, "Of course. We certainly do not wish you to forsake your charge. Rollet, I'm sure Roman would find the Rooms most interesting also." He gave Rollet a look that Deirdre could not interpret, but Rollet suddenly understood. It was something that made him smile. Tremaine stood, signaling the end of the meal.

The others stood, and Rollet said, "Come with me, then." He held out his arm to Deirdre. Roman moved to her side. Then Rollet took a torch and led them to a back room of the palace. He walked right up to the far wall of the room and pressed a panel. The wall opened, and Deirdre saw a narrow flight of crude stone steps. Roman took her arm.

Rollet turned in the eerie glare of torchlight and whispered, "Climb them carefully." He began to ascend them first; behind him, Deirdre gathered her skirts nervously and proceeded. Roman followed her closely. They were treacherous steps, steep and slippery, but he kept a steadying hand at her back.

At the top was a rough-hewn wooden door. Rollet produced a silver key from his coat and unlocked it. "This is the blue room," he whispered. He pushed open the door, and Deirdre felt a waft of cold air. They entered a small room completely of blue—a blue so intense it seemed to vibrate the air.

Deirdre stood rooted in a confusion of senses. The light in this room did not come from Rollet's torch—it was a blue light, and colored everything vivid blue. The room had two doors—the one through which they had entered and another opposite it—but no windows. It was empty except for a small table and chair. The table held a thick, old book and a statuette of a naked man with the head and feet of a goat.

Deirdre looked up at Roman. His skin was deep blue and his hair was blue-black. His brown soldier's uniform had also taken on varying shades of blue. He was staring at the statuette.

"Blue is the color of power from knowledge of secrets locked deep in the heart," whispered Rollet, his face as blue as Roman's. "Blue is the key." He held up the key, and it shone a bright silver in the blue light. It alone kept its natural color in the room.

Rollet took her arm and guided her to the opposite door. "This is the green room," he whispered, taking the handle, but she felt something amiss and turned back to Roman.

He was standing in the same spot, motionless as the statuette which held his eyes. "Roman," she said. He did not move. "Roman!"

His head snapped toward her as if he were coming out of a trance. "What—? Chataine." He blinked and shook his head, hastening to her side.

Rollet appeared irritated with the disturbance. "The green room!" he insisted, opening the door. The air that wafted from it was heavy and perfumed. Inside, it vibrated with green—lush, rich green. The room had in it a couch, on which was placed the nude figurine of a woman.

Deirdre felt Roman suddenly step away from her side. He was drawing deep breaths, keeping his eyes off the figurine. She gaped at him, wondering what could be troubling him so. He looked disturbed and anxious, yet his eyes were drawn irresistibly to the couch.

"Green is the color of desire," Rollet whispered, "and of all sweet things of the earth."

123

Deirdre looked again with real concern at Roman. The agony of resisting forbidden desires was painted vividly in his face. He looked at her, then shook his head, anxiously muttering, "No, no." He was glancing repeatedly at the figurine as if engaged in a blind struggle with it, the effort of which made him sweat. He tore his eyes away and breathed out one word. Suddenly she felt him relax. He released his breath, nodding to her in reassurance.

But Rollet had his hand on the next door. "This is the red room," he chuckled. He swung open the door, and Deirdre felt herself immersed in hot, sticky air. This room had in it a table which held a sword and shield. "Red is the color of blood, of war, and of death," said Rollet.

"Oh, no!" Deirdre wheeled to Roman. He looked as if he were bathed in blood—trembling and sweating, clenching and unclenching his fists. She could almost see the violence raging inside him. "Roman!" She grasped his arms and felt his tense muscles hard as iron.

He wrenched free of her grasp and staggered backward, covering his eyes as if to gouge them out. Whatever horrors he was seeing were invisible to her. His lips moved, forming one word over and over again. Then all at once he calmed and lowered his hands. Control had been restored to him. Although drained, he nodded at her.

"Rollet!" She spun on him angrily. "I don't know what is happening, but I don't like it. You get us out of here!"

He restrained his satisfaction. "There is only one room left. We can go through it, or return the way we came. Do you wish him to repeat what he has just been through?"

She turned her eyes to Roman's blood-red face. He looked numbly at her. "No," she said.

Rollet put his hand to the last door. "This," he said slowly, savoring the moment, "is the black room." He pushed the door open into a black, yawning abyss. His torch died suddenly. The room was utterly black and still—yet, she sensed something building from its corners. Rollet's voice came in an echo: "Black is the color of hell."

With a mighty rush something gathered and threw itself full force on Roman. The odor of it made her gag. She felt Roman thrown back and heard him choking. She opened her mouth to scream, but heard him cry, "Jesus!"

At once Rollet's torch blazed fiercely to light. He dropped it. The outer door flung itself open and pure white light poured in. Deirdre stood blinking in the middle of a small, plain, unremarkable room.

She bent beside Roman, who was raising himself from a sprawl on the floor. "Roman, are you hurt?" He shook his head. Rollet looked dazed.

Roman got himself up and took Deirdre's hand. As they exited the room into a normal sitting room, Tremaine turned to greet them. He startled to see Roman leading them out.

Deirdre, forgetting her fear of Tremaine, furiously rebuked him, "Your Sorcerer's Rooms are not interesting! They're horrible! Who are you to abuse your guests this way?"

He seemed taken aback. "I am sorry to cause you unpleasantness, Chataine—you should not have been affected by the little spells they contain. They are harmful only to persons with a certain weakness."

"What weakness?" She could not imagine a flaw in Roman that she did not share.

"Those who claim God," he said evenly.

Deirdre stared at him in silent astonishment, hardly able to comprehend the import of what he said. Roman replied, "You have no power over us but what God allows, to serve His own purposes."

Tremaine narrowed his eyes. "You tread dangerously, young man."

Deirdre said stonily, "I have had enough entertainment for the evening, High Lord. I wish to retire."

He inclined his head. "I shall summon a servant to show you to your chambers, Chataine. My profound apologies that your guardian suffered ill in our little rooms," he uttered.

They were taken to a stately suite where Roman made clear his intentions to occupy the small room adjoining hers. Before retiring, he searched carefully around her room, examining in particular the carved paneling on the walls.

He pushed and poked and knocked all around them, then stood back, shaking his head. "This is not to my liking at all," he muttered. "Bolt your outer door, but not the one between us." With a last look around, he withdrew to his room.

She lay down to sleep, but could not relax for fear of the darkness of the room—how much it was like the black room! And the grate in the fireplace was empty. Eventually, Deirdre closed her eyes to uneasy dreams.

Later in the night, she roused half awake. In the darkness, the wall of her room seemed to be moving. Then she heard muffled footsteps and sensed someone coming toward her. In an instant she was fully awake, screaming, "Roman!"

The intruder lunged for her but was too late to stifle her scream. The door to Roman's room banged open to admit him. When he paused in the darkness, two forms materialized from nowhere to cover his face with foul-smelling rags. He recoiled blindly, but they needed to wait only a moment before he collapsed to the floor.

A flickering light appeared, revealing an opening in the wall. Tremaine stepped into the room, carrying a torch and swearing at his guards. He glanced down at Roman crumpled on the floor and muttered, "That man is a thorn in my eye!"

"What did you do to him?" Deirdre cried.

"Oh, it's only something my alchemist discovered quite by accident. He will come around wholly in the morning. Except for a slight headache." Tremaine brightened. "No harm done, Chataine. I only required a private conversation with you. Since your pet here gave me no opportunity for that, I had to put him to sleep for a while—which *should* have been done first!" he added, glowering back at his guards.

"What do you want from me?" she gasped.

"It is very simple. I decided it would be wasteful—and unnecessary after all—to kill you. Your father's province will join our alliance in the end, regardless. But you have the power to decide if it shall be done forcibly, with much blood-shed, or peaceably."

"Me?" she choked.

"You. And you shall have a choice about it. If Rollet does not please you, you may marry Merce's son Caspar or Savin's son Artemeus. Our purpose for your country will be accomplished whichever of these three you choose. Your province will be left intact, though of course it will no longer be—independent. And no lives shall be wasted," Tremaine said.

"What if I want none of them?" Deirdre asked quietly.

"Then you will leave us no choice but to attack. It is true that your father has a well-trained army, and Galapos is a fox, but we have five times his numbers. We will crush you. Everyone you know will die. Beginning with him," he gestured to Roman's form on the floor. Deirdre looked down at him.

"I merely desired to give you something to think about before your betrothal fest, Chataine. The lives of many are in your hands."

He turned to leave. "Oh, yes," he said, noting Roman, and gave orders. Roman was dragged back to his bed, and the door between them bolted.

"He will awaken in the morning, and should recall nothing of this incident. If he does, you will tell him he merely suffered nightmares. That is all. After the dreams that potion will give him, he will believe you. For if you tell him—or anyone—what has passed between us tonight, you will start the slaughter early. Should your father move against me, I will spare no one. Not even you. And if you are wondering, there are others in this alliance I have not mentioned. If your father plans a strike, we will know. Goodnight, Cha-taine." Tremaine and his guards exited through the passage, and the panel slid smoothly shut. Blackness engulfed the room once again.

8

Before daybreak there was a rustle and groan from Roman's room. Instantly he was pounding on her door. . . .

✥

"Chataine, are you in there? Chataine!"

She hastily opened the door before he could break it down. "Are you all right? What happened? Why did you bolt the door?" he demanded.

"Nothing happened, Roman," she said uneasily, lighting an oil lamp on the table. In her nervousness, she had to strike the flint several times before it would spark right. "I bolted the door because I became frightened." She cursed herself for not noticing they had bolted it.

He sat on the bed, holding his head, trying to gather his thoughts. "I heard you scream. I opened the door, and— and—"

"No," she said. "You must have been having a nightmare."

He studied her face, and she looked away. "If you were frightened, why didn't you come to me? Why did you shut me out?"

She stammered, "I—was not thinking clearly. I—"

"You are lying, Deirdre," he said softly, then anxiously, "What happened? I remember now—I was attacked—they put something on my face, and I couldn't breathe. . . . Deirdre, what did Tremaine do to you?"

"I don't know what you mean!" she cried.

He grabbed her shoulders. "Deirdre, don't play games with me now! You're in danger here. You must tell me what happened!"

She sat on the bed and began to cry. He held her tightly and said, "Listen to me. If you don't trust me, I can't protect you. I may unwittingly play right into his hands. You are not strong enough to carry this burden by yourself. Let me call on my resources to help you. Let me be your defense!"

She broke. In a hushed voice, she told him everything the Surchatain had said. When she finished, he sat in silence for a minute. Then he said, "We'll let Tremaine think his threats have kept you quiet. He is right about one thing: If your father knew, he would be likely to charge unthinkingly, and that would be fatal. You have told me; that's enough. Don't tell anyone else."

"Yes, Roman," she said, relieved.

"Go back to sleep now. We're not supposed to be up for hours yet." He rose with a wobble and returned to his room. She soon dropped off and slept as one of the dead.

Late in the morning, she awoke with a start from a dream in which she had been suffocating in thick blackness. After a moment of coming to, she realized the room, now dimly lit, was rank and stuffy. With a wary glance at the paneling she went to the window.

The heavy draperies refused to open at first, so she gave them a mighty yank. As they parted, she stifled a scream to

see the ornate iron grill which barred the window fast. It was
wrought in the shapes of tortured faces.

Deirdre closed the draperies and dressed with remarkable speed for shaking so. She opened Roman's door, but
he was gone. Whimpering, she flung open the corridor door
to see him standing outside, waiting. She threw her arms
around his middle and he squeezed her shoulders. "How
long have you been standing here?" she whispered.

"Not long, Chataine. But I would not go down without
you," he murmured, blinking heavily.

With a grateful sigh, she laced her arm through his to
start downstairs. "Does your head hurt?"

"Not at all," he winced.

On the way down, she observed artwork hung on the
paneled walls, which she had not noticed the night before.
Tremaine had not only needleworks, but paintings, many
rare and costly. He had greater wealth than she had ever
seen or even imagined. The thought crossed her mind, *I
wonder why Roman's God can't do all that for him*. She
also considered that if she accepted Rollet, she would share
in this wealth. But this prospect could not make itself appeal-
ing to her after what she had seen here.

When they appeared in the mirrored hall for breakfast,
Tremaine turned from the table to greet them. He was cour-
teous and casual—the perfect host. "Did you sleep well,
Chataine?" he inquired.

"Not really, High Lord. I had nightmares," she said stiffly.

"Ah, that is a pity! Your guardian here said the same thing.
Faithful servant that he is, he would not be persuaded to
come down until you had awakened. Well, now—be seated,"
Tremaine invited, extending his arm.

Roman seated Deirdre and took the chair beside her,
unconsciously stroking his brow. "Your head does hurt," she
whispered. He looked at her with one eye. "Well, we won't
go riding today," she said firmly, then turned to Tremaine.

"May we have a cold cloth for his head?"

"Of course, Chataine." While they ate, Tremaine had a servant bring the requested compress. "I should have known better than to put you in that suite," Tremaine noted regretfully. "It is haunted by the ghost of a soldier who tried to betray me. He hid in the lesser room, waiting to escape. But of course, we found him and severed his head on the spot. So his spirit lingers, seeking revenge on anyone who sleeps in that room."

"He is satisfied now, High Lord," muttered Roman, quaffing from the goblet before him.

Tremaine beamed. "Is he now? Well. Come to the lower pasture, Chataine; we have captured some wild horses I wish you to see. Perhaps your guardian will show us how well he can ride."

Deirdre opened her mouth to decline but Roman was already standing: "Certainly, High Lord."

Before they had reached the door, Rollet hurried up. "High Lord—" he drew his father aside without a word or glance at Deirdre. They talked in whispers a moment, then Rollet disappeared and Tremaine turned to Deirdre. "Chataine, something most inconvenient has come up. Some northern villages have gathered soldiers and revolted, headed by an insolent fellow who requires my personal correction. Rollet will be accompanying me. I cannot say how long we will be gone, but you are welcome to remain here in our absence."

"No thank you, High Lord," Deirdre said quickly. "We must return to Westford. I think that our purpose in coming has been met."

"It has," Tremaine said with a tight smile.

"Then we'll take our leave." Roman was as relieved to hear it as she was to say it.

"As you wish. Farewell, Chataine." Tremaine nodded.

"High Lord," she bowed in response. He directed his eyes to Roman a moment, but turned on his heel without a word.

Roman and Deirdre were out of the palace within a quarter hour. "Whew!" she breathed as they galloped up the thoroughfare. "I feel as though I'm coming out of a bad dream!"

"I also," Roman said with a trace more intensity than usual.

"But what's to be done about his threat? I will not marry into that alliance!" she declared.

He shook his head. "I don't know what to tell you. I'll discuss it with the Counselor, first. He will know best how to advise us and your father."

"Are you sure you should tell him?" she asked doubtfully. "Yes."

They stopped at the same inn as before to don their disguises. Deirdre thought it unnecessary, since Tremaine was no longer trying to kill her, but Roman overruled.

After they had changed, he led her out through the dining room of the inn. It was crowded even at this hour, and a number of patrons were already drunk. One man they passed made an obscene comment to Deirdre. Roman shot him a black look but did not stop.

The fellow's drinking companion, however, took umbrage at the remark. Reeling up, he swung his fist at his partner's face. He was way off mark and came instead within inches of Deirdre's nose. Roman intercepted his arm and flung him against the wall. His fellow jumped Roman from behind, and suddenly everyone was fighting.

Deirdre looked around in astonishment. She had never been in the middle of a drunken brawl before. Men were punching, kicking, and gouging each other, overturning benches and crashing onto tables. When a fellow close to her was smashed over the head with a bottle, a little wine spilled on her old peasant dress. She absently wiped it with a cloth as she watched the melee.

Roman kept trying to get close enough to shove her out the door, but was too deeply embroiled in the fracas.

133

Everyone seemed to want a shot at him. As soon as he knocked one man away another would jump on his back or swipe at his legs.

Then Deirdre realized he was in trouble. They were ganging up on him. She had to help. Looking around, she spotted an iron skillet hanging on the wall. She ran over and took it down. Gripping it with both hands, she started swinging it at everyone around Roman. Wham! Blap! "Ow, ow!" "Hey, girl—what?"

The instant they began falling away Roman caught Deirdre's hand and rushed her outside. They leaped to their horses and spurred hard away. When they had reached a small hill safely out of Corona, they paused to catch their breath.

"I had no idea you were so dangerous," panted Roman. He gingerly touched his bleeding lip. "Thank you, Chataine." She beamed at him. Then he said, "Fix your stomach."

"My stomach?" She looked down. Her pillow was sitting crazily off to one side. "Oh," she laughed, and straightened it. They smiled at each other.

Then Roman's face darkened and he said, "We must get back to Westford without delay." She nodded, and they kicked their horses to a gallop. They spoke little on the return trip, intent on making good time, and reached the palace by afternoon of the second day.

Before she even had a chance to bathe or change, Deirdre was immediately summoned to the Surchatain's chambers. As she entered and bowed, he looked up in displeasure and demanded, "Why are you back so soon?"

Startled, she answered, "Ah—Tremaine and Rollet were called away by a revolt along their northern border, Father. I saw no reason to stay, with them gone."

"Well . . ." he looked irritated, then softened his tone to ask, "and how do you like Rollet?"

She hesitated. "I don't, Father, not at all. Nor Tremaine— he scares me."

"Well, he is a powerful man, and you are just a little girl. I'm sure he would awe you at first," Karel said.

"It isn't that," she insisted. "He is cruel and—devious."

"Is he now?" Karel raised his eyebrows as if she had just insulted him personally. "You are hardly competent to make these judgments, daughter. Perhaps I should explain our situation to you: We are a small country surrounded by others who would swallow us whole if they could. Now, that means it is crucial to our survival whom you marry and thus form an alliance with. Tremaine has given me his personal assurance that an alliance between our two families would honor the integrity of our province—"

"And you believe him?" Deirdre asked, amazed. "Father, he told me outright that one way or another he is going to annex our province to his own!" she blurted.

He glared at her with fire building in his eyes. "Deirdre, I have endured enough of your lies and disobedience. You will not risk the future of our province to have your own way. You will do as I tell you!"

"I will not marry Rollet!" She defied him squarely, relying on that blessed law to back her up.

He hesitated, then retreated. "Perhaps not. Your coming out is two years away and your betrothal fest a year after that, so we have time enough to discuss it."

Giddy at his sudden concession, she soaked up the feeling of power before a little pain hit. "What will happen to Roman when I marry?"

"He will be retired from the army—with honors, of course." As he had lost interest in the conversation, Karel returned to stand over papers on his secretary.

"Couldn't he come with me?" she asked, missing Roman already.

"Of course not. He will no longer be necessary. Your husband will provide guards for you," Karel said absently.

She suddenly recalled the conversation she had overheard between Roman and Galapos. "He doesn't want to retire. He wants to go fight with Galapos."

"What you think he wants is not important," Karel replied impatiently.

"But won't you even consider letting him go?" she pleaded.

He glanced up. "The Counselor believes he should be educated in the law, to train for a counselorship."

Deirdre was astonished. "Why should the Counselor care what Roman does? Is he now responsible for charting the soldiers' careers?" she asked sarcastically. She could not conceive of Roman draped in those pompous crimson robes, studying those boring books. He was too real, too alive to play that tired old role.

"You are dismissed, daughter!" Karel ordered, his patience exhausted. Deirdre swallowed her resentment, bowed, and retreated to the welcoming arms of Nanna.

Late that night, Roman slipped quietly into the Counselor's chambers. Half an hour later, a messenger was dispatched. The Surchatain was not awakened.

The following day as they rode out to the hills, Deirdre told Roman of her conversation with her father. When she mentioned his defensiveness about Tremaine, he frowned. "I'm surprised your father puts so much faith in him. Obviously, he doesn't think Tremaine could ever be a threat. That is most disturbing."

They dismounted to lead the horses up to a grassy knoll. Roman sat heavily, and the Bay Hunter nosed him to get off the tasty little patch of grass beneath him. Roman shifted as Deirdre sat beside him. "What does the Counselor say?" she asked.

"He says to bide our time and build up our defenses. He has sent word of the situation to Galapos," Roman said, glancing up in irritation as his horse nudged him insistently.

"What is the Counselor going to tell Father?" she asked.

"I don't know," Roman replied, brow down.

That prompted a new question: "Roman, I don't understand the Counselor. Why does he do the things he does?"

Roman shrugged. "I don't understand him either. At times he has helped me . . . other times he has not."

"Do you think he can be trusted?"

"With matters of state, certainly. He is loyal to your father. But I wouldn't put my life in his hands," he replied bitterly. Remembering how the Counselor had killed the assassin at the Fair, she began to ask another question. But for once, seeing his face, she did not.

At that very moment the Counselor was in private conference with the Surchatain. "High Lord," he was saying, "a most disturbing report has reached me. It seems that Tremaine himself was the one who hired Stase to kill your daughter."

Karel was incredulous. "That is absurd. Who told you that?"

"Deirdre said he admitted it to her freely—"

"Deirdre!" Her father laughed and relaxed. "She has an untameable imagination."

"Apparently, High Lord, there is some truth to it. Roman says Tremaine took extraordinary measures to detach him from her side so that—"

"Did Roman hear it?" Karel asked.

"No, not directly; but he feels she was telling the truth—"

"Young men are prone to believe anything a pretty child tells them. I will hear no more slander of Tremaine, Counselor. Dismissed."

Eudymon paused, reluctant to leave. But under the Surchatain's cool glare, he bowed and withdrew.

❖

Weeks slipped by and the menace of Tremaine seemed to fade into the remote past. One summer afternoon Karel summoned Roman to his chambers. "High Lord?" Roman bowed.

"Roman, I heard just this morning that a daughter of one of the nobles drowned recently in the lake—you take Deirdre to the lake often, do you not?"

"Yes, Surchatain," Roman admitted uneasily.

"Perhaps from now on you should not."

As it was not a direct command, Roman hesitated. "High Lord, haven't I warded her well up until now?"

"Yes, you have," Karel replied.

"Well, Surchatain, you can be assured that I am most watchful of her near the lake—"

"I have heard her talk about how you take her boating. That too must stop," Karel said abruptly. He began peering distractedly at something outside his window.

For Deirdre's sake, Roman began a reluctant argument with the man who could put him to death: "As you wish, Surchatain. But . . . there are so few enjoyments we allow her, and the lake is one of her greatest pleasures. . . . As her father, will you be the one to tell her she is now forbidden that, also?"

Karel looked alarmed at the prospect of inciting a tantrum. Eyeing Roman, he changed his mind: "She will not be forbidden it. You will teach her to swim. Today."

Roman's eyes widened but he bowed quickly. "Yes, Surchatain."

Deirdre, summoned with her nursemaid, squealed her agreement when told of the plan. She hugged her father gratefully and Nanna went into shock. Nonetheless, she found the Chataine some modest bathing clothes while Roman stopped by his room to don old sparring breeches. Nanna asked to go watch, which Roman encouraged but Deirdre denied. So he took her alone to the lake for her first lesson.

First they waded out into shallow water, where he made her practice holding her breath and going under. Then he took her out in water up to his chest. "No, Roman—don't let go of me," she said anxiously, clinging to him.

"Don't be afraid, Chataine; I'm right beside you. I want you to learn to keep yourself afloat."

"Roman, I've decided I don't want to learn to swim after all. You may take me out," she said, straining toward the shore.

"You can get out when you can swim to shore," he said, prying her off him.

"Roman!" She began to thrash in panic.

"Be still!" he insisted. "Just lie still and you'll float!"

She went limp on her back, holding her breath, and her face broke the surface. Roman stood beside her as she floated like a lily pad.

"Now stroke—like this," he demonstrated, "and kick your legs." Trying it, she found to her delight she could swim while looking at the sky.

Then he turned her over and showed her how to swim face down. Soon she was splashing all around the gentle lake, as far out as he would let her go.

Too soon he called, "Lesson over. Come out now."

"Oh, Roman, I was just getting good at it! I need to practice more," she balked.

"You've done well. Come out now before you get tired," he insisted. She splashed to him in a circuitous manner, and they climbed up on the shore.

She turned to him dripping and triumphant but then stopped, staring at him. Frowning, he followed her eyes. His wet breeches were clinging tightly to his body, rendering them translucent. Hastily, he covered himself with dry clothes.

Deirdre looked away in embarrassment. Being still something of a child, she sometimes forgot he was a man. It was a shock to rediscover it.

Her attention was drawn to him again as he attempted to untie the horses. He had to fumble considerably with the reins before he could get them untangled from the bushes.

She stared at him in amazement—his face was crimson. He glanced sideways at her and muttered, "Get on your horse."

She quickly obeyed, and they turned silently toward the palace. The novelty of seeing him embarrassed caused a mischievous little smile to appear on her face. Dare she press it? "Roman, I am ignorant about many things . . . there is so much you could teach me—"

"And there is much I cannot teach you," he interrupted. "Do not even ask." With that, he spurred to a gallop.

When they reached the back gate of the palace, he ordered, "Get yourself upstairs and dry off. I am through with you today." She searched his face anxiously, fearing she had angered him, but saw a slight smile. She bowed low to him and ran upstairs.

At dinner the Surchatain asked how her swimming lesson went. "Very well, Father," Deirdre answered innocently. "I learned much more than swimming." Roman's fork clattered to the floor.

"Oh?" said Karel.

"Yes," said Deirdre. "I learned that I must get out of the water before I get tired, and that I must not ask Roman to show me things he cannot." Roman stared at her. She alone could see his panic.

But the Surchatain only muttered, "Amazing someone could quash your curiosity." No one else at the table noticed anything awry, and her father addressed another.

But afterward Roman caught her before she could escape up the stairs. "What did you think you were doing?" he asked menacingly.

"Oh, no harm done," she said casually. "No one pays any mind to what I say."

"Nonetheless, if you ever try an experiment like that again, I will—I will—" (she was smiling at him) "I will not take you to the lake again." He finished the threat in some confusion, but she put on a sober face.

"I won't, Roman. I promise. Provided, of course, you take me swimming tomorrow," she bargained slyly.

"No!" he barked. She laughed, and he left shaking his head.

Over the next few days, Deirdre noticed a slight change in him. He talked little when they rode and seemed to lose interest in exploring the hills. He was often preoccupied and occasionally inattentive.

One morning she abandoned her lessons and went to the window overlooking the practice grounds to watch him. She did not see him at first, then spotted him off to the side by himself. He was fidgeting with his longbow, apparently tightening it. Suddenly he threw it down in exasperation and walked away.

When he came at her summons later, she asked, "Ready to go riding?"

He sighed. "Must we today, Chataine? We go every day."

Her stomach tightened. "I thought you enjoyed it."

"I do . . . but, every day. . . ."

"What is wrong with you, Roman? Why are you behaving so strangely? Are you sick?" she demanded.

"No. I am sound. We'll go riding if you wish," he said stiffly.

She became angry. "I want to know what is wrong with you!" He crossed his arms on his chest and just looked at her. At that instant she knew. She had felt that way too often herself. "You're bored," she said slowly. "You are sick with boredom."

He inhaled and looked away, resting his hand on the balustrade. "It's not only that. I have been your guardian for over four years now, and still have years to fulfill my vow. It's not that I don't enjoy your company—I do—but I wish I were . . . *doing* something. I feel as though I'm just waiting around for the next time you get into trouble. There is so much I could be doing now to help Galapos . . . so much I could be accomplishing . . ." he trailed off, and Deirdre was silent. Although she knew he was right, his words stung.

After some moments he said, "Forgive me. I have no right to burden you this way. It's something I must work out for myself. Come—let's go riding." She looked up at him dubiously, but he smiled and cocked his head, extending his hand to her. She took it.

❖

The coming of autumn brought the Fair, and Deirdre was allowed to go for the first time in two years. Roman had little trouble assuring her father that she would be safe enough with him.

It was like going home again. A number of the merchants remembered her and welcomed her back. As her father had given her an extra amount to spend, she resolved with gusto to spend it all.

Walking among the booths, she recalled the penury of Roman's room and asked him repeatedly what he would like to have. He kept saying he had no needs, but weakened when they came to a booth of fine woolens. As they were making selections Deirdre heard a shy voice at her side: "Hello." She turned to see a pleasant-faced, well-dressed girl about her own age. She had dark, curly hair under her cap and green eyes fringed with black lashes.

"Hello," Deirdre said eagerly. "Who are you?"

"I am Laska, Chataine of Calle Valley. And you?"

"I am Chataine Deirdre of Lystra. This is my guardian, Roman." He nodded, glancing at the Callean soldiers who accompanied Laska.

There was a momentary silence. Then Laska asked, "Have you been to Anson's jewelry booth yet?"

"No!" Deirdre said. And they proceeded with haste to

Anson's booth. By the time they arrived, the girls were talking and giggling like old friends. They compared notes on almost every item on display.

Eventually, Laska selected several pieces. "I'm going to wear these at my coming out year after next. When is yours?"

"The same time!" Deirdre exclaimed.

"Oh, we'll be there together! Won't that be splendid? Caspar, my older brother, went to his first fest this past spring and told me all about it," Laska confided.

"Well?" Deirdre cried.

"Oh, it's so exciting—so many men! You spend the days playing and meeting young men, and Corneus has a beautiful garden where—" she broke off and glanced at Roman, then whispered in Deirdre's ear.

"Really?" she squealed.

"Yes," breathed Laska. "If you are really beautiful, a man might fall in love with you the first night. And then he won't be able to look at anyone but you, and he'll always want to be near you. Best, he will do anything for you. Anything!"

Deirdre sighed, "It must be wonderful to have someone love you like that."

"Oh, it is!" Laska said it so confidently that Deirdre looked at her in surprise. "My older cousin got married this past spring. She told me all about it," she hastened to explain.

Deirdre's eyes glazed over. "What does a man do when he falls in love with you?"

Laska the expert said, "First, he asks you to dance." Deirdre made a mental note to pay more attention to her dance instructor. "He holds you close and gazes into your eyes and never once has to look at his feet. Then he tells you how beautiful you are and that he must have you forever. And that's it."

Deirdre blinked. "That's all?"

"Well, sometimes they go about it a little differently, but usually that is what happens," Laska explained.

Deirdre watched the crowds with unseeing eyes, dreaming. A handsome young seaman passed by and winked at her, but catching Roman's cool glare, did not stop. She immediately put the seaman's face on a royal body and imagined him fighting his way through a crowd of suitors to beg her to dance. She sighed, taking Laska's arm. "Tell me more."

The girls spent the next few hours in secret conversations, giving cursory attention to the booths they passed. Roman followed unobtrusively. At one point, when Laska mentioned that Caspar would be at the fest with them, Deirdre said, "But, I thought you said he has already been."

"He has," Laska replied. "But Father won't let him marry until he goes to our betrothal fest. And the men can go as many times as they wish until they find their choice."

"Why is your father making him wait?" Deirdre wondered.

"I don't know," Laska frowned. "Caspar said he understood, but he wouldn't tell me." No insights struck Deirdre, either. She seemed to have forgotten what Tremaine had told her.

For the remainder of the day, the girls shared their treasured secrets. Laska confided, "I dream sometimes of what it will be like to be Surchataine. To have everyone do exactly as I tell them. To make laws and appointments and execute people who displease me. To be the most important person in the country! Why, you could have any man you wanted, just by saying so. As many as you wanted!"

Deirdre nodded, absorbed in her own thoughts. "I dream of being Surchataine, too. . . . I dream of being favored by someone who would love me more than anything he had, and prove it. I dream of being free to go where I want . . . to see new places, learn new things. . . ."

Suddenly she caught a vision of freedom. How would it be to go anywhere she wanted, whenever she wanted, with no one hanging over her? The possibilities dazzled her. At once she wanted that freedom intensely.

Roman was speaking to her: "Chataine, it's time we left. Your father expects us for dinner."

And Laska was saying, "Oh, Deirdre, this has been so nice. I wish you could come visit me. It's a long time until the fest."

"Perhaps I will come see you soon," Deirdre said. Then she whispered, "Are you leaving Hycliff tonight?"

"No," Laska answered in a whisper. "We're staying at the inn here and leaving in the morning. Why?"

"I may go with you tomorrow, if I can get away," Deirdre whispered. Laska nodded excitedly.

"Goodbye, Deirdre!" she called as they mounted their horses.

"Goodbye, Laska," Deirdre winked.

As Roman and Deirdre rode easily side by side up the broad market road to Westford, Deirdre was quiet, making plans. Roman said, "It was good to see you finally able to spend time with a girl your own age." When she did not reply, he said nothing more.

She was preoccupied at dinner, also, and asked her father if she might speak with him in his chambers following the meal. "What is it? Tell me now," Karel said at the table.

She inadvertently glanced at Roman as she said, "No—in your chambers, please, father." Karel shrugged, and Roman sat back, looking at her.

After dinner, Karel strode to his chambers with her hurrying behind him. Inside, he closed the door and said, "I only have a moment. What's on your mind?"

Deirdre began her considered request: "Father, I met Laska today, Surchatain Merce's daughter. She asked me to visit her in Calle Valley. She's staying at the inn in Hycliff tonight, and leaving tomorrow morning. . . . I would like to go with her."

The Surchatain deliberated out loud, "Merce, eh? His son is Caspar. . . . Well, I see no reason to deny you this. You and Roman may meet her party in Hycliff early tomorrow."

Deirdre sprang her next request: "Father, I want to go alone. Without Roman. I'll be safe—she has guards traveling with her."

Karel looked as though she had asked to fly there. "You cannot go without Roman. He is your guardian."

"Father, I don't need him anymore! I'm fourteen years old and I can take care of myself! I'm sick of seeing him everywhere I turn! Please let me go without him!" she pleaded.

"What possesses you to demand this?" he queried sharply. "You are not going anywhere without Roman! Dismissed!" After she had left, Karel stood shaking his head in confusion, then summoned the Counselor. Deirdre stomped to her rooms and dismissed Nanna curtly, then undressed and lay in bed. It wasn't fair! She wanted to be free only a little while.

In sudden resolution, she threw off the covers and found her clothes. She packed a small bag, fastened on her cloak, and opened the door to peek out.

She paused. Roman might be punished if she just disappeared. She would leave a note. Deirdre stepped back inside, then thought, no, a note would let them find her too quickly. Her father would reason out where she had gone. It gave her some dark satisfaction to imagine him moaning, "I should have let her go when she asked!"

She opened the door again and quietly slipped down the stairs. Catching a glimpse of red from the corner of her eye, she hastened through a corridor—it was either the Counselor or a palace guard, and she didn't care to explain herself to either. She passed through the kitchen corridors and unlatched the courtyard door—it squeaked so loudly! Hastily, she shut it and slipped into the darkness.

There was the guard, occupied with a bottle. It was not difficult getting past him unseen to the rear gate. She drew it open.

"Chataine, where are you going?" She whirled, heart sinking

to see her guardian, arms crossed and face reproachful.

"I am leaving. Alone." Deirdre took her stand, knowing it was futile.

He shut the gate and took her hand. "I think not. Come back inside."

Furious, she yanked her hand away. "I want you to stop ordering me around! I don't need you anymore, and I am indeed leaving!" She shoved him with all her meager strength and spun around to the gate.

Exasperated, Roman caught her and lifted her over his shoulder. As he carried her thus through the courtyard, she kicked her legs and beat his back. "Let me down! Let me go! I hate you, Roman! I hate you!"

"If you must, but you still cannot leave," he said calmly. He carried her into the palace, where servants and soldiers gathered snickering while she burned with humiliation. Worse, when the Counselor saw and nodded in vindication, she realized he must have seen her leaving and tattled to Roman.

"Put me down!" she demanded, but he carried her all the way upstairs and pounded on Nanna's door. The nurse-maid opened it and gave a weak scream.

Roman put Deirdre down, saying, "The Chataine attempted an excursion alone. You had best watch her tonight."

As he turned away Deirdre shouted, "I will never forgive you for this, Roman!" He paused, but she flung herself into her room.

The next day she refused to go riding or even speak to him, and frostily ignored him at dinner. Everyone else thought it amusing, and Karel was downright pleased, but Deirdre was determined to make Roman suffer for the rest of his life.

After three days of her unyielding coldness, Roman respectfully requested an audience through Nanna. "You should hear him, dear," Nanna urged. "Perhaps he intends to apologize."

So Deirdre gave leave for him to enter her receiving room. When he bowed, she asked, "What is on your mind, Roman?"

Deirdre was gratified that he stood at attention with his arms behind his back, as he would for a formal hearing with the Surchatain. "Chataine, I spoke with the Counselor. He told me you had requested to go to Calle Valley without me."

"So?"

He hesitated, searching for words. When he spoke again it was not guardian to charge, but friend to friend. "I know how you must feel—almost like a prisoner, bound in chains to me. I feel that way myself at times. But there are some things we have no control over. These circumstances are beyond our choosing. We just must live the lives given to us as best we can—otherwise we will make ourselves miserable . . . as I was doing, wanting to go with Galapos when I could not."

She lowered her head. He continued, "I want you to be happy, Deirdre, but I can't forsake my vow just to please you. Don't punish me for doing what I must." He stood watching her as she studied the floor for several long minutes. "I've missed our riding. Will you go riding with me today, Chataine?" he asked quietly.

"Let me get my jacket," she said, turning to her inner chamber. When she came out again, she added, "You know I don't hate you."

"I know, Chataine."

Outside, as they led the horses from the stables, she noted unusual activity in the courtyard. The palace overseer was vainly trying to organize servants and villagers into groups. A large cart filled with empty bushels stood nearby. "What is all this?" she asked Roman.

"It's time to harvest the orchard—the apples are falling

off. But your father is shorthanded for workers," he said, glancing up.

"Oh." She stopped to watch, then looked beyond the courtyard to rows and rows of heavily laden trees. "We could help, couldn't we?"

He almost fell down in surprise. "Yes, of course!" Leaving the horses, he escorted her proudly to the overseer. Roman took up a basket and informed him, "The Chataine has offered her assistance in the harvest." While the official stared after them, Roman led her to the first tree in the first row. "I will climb up, and—"

"No, no! Let me climb, Roman!" she insisted.

He shook his head in hapless bewilderment. "As you wish, Chataine, but take care. I'll stand beneath you."

Eagerly, she thrust her skirt aside and let him lift her to the lower branches. He began instructing, "Pick only the ripe ones and throw them down to me one at a time—"

"I know, I know," she said impatiently. She began to pick and toss. He caught them and placed them in the basket. Then she decided that was too easy. She began throwing them down more rapidly, sometimes two at a time.

"Deirdre—wait—" he sputtered. One caught him perfectly on top of the head. She shrieked in laughter and he made a sudden rush at the tree. "Do that again, and I'll come throw *you* down!" he threatened with appalling familiarity. She suppressed a barrage of giggles.

They filled the entire bushel and carried it back to the courtyard together. Deirdre lifted out another empty basket. "We need to help until they finish," she said sternly.

Roman stared at her open-mouthed, yet in his face was something else besides astonishment, something unreadable to her—a look almost of pain. He blinked and said, "That will take several days. It will be enough for us to pick one more bushel." They took it to the trees and worked in earnest silence.

From the branches, she caught him looking at her again with that same sad expression and asked, "What's wrong?"

He caught the apple she tossed down. Clearing his throat, he said, "You are changing—growing so. You surprise me every day with something new. . . ."

"What do you mean?" She leaned from the tree, reaching down to him.

He carefully lifted her down. "I mean, soon you will be grown, and I will no longer ward you. . . ." He turned his back on her, and she wondered why that would disturb him so.

❧ 9 ❧

Sixteen-year-old Deirdre stood before the looking glass and carefully combed her long hair. She studied the reflection and smiled. Some of the guards were looking at her appreciatively now. And she drew attention whenever she went into town. It was a little overwhelming to be noticed so suddenly. She took an overall survey in the looking glass and, after smoothing a stray curl, decided she presented an acceptable sight. She stepped out of her chambers. . . .

❖

The guard in the hall stood at attention as Deirdre passed him. He looked younger than most. She smiled, and he nodded. "What is your name?" she asked sweetly.

"Arin, Chataine," he responded.

"Are you required to stand here all day?" she wondered, wide-eyed.

"Unless I am ordered elsewhere, Chataine," he smiled.

She began to reply but Roman's voice to her left said, "Guard, you will stand at attention at all times in the presence of the Chataine" (he snapped to) "and if I ever see your eyes leave the wall in her presence, I will put you in charge of cleaning the stables for the next six weeks. Understood?"

"Yes, Captain!" The guard became a statue.

Deirdre turned to Roman in exasperation. "Are you everywhere?"

"Only where I am needed, Chataine. Would you care to go riding now?"

"No, Roman. I am much too busy today." She returned to her room and checked herself in the glass again as Nanna came bustling in.

"Here it is, darling! Isn't it beautiful?" Nanna held up a long, full gown of creamy silk and lace.

"Oh, yes!" Deirdre exclaimed, holding the dress under her chin in front of the glass. Her first fest—her coming out—would be next week in the palace of her Uncle Corneus.

Nanna clapped. "You are so beautiful! No girl there will be lovelier than you! And who knows"—she rolled her eyes with a naughty smile—"but that some young Chatain will decide he cannot wait until your betrothal fest to ask you to wed!"

Deirdre startled, suddenly remembering Tremaine. His threat had been sleeping peacefully in her mind, but now the imperative of that decision loomed near. "Oh, Nanna, I don't want to get married yet!" she said, thinking, *I have another year before I must face that*. "Nanna, I want to be free now, to live for myself. I don't want to think about being someone's wife, and—and—" An unplanned rush of tears came.

Confused, Nanna gathered her in. "Dear, of course you are free to do as you please. No need to run ahead of ourselves here. You are the one to say when and whom you will marry. No one can say that for you—not even the Surchatain."

Deirdre groaned and fell on her bed. "Tell Father I don't feel up to dinner tonight."

She was there, nonetheless, at the dinner table that evening. Roman glanced at her from time to time as she picked at her food, but no one else seemed to notice her malaise. She smiled at him. Good old Roman. He was always there. He always cared. A thought struck her: *I wonder how much I can make him care?* She finished dinner smiling and laughing as she planned the assault.

Late that night, when the palace was quiet, Deirdre rose from bed and pulled on her overrobe. On second thought, she loosened it somewhat around the neck. She stuffed pillows under the quilts to resemble her sleeping form—it would not do for Nanna to come searching for her. Then she took up a candle, slipped out of her chambers, and descended the cold stone stairs. Cautiously, she found her way to the corridor by the kitchen. Remembering when she had done this before almost made her giggle, but she hushed herself and went on.

She came to Roman's door and listened. Not a sound within. Trying the door, she found it bolted. She hesitated, then knocked softly. No answer. She knocked again, louder.

There was a shuffling within, and Roman opened the door sleepily. When he saw her, he woke up fast. "Chataine! What's wrong? What is it?" She came in and he shut the door. As she placed the candle on the small washstand, he peered at her. "Why are you here, Chataine?"

"I wanted to see you, Roman." She opened her overrobe.

He watched her. "My life is worthless if you are found here."

"Don't be silly. I only want to talk." She looked him over appreciatively. He had a soldier's taut, muscular build. He was wearing only lightweight breeches, which sagged loosely around his hips.

As he started to shift uneasily, she came up close and

put her arms around his neck. Her touch struck him immobile. "Why are you doing this?" he whispered.

"Because I care for you, Roman." She reached up to kiss him.

That brought him around. "No," he said, backing off. "If you cared anything for me, you wouldn't put my life in danger just for your fun."

She looked at him crossly. He was spoiling everything. "Father isn't going to do anything to you."

"No? Remember the horse?" The scars showed plainly on his chest.

"If you don't want me, just say so," she huffed, throwing her head back.

"That's not the point. I can never have you, Deirdre; we both know that. Why are you tormenting me?"

"Tormenting you! Is that what you call it?" she asked indignantly. Yet even as she said it she could see he was really in pain. "Very well, I certainly will not torment you!" She stalked out and slammed the door. Hearing it echo all over the palace made her scramble for her chambers.

Safe in bed, she buried her face ashamedly in a pillow. That was foolish and she knew it. She should not try to use him like that. He had taken enough abuse from her, and for her. She would apologize to him in the morning.

Accordingly, after breakfast in her chambers, she sent the errand boy for him and waited. As the minutes passed and he did not come, she grew uneasy. At that point she received a summons to her father's chambers. When she entered, she saw to her alarm Roman standing stiff and stony-faced before the Surchatain.

"Deirdre," her father began, "Roman has requested to be removed from service as your guardian. He says he is no longer effective in his duties. Do you know of any reason this should be so?"

She gulped. "No, Father, none at all."

"Do you see that he is losing his effectiveness?"

"No, of course not, Father. He has always been faithful and capable," she said.

"Has he behaved improperly toward you?" Karel asked.

Her eyes stung. "Never, Father."

The Surchatain raised his shoulders. "Well, Roman, since I cannot determine exactly what fault there is, I must deny your request. You have proved yourself too useful. Whatever the trouble is, I trust you will work it out yourself. You are both dismissed."

As they exited into the corridor, Roman neither spoke nor looked at her. She caught his arm, and he glanced at her sharply. She let go. "Roman, please, I want to apologize for last night. I don't know why I did that. I didn't realize it would affect you so. Please forgive me," she whispered.

"Done," he said, then added, "but you must never touch me again."

Deirdre's chagrin over the incident was forgotten in the next few days of preparing for the fest. Her finest clothes were packed for the three days of festivities that would precede the gala event on the final night. Even Roman, going as her chaperon, was offered splendid new clothes, which he refused. "I will wear the shortcoat made for me by the Chataine," he said. Nanna was particularly grieved that she would not be going as chaperone, but the Surchatain's decision was final.

The party departed for Ooster in the morning, escorted by an armed guard. Deirdre's anticipation mounted with every mile they covered. No need to waste time trying to flirt with Roman—Uncle Corneus's fests were notorious for the romancing that went on. And instead of the Cohort to admire her, there would be a palace full of royalty. Envisioning herself in her new gown surrounded by a crowd of suitors, she could hardly endure the slow pace of their travel to Ooster—a pace that had once left her dizzy.

155

When at last they came within sight of the palace, Deirdre spurred her horse to a gallop, surprising the soldiers who rode with her and forcing Roman to spur after her in pursuit. She arrived at the gates with him a handbreadth behind her, where servants took their horses. She and her luggage were then taken to a guest suite so she could bathe and change. Roman followed to stand outside until she came out. Throughout the whole three days there she never realized he guarded the door whenever she was within, even sleeping on the floor so that no one could go in or out without walking over him.

Dressed and groomed, Deirdre emerged to join the fest. As she entered the audience hall she laughed in recognition of her uncle's flamboyant touch in decorating for the festivities.

At the heart of the hall was a five-tiered fountain that flowed with wine. Long, thin tables circled it like a maze, set with aromatic dishes of pheasant, beef, and ham; fruits and pies; pastries; and more she could not see. Enormous bouquets of spring flowers marked the entrances to the maze. The crowd of guests already there were eating and laughing as they watched several venturous young men attempting to find their way through the maze to the fountain of wine.

Deirdre scanned the room excitedly for familiar faces. She recognized Jason and Colin, and Rollet on the far side of the fountain.

"Deirdre! Over here!" called a voice, and she spotted Laska waving to her.

Deirdre hurried over to greet her. "Laska! Hello!" They embraced. "I received your last message but had no time to send a reply—"

"Don't give it a thought," interrupted Laska. "Have you ever seen anything like this in your life? Oh, hello, Roman." He nodded.

Deirdre laughed a shade too loudly. "No, I haven't. Uncle has—" she broke off as she caught sight of one young man surrounded by girls. He had a perfectly sculpted face and a head full of chestnut curls. Deirdre touched Laska's arm and nodded. "Who is that?"

"You don't know? That's Chatain Artemeus. Do you like him?"

"I certainly do." He was the most handsome man Deirdre had ever seen. Suddenly he looked directly at her. Smiling, he broke from the group of fawning girls to walk toward Deirdre. She felt suddenly panicky.

He took her hand. "Laska, will you introduce me to this lady?"

Laska smiled. "You are greeting Chataine Deirdre, daughter of Karel of Lystra. Deirdre, this is Surchatain Savin's son Artemeus."

He kissed her hand. She said, "I am honored to meet you."

"I am spellbound by your presence," he answered. "I beg you to sit with me at dinner tonight. Please."

"Of course. Thank you." Deirdre desperately hoped she appeared more poised than she felt. Then there were more people to meet, treats to taste, and much laughing and flirting to do. Deirdre began to feel so lightheaded with it all that she had to excuse herself to go back upstairs and rest.

Later, getting ready for dinner, Laska advised her confidently on how to handle Artemeus. "I have heard that he's quite a lover. But don't give in directly—make him beg for it. You'll hold his interest longer," Laska said, standing in front of the looking glass to arrange her dark curls on her bare shoulder.

"Laska!" Deirdre was shocked.

"This is how it's done, Deirdre," Laska insisted.

Something about Laska's hardened tone struck Deirdre as strange. Suddenly she asked, "Where is your brother, Caspar?"

Laska half turned, but did not meet her eyes. "He . . . could not come this year."

"Don't you want me to meet him, Laska?" Deirdre asked.

A look akin to fear came into her green eyes, then she shook her curls and said gaily, "Next year! This year is ours to enjoy!"

"You're right," Deirdre agreed, smoothing the pink folds of her dress.

She came down for dinner in a daze. Two long rows of tables were set up in the dining hall for the guests to sit wherever they chose. As was customary, the girls' chaperons stood behind their charges' chairs during the meal. Deirdre wandered to an empty chair where Roman seated her, then took his place behind her.

Artemeus seated himself next to her and leaned close to whisper, "Deirdre, you look lovelier than all the flowers in the palace." She blushed at the look in his smoky grey eyes, and he added, "I am sure that any other chataine would be ashamed next to your beauty."

"Artemeus, there are many lovely girls here," she protested happily.

"Not as you are," he countered firmly. "Your skin is so fair and perfect—your hair is like silk—your eyes are so wide and deep a man could drown in them."

She giggled. "Please—you will turn my head."

"I hope to turn it my way," he said earnestly, taking her hand. A servant set two full plates before them and Deirdre drew her hand away to eat.

"So you are Savin's son." As she said it, she suddenly recalled he was one of the choices Tremaine had given her.

"Yes," he said proudly. "My father is the greatest ruler on the Continent, next to Tremaine."

"And my father," Deirdre corrected.

He smiled. "We rule Goerge from a palace built high on cliffs of solid rock—Diamond's Head. Have you ever been there, Deirdre?"

"No," she said, dipping a strawberry in sweetened cream.

"You must come soon. It's one of the wonders of the world—a fortress worthy of housing the most desirable Surchataine." Gazing into her eyes, he had not even touched the aromatic dish in front of him.

As she raised the goblet to her lips he drank in her every movement with longing eyes. She was thinking hard. What would it be like to marry him? If she did, she would save her country from invasion by Tremaine. But. . . .

"I could not leave Westford. That is my seat to rule Lystra," she reluctantly objected.

He laughed. "Deirdre, my love, why should you worry about things like that? Lystra will be well in hand."

"In whose hand?" she asked seriously.

He laughed again. "Oh, I love a clever girl! You are so entrancing. . . . I must have you, Deirdre," he ended in a murmur.

She felt Roman, behind her, shift. *I have time yet*, she thought. *I need not think about marriage, only the pleasure before me now*. "Perhaps you shall," she smiled enticingly, and his eyes lit up with anticipation.

As dinner ended he stood and took her hand, kissing her fingers. Wordlessly, he led her out to the palace garden. Roman followed. Artemeus swung open the wrought-iron gates, and Deirdre stepped into a paradise of color and fragrance. She detected scents of jasmine and honeysuckle, but before finding them stumbled upon a trellis of climbing roses in blazing yellow-orange. The pebble-lined paths into the garden curved in a circular fashion, some of them ending abruptly. It took her a moment to recognize that the garden mimicked the maze of the food tables in the audience hall, or vice versa.

Artemeus led her to the end of one path, and they sat on a velvet-covered couch. "Deirdre," he whispered, "you are the one I must have. Will you give me your love?" He bent forward to kiss her lips.

She hadn't time to answer before seeing Roman step from the shadows toward them. Obeying her guardian's steady gaze, she avoided Artemeus's embrace and he almost toppled off the couch.

"Deirdre!" he complained, regaining his balance, then followed her glance to Roman. Artemeus swore under his breath. "You are dismissed. You can go," he called to Roman. Her guardian did not move.

"Let me speak with him," said Deirdre, embarrassed. She rose and walked over to him. "Roman, you really don't have to stand over me this way. I'm not a child and my life isn't in danger here," she said softly.

"No, but your honor is. Your father made clear to me what my duties are," he replied. The hair on his forehead had parted in such a way that the scar was plainly visible. Its existence rebuked her. Humbly, she nodded and returned to Artemeus's side.

"I'm sorry. He's not leaving," she said.

Artemeus looked toward him darkly. "No?" He got up and sallied up to Roman, who looked down on him without expression. "Well, there's no doubt you're a good chaperon. The finest. I know you earn your pay. As a matter of fact, I'm sure you're not paid near your worth. So listen"—he drew out a bag of coins—"I have twenty royals in here, and they're all yours if you'll leave us for an hour. One hour. Here." And he held them out.

Roman did not move, nor even answer. "Go on, take them," urged Artemeus. No response. "Damn you!" he burst, and strode back to Deirdre.

"Is it so important that he leave?" she asked. "We can talk, and he won't eavesdrop—"

"Be quiet and let me think!" Artemeus snapped. Deirdre was stunned. His face smoothed. "I'm sorry," he said tenderly. "You wait here. I'll return right away." He left her standing by the couch. Uncertain as to whether she should wait or not, she looked toward Roman. He was as still as the stone walls around them, his face unreadable in the darkness.

In minutes Artemeus was by her side again, smiling and relaxed. "Everything is taken care of," he whispered.

Deirdre felt vaguely alarmed. "What did you do?"

"Just arranged some entertainment for your friend," he murmured darkly.

Without warning two young men armed with clubs sprang over the garden wall onto Roman. But he merely side-stepped their attack, shaking one off into the rosebushes and throwing the other up against the wall.

Roman paced over and took Deirdre's hand, but Artemeus held on to the other. "Release her," Roman warned. When Artemeus did not, Roman punched him beneath the ribs just hard enough to set him gasping onto the couch. Then he firmly led Deirdre back to the well-lighted banquet hall.

"I see why Father wouldn't send Nanna," she said, sub-dued. "I'm sorry that happened, Roman."

He smiled. "Don't apologize. It was quite satisfying."

Later in the evening she spotted Artemeus with some of his friends. She took a deep breath and approached him, intending to make amends, but he eyed her coldly and turned his back. "Do you know what I really hate?" he asked his friends. "A wench who won't deliver what she promises!" They laughed, and Deirdre turned away in tears.

❖

Deirdre began the next morning with the resolution to for-get Artemeus and start all over. After breakfast, she found most of the other guests gathered on the grounds. She brightened to see the men showing off their archery skills. Boldly, she approached the weapons stall to select a bow and quiver. One of the young men saw her and laughed,

"Hey, fellows, move up a target!"

"That isn't necessary," she smiled, taking a place on the firing line. She nocked the arrow to the bow, drew back smoothly, and shot. The arrow planted itself in the bull's-eye. The men around her gaped.

"I'll wager you can't do that again," one of them said.

"You lose," she answered, and shot again.

"Pure luck," another man scoffed.

"How about a little competition, then?" Deirdre proposed. "Who would like to . . . ?" She trailed off as the crowd quickly dispersed, both the men who had been shooting and the girls who had been watching them.

Deirdre looked around. "Where did they all go? You would think I was shooting at *them!*"

"You might as well have been. No one wants to risk being bested by a girl," Roman said, then beamed at her. "I'm proud of you. Your practice paid off."

"How?" she muttered, looking across the deserted grounds.

That afternoon a mixed group set off for a short excursion on horseback, Deirdre and Roman with them. But Deirdre grew impatient with the slow, timid riding of the other girls and shot ahead with the men. Roman passed her in a show of horsemanship, so she jumped Lady Grey over a briar patch and took a shortcut to come out ahead of him. He passed her again with sheer speed. By the time they had finished their little game of one-upmanship and stopped to look around, the others were nowhere in sight.

At dinner that night Deirdre made another resolution to start all over. So she listened bright-eyed as her dinner companions told of their exploits. Otto, seated across from her, was saying, "It was a dangerous plan, but we had to recover the money those villains had taken. So we—just my brother and I—lay in wait in the forest until we heard them riding up. We gave chase to the edge of a cliff, where they had to stop and fight us. There were three of them, and we had only our hunting knives to their swords. It was very bloody—my brother lost a finger. But we overpowered them and threw them off the cliff, then took their horses and money."

"How exciting!" exclaimed Deirdre. "When I was ten, we were traveling here to see Uncle, and I was kidnaped by two men who took me to an assassin. He tried to throw me over a cliff, but my guardian Roman caught me . . . and . . ." she faltered as Otto turned to speak to a girl seated next to him, "saved me," she mumbled into her goblet.

A fellow next to her spoke up. "Deirdre, have you ever been to Corona?"

"Yes! Tremaine invited me—"

"Well, I stopped there on my way here. I was traveling alone, you know. I told Father, I said, 'Father, I don't need guards traveling with me! Just give me expense money and I'll be off!' So I stopped in Corona to see Tremaine's palace. You should see his audience hall!"

"I have! He invited me to visit Rollet there two years ago. Roman thought someone might still be after my life, so we traveled disguised as peasants! He put me in a tattered old dress, with a pillow underneath to make me look pregnant!"

She paused to laugh, and he resumed, "Yes, well, as I was saying, Tremaine's audience hall is something to behold! The floor is set with diamonds and rubies . . ." he continued to talk, but Deirdre shut out his voice to concentrate on the delicious quail.

Later, one young man named Morin asked her to walk through the gardens with him. "No, thank you," she said quickly, glancing toward her guardian shadowing them. "I would rather stay in here and talk."

"Very well," he said, and a tentative silence ensued while they searched for something to talk about. He finally said, "Do you ride?"

163

"Yes, fairly well," she answered cautiously, mindful of leaving all her potential suitors in the dust that afternoon.

"I train wild horses to the saddle and bridle," he remarked. "I suppose I have trained fifty horses in my life."

"How interesting! I know that is difficult. I thought I would try it once, but the horse reared and knocked me down before I ever got on him. He would have trampled me if my guardian hadn't saved me. He threw himself over me and let the horse strike him instead. It was so brave of him. . . ."

"Really?" Morin asked, peeved. "Isn't it his sworn duty to protect you?"

"Well, yes," stammered Deirdre. "But that doesn't make it easy."

"Or interesting," he said, taking his leave.

At that point Laska drew her aside and scolded her, "Deirdre, you must stop talking about Roman. They are not interested in him."

"I can't help it," Deirdre said. "He's been with me in everything I've ever done."

"Then don't talk about yourself. Just listen to them," Laska instructed, then went off to join in the general pursuit of Artemeus.

So Deirdre listened. All night long she listened, and went to bed very tired.

In the morning she awoke with a headache. Tonight was the night of the fest—the grand finale. This was her last chance to make good. She invested her time that day admiring the men in their activities, and so managed to gather several beaux for the fest that night.

But when the guests gathered in the banquet hall, and she talked and danced in her elegant silk dress, she found she could not really concentrate. Her eyes kept drifting past her partners' faces and her ears just barely caught what they said. For some reason she kept glancing toward Roman, who was watching from his position against the wall.

The festivities wore on interminably. Deirdre stopped dancing to stand apart and watch. This was the night she had been dreaming of ever since talking with Laska at the Fair. *Why did I believe it would be so wonderful?* she mused.

Laska paused between dances to encourage her: "You're doing much better tonight. I think Gastin is interested in you."

"I wonder if he can dance," Deirdre murmured.

Laska frowned. "You tell me. You just danced with him!"

Deirdre glanced at the young man raising his goblet to her from across the room. "Not him. Roman."

Laska grabbed her shoulders and almost shook her. "Deirdre, you stop that now! Remember who you are and why you're here! You're going to marry one of these men soon!"

Deirdre looked at her vacantly, then left the fest behind and went up to bed.

The following morning they departed for home under heavy grey skies, riding in utter silence. Roman kept glancing at her.

I tried, I really tried, she thought. *What went wrong? You expected them all to be like him.*

Her eyes went quickly to Roman. He returned her look quizzically. *It's true; there is no one like him*, she thought. And she considered how she felt about him.

In the afternoon the clouds grew darker and the rain came heavily down. The travelers stopped to don their thick cloaks, but still got wet and chilled as they rode. The rain slowed their pace to a walk as the horses lumbered through muddy streams that used to be roads.

Deirdre shivered, then laughed, "Remember when you used to carry me in front on the Bay Hunter?"

Roman reined the horse to a sudden halt. The soldiers halted. Deirdre stopped beside him. He reached over and lifted her onto his horse as easily as if she were still a child of ten, then wrapped her up in his cloak. She snuggled down in its musty warmth, laying her head against his neck. Roman took up the reins and clucked to the Bay Hunter.

They continued homeward to the sounds of rain beating lightly on leaves, creaking leather, and hoofs pulling rhythmically from the sucking mud. "Roman," she murmured, "the night after I was snatched, on our first trip to Uncle's—you remember?" He nodded. "That night, I opened your door and saw you on your knees. . . . Were you praying to God?"

He cleared his throat. "Yes, Chataine."

"Do you pray often?"

"Every night, Chataine."

"What do you say?" she wondered.

"Whatever is on my heart."

"Does God answer you back?"

He shifted, pulling his cloak further over her head to keep the rain off. "At times. Not in words, but impressions, usually. I find insights."

She sat up. "Like someone speaking without a voice to you?"

"Well, sometimes. Most often when God chooses to speak to me and I am listening, I am given peace, or new understanding, or just the certainty that He is in control. And often I think God has given me a guardian, like I am guardian to you," he said.

"Why do you think that?"

"Because we are both still alive," he said wryly.

She laughed. "Do you suppose I have a guardian too, besides you?" The thought of a heavenly being scrambling around keeping her out of trouble amused her.

"'The angel of the Lord encamps around those who fear Him, and delivers them,'" he quoted. That turned her thoughts serious again.

"Roman . . . could God speak to me?"

"He speaks to whomever He wishes."

"Even if I had not asked Him anything?"

"Sometimes He has to get your attention first, Chataine." He glanced down as the Bay Hunter balked at a rivulet in the road.

She considered all this, then asked, "Roman, do you pray for me?"

"Every night, Chataine. You are always on my heart."

She looked up at his face. It was the most handsome face she had ever seen.

10

Only days after they arrived home, Deirdre's father informed her at dinner that she had received a marriage proposal. . . .

❖

Karel opened a letter and said, "It proposes your marriage to Chatain Gastin. What province does he rule, Deirdre?"

"Gastin?" she frowned. "I don't know. I don't even remember who he is. Send him a refusal." He nodded, apparently relieved.

The entertainment after dinner that evening was a group of singers who favored sighing love songs. Deirdre listened enthralled:

You have bound me with your eyes;
I am captive to your smiles;
Your tears rend my heart

169

You are such a part
Of me, my dove, my love.

If I loved you when we met,
I will love you ever yet,
For that love of mine
Was naught as it is
Now, my dove, my love.

What then shall I do
To win such a maid as you?
Is there hope for me
To ever touch your
Heart, my dove, my love?

Her rapture with the beautiful melody was marred only
by Roman's fidgeting. He was drumming his fingers and shifting all over his chair during the song. "Shh!" she hissed. He
glanced at her and stilled, but a moment later leaned back to
whisper to the Counselor. Deirdre glared at him, and he sat
quietly through the remainder of the performance.

When Karel dismissed them she meant to take Roman
aside and upbraid him for his uncharacteristic rudeness, but
he left the table immediately with the Counselor.

❖

An hour later Roman emerged from Eudymon's chambers
and stopped in the corridor to think. Hesitantly, he headed
toward the servants' dining hall and looked in. They had all
finished eating, and only scattered groups remained. He
scanned the groups from the doorway.

A healthy-looking serving girl approached smiling: "Good
evening, Captain! Who are you looking for?"

"Ah, in fact, you, Angelina," he said, apparently deciding.

"Yes?" her smile brightened.

"When you are finished, I thought—you would perhaps walk with me out to the orchard," he said tentatively.

"I am finished now," she said, tossing her apron to a group of maids who giggled and waved her out. She left the hall on his arm.

Over the next several weeks Deirdre grew irritated at Roman's increasing aloofness toward her. He took her riding only when she specifically requested it, and he deliberately avoided the willow grove. He reverted to his taciturn manner of their early months together. Moreover, he began to leave the table every night immediately when dismissed by the Surchatain, not even pausing to say goodnight to her.

She took a careful inventory to see what she might have done recently to offend him, but found nothing. She then determined to take a more direct approach to find out what was wrong. Accordingly, she summoned him one afternoon to her chambers.

When he entered, he bowed formally—something he had rarely done with her. "You summoned me, Chataine?"

"Yes, Roman," she began earnestly, but Nanna suddenly entered with fresh bedding. "Yes, Roman," she took on a formal tone as well, "I require your assistance in the garden. Will you be so kind as to help me?"

"Of course, Chataine." He bowed again, to her aggravation. They walked with three feet of space between them to the small courtyard garden. He unlatched the gate and she entered, then directed him to the corner of the garden where new rosebushes had been planted the previous spring.

"I am in a quandary as to whether the pink or the red roses complement this dress best. What do you say?" she asked. He just blinked at her. Then she dropped all pretense and asked earnestly, "Roman, what is wrong between us? Why are you suddenly so distant?"

He gazed at her and replied, "I believe the pink favors your complexion more."

"Thank you," she said, breaking off a pink bud and placing it in her hair. "And I believe the red favors yours." She broke off a red bud and tucked it in the top eyelet of his shortcoat. It was his old one—not the one she had made for him. "Now—"

"Cap'n Roman! Captain!" They heard the voice of the errand boy outside the garden gates.

"Here!" Roman called. As he turned, he withdrew the bud.

"Captain, the Surchatain has granted your audience now."

"Thank you, Kevin." Roman bowed to her: "Excuse me, Chataine," and she nodded.

Deirdre stayed in the garden a few moments after he had departed, smelling the roses and lilac. On her way out, she saw the little red bud lying crushed on the path.

The following morning Nanna wakened her cheerful and singing: "Up, up now, Chataine! It's going to be a lovely summer's day!" Deirdre groaned and rolled over. "I heard an interesting bit of gossip from the servants today," Nanna said enticingly. "Do you want to hear it?"

Deirdre mumbled something. Nanna teased, "One of the housemaids is getting married—Angelina. Do you know her?"

"Umm. She's very sweet."

"Do you know who she is marrying?" Nanna asked, eyes bright.

"No," yawned Deirdre.

"Roman!" Nanna said triumphantly.

Deirdre came wide awake. "He can't get married!"

"Yes, he can. They said he went to the Surchatain and asked permission to marry, since you will soon be married and need him little now anyway. Your father gave him leave."

Deirdre felt sick. "When are they marrying?"

"As soon as possible, from what I hear," Nanna chuckled.

Deirdre put her head in her hands. So there was the cause for his coolness! He had fallen in love with someone

172

else, and wanted no more part of her. The thought of losing him—her battle-scarred babysitter and confidant, teacher and protector—made her heartsick. He could not marry! She must stop him. How? She could get Angelina sent away from the palace. She could send her to Laska as a gift.

No, that would not do. Roman deserved better treatment than that. The only thing to do was talk to him. Right away. She dressed in urgent haste and ran down the stone stairs to summon him. He was gone—away from the palace. One of the soldiers said he thought Roman had gone to the village, or the town.

Was she too late? Had he already taken Angelina to the town notary? Deirdre waited at the front gates for him, pacing and chewing her lip. But when she saw the soldiers glancing toward her and whispering among themselves, she turned to go back inside.

In another moment Roman came galloping up and dismounted with a leap. As he threw his reins to the stable hand and ran up the steps, she paused at the palace doors. He saw her and startled guiltily. "Chataine—did you summon me while I was away? Forgive me—I returned as soon as I was able."

"Where have you been?" she asked softly. Angelina was not with him.

"To the village. Taking food and medicine to the villagers." He rushed on to explain, "They are having another plague—each is worse than the last. I am afraid they will have to leave the branch of the river altogether, it is becoming so foul. But they just will not listen."

She felt a flood of relief. "May we go riding now?"

"As you wish, Chataine."

On Lady Grey, Deirdre headed for the lake, and Roman followed reluctantly on the Bay Hunter. They dismounted by the willow trees. As they tied the horses she watched him, waiting for an opening, but he never looked up. He turned idly to the water and began skimming stones. She walked to his side and watched the little rings widen on the glassy surface.

Then she opened her mouth and forced out, "I heard you're getting married." He nodded, flinging a rock. "Roman! Why?"

"I am a man. I need a wife, Chataine," he said grimly. Hardly like someone in love.

"I need you, Roman!" she cried.

He stopped throwing and gripped the stones in his palm. "I will be here when you need me. That will not change. But in the short time left before you marry, there is little I can do for you."

"You swore to guard me until I marry," she accused.

"And I will." He looked her in the eye.

"But if you are married, you will have other—concerns," she argued. He weighed the stones in his hand without speaking. "Roman, I ask one thing of you. If you do this, I will not burden you with any more demands." She paused to meet his eyes. "Wait until I marry before you do." The heaviness of her request sagged his shoulders. "Please! Roman, I beg you."

"As you wish, Chataine. I'll wait," he said quietly. Deirdre closed her eyes in sweet relief.

But Roman was moving toward the horses. "Where are you going?" she asked.

"*We*," he said. "Back to the palace."

"Already?"

"I must tell Angelina immediately. She deserves that much consideration," he said tightly. For the first time, Deirdre came face to face with her own selfishness, and she lowered her head in humiliation. But she would not relent. He was too important to her.

They arrived at the palace. Roman turned over their horses to a stable hand, and they parted wordlessly in the foyer. This was one scene she had not the slightest desire to overhear.

Roman trudged to the kitchen and looked in. "Angelina?" She turned from a large kettle to smile warmly at him. Glancing at the cluster of maids nudging each other, he asked, "Can you come away for a moment?"

"For you, yes." She took his arm with a smug glance at her friends. He hesitated, then led her to the empty chapel. He shut the doors and turned toward her, but before he could speak she clasped his neck and pressed her lips to his.

When he held her lightly she opened her eyes and drew away. "What is it?"

"Angelina . . . I, uh . . ." he stammered as she tightened her lips, sensing bad news. "The Chataine has asked me to postpone our marriage."

"She has?!" Angelina exclaimed. "Why?"

"Well, she fears I will become lax in my duties toward her," Roman uneasily explained.

Anger crossed her face. "That is hardly likely, knowing you. Anyone can see how faithful you've been. Almost anyone."

"I tried to reassure her of that, but she still had fears . . . of being abandoned, I believe. I am her only friend in the palace, other than her nursemaid."

"Small wonder," muttered Angelina. "Roman, you are not her slave. She has no right to order your personal affairs. The Surchatain gave you permission to marry—isn't that enough?"

"Ordinarily, yes, of course," he said anxiously. "But as she felt so strongly about it, I felt . . . I should . . . accede. . . ." He could not meet her gaze.

"Roman." She turned his face to make him look in her eyes. "Is it really me you want?"

"Certainly!" he insisted. "I would not ask you if I didn't mean it." But his eyes wandered from her face again. "Besides, she will certainly marry next spring, then I will be free."

"I will wait, then," she said softly. "Until the spring." She left the chapel to return to the kitchen.

He remained a moment in thought, then sighed and shook his head. "I need never fear dying by the sword," he muttered. "These woman will tear me apart long before then."

The following day, Nanna brought the noon meal to Deirdre in her chambers, setting the tray down with a thump. "I heard more gossip today, dear," she said darkly. "Do you want to know what they are saying?"

"I don't care what they are saying," Deirdre replied, averting her face to the window.

"They say you forced Roman to postpone his wedding. Is that true? Deirdre, look at me!"

"What is it to you? Why are you so angry?"

Nanna sat her down. "Deirdre, they say you are in love with him. Tell me that isn't so!"

"What difference does it make? Why are you so upset?" Deirdre asked stonily.

"If this gets around to your father's ears, it will make a great difference! You know what will happen to Roman! And you—why do you risk your future for the sake of a— an illegitimate soldier?"

"Stop it!" Deirdre cried, leaping up. "I don't ever want to hear you say things like that about him again!" She ran from the room, knocking over the tray.

That day as they rode, Roman was quiet and Deirdre downcast. She longed to talk to him, to make him understand. *I don't want to run your life, Roman. I just want you near me.* But she could not put her feelings into words. Nor did she feel the slightest curiosity to know Angelina's reaction to his news. She did not want to hear of Angelina nor talk of her.

He found a nice grassy hill and they dismounted, releasing their horses to graze. Then he wordlessly threw himself down on his back in the sweet green grass. She sat beside him. As he lay gazing up at the sky, she leaned over and began rubbing his temples. He closed his eyes.

On impulse, she kissed him on the forehead. He did not push her away. "Roman . . . do you care for me?"

His eyes opened, but not toward her. "I care for you greatly, Chataine. I have a strong interest in your welfare," he said dispassionately.

"No, I mean, besides being my guardian. How do you feel about me just . . . as me?" she pressed softly.

It was a minute before he answered. "I am interested in only the best for you, Chataine. And that's all I am allowed." He stood and helped her to her feet. "Time to go."

She studied his face. There was a tenderness, a vulnerability in it she had never noticed before. Had it always been there, and she just had not seen it?

Suddenly she realized she finally had it. She had power over him—not to make him do what she wanted, necessarily, but to affect him. To change his life. To possibly destroy it. Moreover, she had not gained it by manipulation or cunning. He had given her that power himself, of his own accord.

It was a different, older Deirdre who returned with him to the palace. Roman was different, also. He dropped the formality and no longer attempted to avoid her, but things were not the same. He was quiet and withdrawn, carrying a habitual countenance of sadness or resignation. It baffled her, but the more she tried to solace him, the more he withdrew. She began to yearn to understand him better.

Some days later, she coaxed him out to the lake again. As they stood at the shore looking over the water, she asked brightly, "What shall we do today? Go swimming?"

"No," he said quickly.

"Then take me out in the boat," she demanded. "Roman, why won't you ever take me to the far shore? What's over there?"

"Nothing that's not over here," he said, then squinted across the water. "On second thought, let's do go have a look."

"Well said!" she agreed. He held the small boat steady

while she clambered in, then he took up the oars and began stroking strongly. Deirdre leaned over the prow and trailed her fingers in the water. "How fast you're rowing! This is fun!" she laughed. He grunted.

After a few minutes the boat scraped ground, and he leaped out to drag it up on shore. Then he sprinted to the nearby trees, leaving her sitting in the prow. By the time she managed to climb out and find him, he was studying the remains of a little camp. A fire still smoked on the ground. "What's this?" she exclaimed.

"An unwelcome guest," he said grimly. Deirdre then saw strange markings in the dirt and pebbles arranged in patterns. A figurine with a grotesque face was lying as if abandoned in haste. Roman began obliterating the designs with his foot, scattering stones and ashes. He broke the figurine in pieces and threw them out into deep water.

Deirdre watched in amazement. "What are you doing? What is that?"

"A sorcerer has been at work here. He must have seen us, also." He spat out a curse.

"Roman!" She was profoundly shocked.

"I'm sorry, Deirdre, but this is an evil omen. Sorcerers at work in the land are like leeches sucking the lifeblood. They are extremely dangerous—they can bring a whole country to ruin in short order if they influence the right people. God has forewarned us." She listened soberly, but wondered at the intensity of his foreboding.

❖

The winter of that year was the worst Deirdre could ever recall. The cold and snow were unrelenting as wolves. Although every fireplace in the palace was kept loaded with wood, an icy chill pervaded the palace. Everyone wore heavy outer garments even while inside. Deirdre was not permitted even to leave the palace proper in such weather. And she soon found that Roman would not be there for a time, either.

Early one morning Nanna brought her a note given her by an errand boy. In bed, Deirdre opened it and read: "To the Chataine. From Roman. I wished you to know that I have been accepted to carry communications between the palace and the outposts for a short time. I had to leave before you awakened. Please pray for my safety. I am ever your respectful guardian." She closed her eyes to hold back the tears. What idiot would volunteer for such dangerous riding?

There were four outposts positioned around the border, not including the soldiers stationed in Hycliff and Westford. Each outpost was a fortress in itself, well stocked and buttressed to withstand attack or siege. All scouting and patrolling parties were dispatched from these, and all units were coordinated from Outpost One, Galapos's field headquarters. In fair weather, covering the distance from one outpost to the next closest might require half a day, given a strong horse. But in the killing cold and obscuring snow, a rider who made it within a day was considered superb. Those who did not were dead.

But communications were the lifeblood of the army. Galapos could not command if he did not know what was happening elsewhere. And Roman thought so little of expending his life for Galapos. "Please pray for my safety," he had written. He knew the risks. Then why, oh why did he go?

Resigned to waiting, Deirdre set tasks for herself to consume the time while he was gone. There was a quilt to be sewn and many books to be read. Immediately following breakfast, she set herself to busyness.

❖

Dressed in layers of woolens under his thick cloak, Roman pushed the Bay Hunter to the limit of his endurance, galloping through thick snow. He felt the cold sear through him as he plunged over the East Passage toward Outpost Three. At length, it seemed unbearable—the wind never let up. And what would it be like to perish in this barrenness? *Oh, Lord, that may be best—to die out here and not have to face her again.*

His horse suddenly hit a hidden hole and fell sideways to the ground, pinning Roman's leg. Sharp pain shot through his knee as the Bay Hunter thrashed about, unable to regain his footing. In the distance, Roman heard the howling of hungry wolves.

Lord, I was wrong—I do want to see her again, he quickly corrected himself. The horse staggered up, snorting indignantly. Limping to remount and push on, Roman considered himself reminded to pray as sincerely as he wished to be heard.

❖

Deirdre sat at dinner staring at Roman's empty place. Why had she taken for granted his being there night after night? Why had she assumed he would be around forever? She picked up her fork, sighing. This was only the first day.

Glancing up, she saw the Counselor regarding her with a look almost of compassion, so she murmured, "How long do we expect Roman to be gone, Counselor?"

He furrowed his brow and inhaled thoughtfully. "Well, to make two full circuits between the outposts . . . I would say a week, at the outside two." She nodded. He whispered, "I miss him also."

Day after day, Deirdre worked to exhaustion on the quilt, but that gave her too much opportunity to think about him. Her fingers would freeze with the needle halfway in as she thought back over their hours together. He did so many things out of simple kindness, things that were not required of him. For instance, ever since she had complained that first summer about his rough hands snagging her silk sleeves, he had begun smearing lard on his hands at night. He never said a word about it, and she would not have known had she not recently overheard the maids giggling about his having the softest hands of any soldier. And even though Deirdre had stopped wearing silk on their outings years ago, he continued to do it. Did he like for her to hold his hand so much?

Sighing, she laid the quilt aside to search out the required books from her father's library. But since she could not concentrate enough to read for long, she gradually began to pass the hours wandering through the palace and peeking out the shutters.

❖

On the Bay Hunter, Roman pounded with weary relief through the gates of Outpost One. Galapos greeted him joyfully: "Well done, well done, my boy! Come in, get warm and fed, and give me your messages."

They hustled him blue and shivering into the dining room of the fortress where he stood almost on top of the fire to thaw. A soldier broke out a keg, and Roman drank great gulps of ale by the fire. Then he sat to devour a plate of stew under Galapos's shining eye. "What do the outposts say, Roman?"

He swallowed his mouthful. "Outpost Three has been able to recruit eight hundred men from Hycliff, Westford, and the country villages, but they are short on arms—particularly bows and broadswords. They have leather jerkins, but few chestplates. Outpost Two is meeting resistance from the villagers in recruiting men—they are largely sympathetic to Savin, as opposed to Karel or Tremaine. Also, the outpost lost forty horses to lameness from the rocks. They have not arms to send elsewhere, either. What does Four say?"

"They are gaining strength under Basner. But still, they are the most vulnerable, in the valley." Galapos paused to calculate, watching Roman eat. "It is strange," he resumed thoughtfully, "that I have received no directive from the Surchatain regarding our defense against Tremaine—only from the Counselor. What are the High Lord's thoughts on this?"

Roman stopped chewing. "I don't know. After our trip to Corona, Deirdre told me he did not believe Tremaine had any intention of attacking us. I thought the Counselor would have enlightened him by now. . . . I wonder, what shadow has darkened his ability to see Tremaine for what he is?"

Galapos shook his head and said nothing while Roman attacked a loaf of black bread. Then Galapos asked, "And how is the Chataine?"

"She is beautiful, Galapos. A beautiful young woman," Roman said wistfully.

"Is she now?" Galapos smiled broadly, then his face clouded. "But not for you, my boy."

"I know," Roman replied.

"Tell me though—do you have any clue as to whom she plans to marry in the spring?"

Roman shook his head. "No. Rollet she refused at the outset. Artemeus has fallen from her favor, I believe. Caspar has not yet approached her, though when he does she may favor him. She is good friends with his sister."

"Was he not at the fest?" Galapos asked.

Roman held a chunk of bread to his lips, thinking back, then said, "No, he was not. I wonder why."

"Perhaps he knew it was . . . unnecessary," Galapos said slowly.

"Or useless?" Roman asked.

Galapos stroked his thick moustache. "We need to know more. I need to get spies into Merce's palace. . . . So little time, and so much yet to do, to be ready to fight. If only we had allies, also." His eyes widened. "Surely a man who values commerce values the freedom to conduct it in!" Roman met his eyes in a flash of recognition. "My boy—can you ride to Ooster today?"

Roman stood. "Give me your message and I'll be gone."

❖

Deirdre sat in her room, staring at the nearly completed quilt. Three weeks. Twenty days he had been gone now. Or was today twenty-one? She picked up the thread with tired fingers.

Nanna entered, lugging more wood for her grate. "Is it warm enough in here, darling?"

"Warm enough," Deirdre sighed listlessly.

"Here—you bought this lovely shawl at the Fair and haven't even worn it yet." She draped it around Deirdre's shoulders.

"Thank you, Nanna," she mumbled.

Nanna stood back and sighed at her dejection. "Angelina tells me Roman has returned, and—"

"He has?" Deirdre bounded out the door before Nanna could utter another word. She raced to the kitchen and flung open the door, but saw only the maid. "Angelina! Where is Roman?!"

"Chataine," she acknowledged, bowing. "He has gone to the villagers with provisions."

"What? After just returning from the border?"

"Well, Chataine, he passed through the village on his way here and saw the need was urgent," Angelina explained.

"Oh—" Deirdre muttered in exasperation, "well—" She backed out of the door and went to the foyer to wait for him.

It proved to be a long wait. She sat and fidgeted, then walked to the foyer fire and threw a stick on it. That accomplished, she sat again to fidget some more.

At last, the heavy wooden doors swung open with an icy whoosh and a muffled figure entered. She stood eagerly, but it was only a bearded stranger. Disappointed, she sat again.

The man paused shivering before the foyer fire and said, "Were you waiting to greet me, Chataine?"

"Roman?" she gasped. He let down the hood of his cloak and grinned at her. Between the black beard and dark circles under his eyes, he was barely recognizable.

She stepped haltingly toward him, wanting to throw her arms around his neck—but not daring. So she took his icy fingers in hers to warm them, and kissed them.

"Deirdre—don't," he murmured. From the corner of her eye she saw Angelina enter the foyer, then abruptly turn and leave.

"I missed you so," she whispered.

"And I you—you will never know—" he jerked his hands away as the Surchatain came into view.

"Ah, Roman, you have returned. Are things well at the outposts?"

"Yes, Surchatain." Roman bowed as Karel passed by.

"Good. I will want a complete report soon. Guard, summon Lord Farquehart to my chambers," Karel instructed.

He remained within earshot as Deirdre asked, "How do the villagers fare?"

Roman dropped his head. "Poorly. The plague worsens with the cold, and many are dying. There is so little we can do for them. The children—" He closed his eyes and leaned his shoulder against the wall. Deirdre understood. He wanted to do for them what Galapos had once done for him.

Deirdre turned to ask her father what could be done for the villagers, but he walked out as she was starting the question. Flustered, she looked back at Roman. He was still leaning weakly against the wall, eyes on the fire. So she told him, "Stay here before the fire, and I'll bring you hot soup." He nodded gratefully.

She hurried to the kitchen and began ladling out thick bean soup from a large kettle on the fire. Then she heard a strange scratching noise at the rear door of the kitchen. Angelina was not around—there was no one in the kitchen besides herself. So she opened the door and looked out.

A shabby child stood knee-deep in the snow outside. He stared at her. She stared back. "I didn't get none," he finally said.

"What?" she leaned down, cocking her head.

"Roman came and gave stuff to the others, and I didn't get none!"

"Oh!" Deirdre said. She pulled the child inside, instructing, "Wait here." While he gazed, she filled a leather bag with victuals and gave it to him. She wrapped her own lambswool shawl around him and hung a sack of coal over his shoulder.

Thus laden, he had begun to stumble out when he stopped and turned to look at her. He pulled on her hand till she bent down, then gave her a sloppy, resounding kiss. She returned it, laughing, and sent him on his way.

She took the soup to Roman, who thanked her and gulped it down straight from the bowl. She almost began to tell him about the child, but then decided, no, this was something she did without looking to him for approval. He handed the empty bowl back to her. "It's good to be home," he said.

At dinner Deirdre was delighted to see him rested and clean-shaven again. He even wore the leather shortcoat she had made for him. He hardly spoke a word, as usual, but she could read contentment—even happiness?—on his face. "Roman," she smiled wonderingly, recalling a question of long ago, "are you happy here?"

"Exceedingly," he said easily.

She felt a thrill run up her spine, and the Counselor said, "Of course! He has just survived three weeks of the most perilous duty in the army! Surchatain, shall we toast this soldier's courage?"

Deirdre stared at the Counselor. She had never heard such praise for Roman fall from his lips. Eudymon caught himself in confusion, as if recalling something crucial that had slipped his mind.

The guests at the table waited, then looked at the Counselor and Roman in embarrassment as the Surchatain made himself deaf to the proposal. Roman did not seem offended, however. He was studying his plate—and the Counselor—with the intensity of sudden appreciation.

❖

Now that Roman was home, Deirdre intended to hoard his time, but found that again he had other plans. Every afternoon he departed the palace with supplies and spent hours at the village. Once, she appeared downstairs in heavy clothes and cloak as he was about to leave. "I'm coming with you," she announced.

"No, Chataine, you are not," he said emphatically. "As I told you, there are many ill. I will not have you down there." He took up his pack and paced toward the door.

She followed, protesting, "But—*you* are going—Roman!" she shouted after him as he hurried out. "Curse it," she muttered, yanking off her hood.

In two weeks' time the weather was unchanged, and Deirdre felt really tired of being kept inside like a prisoner. She listlessly roamed from room to room of the palace searching for something to occupy her. Roman was out for the afternoon, as usual.

At dinner she did not want to eat anything. It all looked like so much mush. She drank, though, for her throat was parched and her head was pounding.

"Deirdre? Answer your father. Are you ill?" It was Roman's voice. He was looking at her intently.

"What? Oh, Roman. Did you address me, Father?" Strange that she could not focus on him. Her own voice sounded far away.

Roman was standing now, coming over to her chair. He was saying something about her face. She felt hands on her forehead and heard an odd buzzing . . . that was the last she knew as she fell unconscious into Roman's arms.

Her skin burned with fever, and for days she drifted in and out of fitful sleep. The physician prepared potions, which they forced down her throat and massaged into her chest, but otherwise he was helpless to succor her. "It is the same disease the village folk are fighting," he reported in distress.

"What?" cried Karel. "How could she have been stricken—she and no one else in the palace? Roman!" He turned on the Captain. "Where have you been taking her?"

"High Lord, she has not set foot outside the palace walls!" declared Roman.

Nanna added timidly, "Surchatain, that is the truth. She has not been out."

As Deirdre's fever burned, there was much pacing and crying, but none of it did her any good. Nanna cared for her continually, hardly eating or sleeping herself. She gave the Chataine water when she could take it, and bathed her forehead with wet cloths. Roman took up his post in her receiving room, looking for entrance, but Nanna would in no way allow him in the Chataine's sleeping chambers. Still Deirdre grew weaker.

For her part, Deirdre was engulfed in feverish nightmares. She dreamed she was in the palace alone. She knew there was a banquet going on somewhere; she could hear the laughter and gaiety echoing faintly through the stone corridors. Roman was there—every now and then she heard him call for her, as if he were looking for her. She was supposed to be there as well, but she didn't know where it was or how to get there.

So she ran from room to empty room searching, unable to find him or the banquet. Her anxiety grew unbearable— she *must* find him; she *must* get there before it ended and

187

they left. Around every corner her hopes rose to think she was almost there, as their voices seemed louder. She could hear the music playing, as well. But, no—rounding each corner she found nothing but emptiness. Yet the echoes lingered to taunt her in her desperate search.

Running endlessly from corridor to corridor, she began crying and calling his name: "Roman, where are you? Oh, Roman, help me find you! Help me! Roman!"

Thrashing on her bed, Deirdre cried out feverishly, "Roman! Roman!"

In the next room, he heard her. Pounding on the door, he shouted, "Nurse! Let me in now! Now! Unbolt this door, or I will tear it off the hinges!"

Nanna surrendered to open the door, but scolded him as he rushed to kneel at Deirdre's bedside. "Chataine, it's Roman. I'm here. Deirdre, I'm here." Unaware, she sank back down to the downy bed in her heartbreaking inward search.

Roman combed his fingers through her damp, matted hair and studied her pale face. "She is worsening," he whispered.

Nanna stood wringing her hands behind him. "What is to be done?" she pleaded. He shook his head. Pressing Deirdre's fingers to his face, he closed his eyes.

A minute later Nanna touched him on the shoulder. "Roman. There is something I must tell you, in case the Chataine—in case she—" unable to say the word, she went on: "You must promise me you will tell it to Galapos when the time is right."

He raised his face to her. "Not here," she said. "In the outer room. Come." Gently replacing Deirdre's hand on the bed, he rose to follow Nanna out, and she closed the door.

❖

When Deirdre at last opened her eyes, she saw nothing at first. The room was blurred, dim and cool. Although terribly weak and thirsty, she breathed out gratitude for release from the nightmares. And she was no longer alone. Without even seeing him, she knew he was there.

He moved quickly over her, then called out, "She's awake! Bring water and gruel! Now!"

Gruel, yes. The food of peasants sounded wonderful right now. Roman was lifting her, talking to her: "All is well, Chataine; you're going to be well. He heard our prayers for you."

A cup of cold water was put to her lips, which she drank shakily. It tasted like nectar. Drinking, she raised her eyes to focus on his face. He had a scraggly beard and dark circles under his eyes. Good old Roman.

She reached up to squeeze his neck with what little strength she had and he enfolded her to his chest. Rushing in with a bowl of gruel, Nanna cried, "Darling!" and threw her arms around them both.

Weeks passed before Deirdre could even leave her chambers. Spring had come, and her betrothal fest would be soon. Yet it was evident she was not strong enough for the trip. She would have to wait until the following spring. Karel dispatched a messenger to Corneus and his guests explaining her illness and giving deep—and sincere—regrets for her absence.

When Nanna reluctantly informed the Chataine that the fest would take place without her this year, she was astounded to see Deirdre only sigh and nod. Nanna proudly attributed the lack of tantrums to maturity, but in truth it was gratitude. Deirdre's near encounter with death, at least, had gained her one more year of freedom.

II

The next months of her life Deirdre lived like a condemned prisoner out on leave. She savored every small
pleasure and practiced every kindness, until even Nanna was
abashed and sent provisions of her own to the villagers.

As always, time with Roman was her greatest treasure.
She ceased laying demands on him and plying him with personal questions. He received full freedom to go where he
wished and do what he needed without answering to her.
Yet there was one sacrifice she still needed to make. She
avoided it, fought it, ignored it, but her irritatingly active
conscience would not let her rest. So she rose from bed late
one evening and summoned him to her receiving room....

❖

"Chataine?" Roman entered and bowed. Seeing her in her
overrobe, he stayed close to the door.

"Roman," she began, pacing and rubbing her hands, "I

have not been fair with you. I have been selfish and demanding." She paused, but was annoyed to see that he did not disagree with her. She resumed, "I have decided to give you permission to marry any time you wish. You have waited long enough, and I thank you for your patience and indulgence." There. It was out.

He silently studied the wall beyond her. Then he cleared his throat. "Chataine, thank you for your gracious permission. I believe that I will not, however—not yet. The time is not right."

"Really, Roman?" she exclaimed joyfully, clapping her hands. Then she stopped herself, feeling her reaction was somehow inappropriate.

"Yes, Chataine." He gave a tired smile. "Will that be all?"

"Yes, Roman. You may go," she beamed. She slept sweetly that night.

But it still did not mean that she would see all of him she wanted. Besides his trips to the village, Roman was intently working with the soldiers at the palace, training and arming them. Galapos had made him unofficially in charge of their development as a fighting unit. Officially, of course, he was still the Chataine's guardian. But the greater part of his time by far was consumed with preparing them to fight, and soon. Deirdre watched for hours from the upper window as he instructed them, sparred with them, and yelled at them.

One day she wandered out to find him sifting dismally through their supply of threadbare, moth-eaten woolens. "How shall we fight in the winter, with men losing fingers and toes to frostbite?" he muttered bitterly.

Deirdre stared at him, then turned and ran back into the palace. "Nanna!" she called urgently, rushing into her chambers.

"What? What, dear?" Nanna appeared in alarm.

Deirdre plopped down before a storage chest, heaved up the lid, and began emptying it of yarn. "Summon all the servants who are not directly engaged in a duty ordered by my father. Collect all the knitting needles you can find. We'll need more yarn—send someone to Hycliff to buy all the finest wool Tweedle sells," she instructed, critically examining a ball of scarlet yarn.

"Certainly, dear," Nanna said faintly. "What . . . ?"

"The soldiers need woolens—socks, gloves, mufflers—everything. We are going to provide them," Deirdre said.

Nanna drew up stiffly in protest, "Dear, that's not—"

"Don't lecture me about proprieties!" Deirdre shouted, turning. "These men are going to be fighting for your life, and mine! Just do what I say!"

Flabbergasted, Nanna withdrew without another word. But she carried out the Chataine's instructions, and over the next few weeks she, Deirdre, and numerous other servants knitted until their fingers ached and their eyes burned.

When Deirdre presented Roman with twelve basketloads of thick woolens in brilliant colors—the first fruits of their efforts—Roman was dumbstruck. He remembered himself to thank her prettily in view of the others, but when they were alone, he whispered, "Now I know you care for me."

And still they went riding. The green summer months were passed in excursions to the hills and even neighboring towns. And still they found their way to the willow trees to rest and talk. During these days Deirdre noticed a new peace and ease in Roman's manner, especially toward her. When she remarked about it, he smiled a little and said, "I believe I have finally learned to lay my burdens on God's shoulders. He has assured me these things will be resolved in His way."

She wanted to ask him if God had been talking to him again, but then thought, *Why do I want to ridicule him?* He cut his eyes toward her respectful silence and smiled again.

She raised her eyebrows inquiringly. He said, "It is amazing to see the changes in you—how you have grown up right under my eyes. Yet you are still wonderfully a child." She could not tell him how much he was responsible for what he saw in her.

Once, when she was able to pry him away from his duties for one of those excursions, they rode farther than usual and became hot and thirsty while yet miles from home. Unexpectedly, they came upon a little hut in a clearing in the forest. Deirdre sighed and dismounted. "At the least we can get water here."

Roman looked around, disturbed. "I didn't know there was a shelter here. I don't know who lives here. Chataine, stay beside me."

He approached the door and started to call out, but before he could, it creaked open and a young woman in grey silk appeared. Deirdre startled, feeling a flash of jealousy. The woman was piercingly beautiful, with blue-black hair falling loosely past her shoulders and grey eyes in a face modeled from the sirens of antiquity. *Why is a woman dressed like this living in a hut?* Deirdre wondered.

The beauty never glanced at Deirdre, but gazed at Roman as if he were the embodiment of desire. "You have done well to come, Roman the Warrior. I knew you would."

Roman evaluated her uncertainly. "Who are you?"

"I am Varela, and I have many gifts for you, Warrior," she said in a sultry voice.

He was silent a moment, as if still trying to read her. "The only gift I desire of you is a cup of water for the Chataine and myself."

She laughed deliciously, reaching out to him. "I have much more to give than mere water." Her eyes began to glow. "It has been given me to make you victorious in your battles to come, Warrior."

Roman gave a start as if waking from a trance. He stepped back in repulsion. "I have no need of your gifts, sorceress." To Deirdre he said, "Mount."

"What about some water?" she whispered.

Louder, the woman said, "You will not succeed without me!"

"My success has already been assured without you," he retorted, mounting. "In Christ the Conqueror."

Her face contorted and she shrieked, "A curse! I have a curse for you, then!" They spurred their horses, but she screamed after them: "I see death around you, Warrior! I see the death of thousands around you! I see death surrounding you!"

Deirdre shuddered, "What could she mean?"

"It has no meaning," he replied. "Don't let it trouble you." Nonetheless, they galloped rapidly away from the hut.

"Roman, I'm thirsty!" she pleaded. At once they came upon a clear brook almost hidden in the forest floor.

"We'll drink here," he said.

As they scooped up water in their cupped hands, she watched him. "Then you will fight with Galapos," she observed.

"That is very likely. I don't need her to tell me that," he said, shaking his hands dry.

"Shouldn't you at least hear her out?" she wondered. "I've heard that they are often right—"

"But not always. And what truth they have is distorted to fit their purposes. You must learn, Chataine, to gauge truth by the source, because not everything that sounds true is really so."

"That sounds reasonable," she mused, "considering it came from you." He just shook his head.

It was on the day following that she really began to notice Roman's chapel visits. She had known for years he attended services there, but she had paid no attention. Her father did not go, nor the Counselor—as a matter of fact, she could not name any who went but him. Now, however, her desire to know him better drove her to the chapel doors.

She found a small, simple hall, with a dais at the front

and behind that a rough wooden cross. There were perhaps fifty people inside, kneeling or sitting quietly on the benches. Deirdre was surprised to see that at least half of them were soldiers—yet not surprised, when she considered how well respected Roman was among them. The rest were servants and a few lesser palace officials.

She picked out Roman quickly. Then her heart sank as she saw Angelina sitting close beside him. They were talking in earnest whispers. Deirdre hesitated, turned to leave, but changed her mind and sat on the last bench.

Presently she saw Angelina rise abruptly and walk back to the door, not a happy look on her face. When she saw the Chataine, she startled and bowed stiffly to her before walking out. Roman had gone down on his knees. Deirdre stayed where she was. A few servants who saw her nodded respectfully, but no one made a fuss over her presence.

Soon, a holy man in a simple brown robe entered, walked to the dais, and greeted those present: "Brothers and sisters, hear the words of our Lord Jesus to His close followers the night before He was crucified." *That is the one they worship,* Deirdre recalled, and felt a little smug in her knowledge of the Way.

The holy man opened a large book and read: "Don't let your heart be troubled; you believe in God, believe also in me. In my Father's house are many great rooms; if it were not so, I would have told you. I go to prepare a place for you. And if I go to prepare a place for you, I will come back for you, to bring you with me. . . ."

Studying the back of Roman's bowed head, Deirdre thought about how nice it would be for someone who loved her to prepare a home for her—building it strong of stone and mortar, with wooden floors and plaster on the inside . . . filling it with lovely tapestries and finely carved furniture . . . and then, sharing it with her. In reality, she did not know where she would be living after next spring—or with whom.

Wouldn't it be wonderful to believe in a future with someone who loved her more than life itself?

Thinking of this, with her eyes fixed on Roman's black head, she missed some of the reading. But then she roused herself to hear: "Believe me when I say that I am in the Father and the Father in me, if only because of the miracles. And I tell you that whoever believes in me shall do the things I have done, and even greater things, because I am going to my Father. And whatever you ask in my name I will do, that the Father may be glorified in the Son."

If that were true, all these people would be rulers instead of servants and soldiers, she reflected. She could not explain why Roman believed it, nor why he was so credible in everything else.

"I leave you peace, my peace, not the transient peace the world gives. So don't ever be discouraged or afraid." At those words, Roman's rocklike stability impressed itself on Deirdre's mind.

"You have not chosen me, but I have chosen *you*, and given you a mission to bring forth fruit that will remain, and in so doing, whatever you ask the Father in my name, he will give you. This is what I command you: that you love each other." *A command to love! As if it were hard. . . . Oh, Roman!* and the desire she had never dared face took shape as a man she had known for years. Deirdre bowed her head in tears: *Oh, God, if you are there, if you will hear me—give me the one I love.* She raised her face, shaking her head abruptly in denial. Some things even God could not do. It was never to be.

The leader finished reading and went down on his knees for prayer. The congregation followed suit—Deirdre too. Her voluminous skirts made a distracting rustle as she knelt. Roman glanced back, but she ducked her head and he did not see her.

The holy man said a prayer full of gratitude and thanks-

197

giving, then stood again to make this announcement: "Brothers and sisters, most of you know this is our last meeting here. The Surchatain has forbidden us to meet anywhere in the palace hereafter. We will . . ." he seemed to be looking at Deirdre, "we will inform you when and where we can meet again. For now: The Lord bless you and keep you; the Lord lift His countenance upon you, and give you peace." He raised his hand in a blessing and the meeting broke up. Roman rose heavily from his seat and went forward to greet him as the others left.

Deirdre slipped from the chapel, disturbed. Why would her father forbid these services? They were surely no threat to him. Yet, this God of Roman's seemed to demand devotion above the Surchatain, and she could not imagine her father tolerating anything that put him in second place. But—there was another contradiction. If this worship were a delusion, as Rory said, or empty and useless as her father claimed, then why would he take such measures against it? He did not prevent other soldiers and servants from far baser activities.

At once, two memories presented themselves vividly to her mind's eye. One was of Roman, stamping out the sorcerer's patterns, saying, "They are dangerous. They bring ruin if they influence the right people." The other was of Tremaine's rooms—the blackness—Roman's cry and the sudden light—Tremaine saying, "The rooms affect only those who claim God."

In a flash Deirdre stood on the brink of a chasm and glimpsed a great war raging on a scale that staggered her. These antagonists fought not for such petty spoil as boundaries and trade, but for lives, human lives, millions of little lights dotting the great plain. Each represented a sphere of dominion, a conquest—a spectacular victory or horrifying defeat.

No! She buried her face in her hands, running hard away

from the chapel. She would have none of this war. Therefore, she made no further attempt to attend services, wherever they might have been held.

❖

The summer melted quietly into autumn. Deirdre loved the autumn—the trees bursting out in brilliant red and orange and yellow, the warm afternoons and cool nights . . . the abundant harvests and the aroma of produce drying in the kitchen for the winter store.

She and Roman sat on the high bluff overlooking the golden brown fields, watching the barley harvest in progress. He began rubbing his brow in the way that signaled pain, so she reached over to pull back on his shoulders and rest his head on her knees. As she massaged his face and forehead, he closed his eyes. "You remind me of autumn," she said. He opened one eye. "You are brown and warm, full of color and life. Yet you can be cool, too."

He contemplated this for a moment. "You are spring," he said quietly. "Bright and delicate and beautiful . . . budding with promise. . . ." She grinned and slipped her arms around his neck to hug him. His hand stole up to squeeze hers.

❖

Then winter was upon them again. Fortunately, it was a mild winter compared to the preceding one, so that Deirdre was allowed out to their usual haunts. And for the first time ever, she coaxed Roman out onto the frozen lake with her. He had always said he needed to watch from firm footing in case she got in trouble. But now she discovered the true reason he stayed on shore: he could not skate! He had never learned. "Roman, I could have taught you," she said.

He shook his head. "I was too proud to be your pupil."

But today he humbled himself to strap on blades in the sleigh. She offered her hand as he stepped out, but he eyed her and alighted by himself. Blessed with strong ankles, he was steady enough on the ground, but the moment he stepped gingerly onto the ice he fell flat.

Circling him, Deirdre bit her lip to keep from laughing as he got to his feet. He was wobbly at first, getting the feel of the ice, but after the first few minutes he skated remarkably well—stopping, turning, even making circles. But when she tried to skate with him, their feet got tangled up and they went down in a heap together. They were laughing, and then all at once they were holding each other close.

For a heartbeat he held her, then let go and scrambled to his feet. "This lesson has ended," he said.

Other times they had the most fun riding in the sleigh, whenever Deirdre could wrench him away from soldiering. She would bundle up in her fur-lined cloak and heap furs in the sleigh, then she and Roman would set off to explore the world in crystal and white.

One day, in a radical departure from the norm, he interrupted her lessons with Olin to take her sleigh riding. "How dare you?" she protested happily, throwing aside the books.

"I want you to go with me now, because there is someone I want you to meet," he said, taking the furs she thrust at him.

"Yes? Who?" She grabbed up her cloak, forgetting about the little velvet slippers on her feet.

"You'll see." He took the armload of furs, and they stole out of the palace to the waiting sleigh. Seating her, he said sternly, "Deirdre, please do not announce at dinner that I took you away from your lessons to go with me."

"I may, and I may not," she teased. "Who are we going to see?"

"You'll see." He clucked Lady Grey to a trot, and Deirdre sang inwardly as she sat close beside him, watching the silver trees glide past. If she looked carefully, she might spot a snow rabbit or silver fox among the trees.

Roman guided the sleigh beyond the far side of the village. There sat one lone hut, removed from the others. Smoke billowed up from its center chimney. Roman guided the sleigh up to its door, jumped down lightly and helped Deirdre out. Then he pulled out a basket filled with dried fruit, venison, and fresh bread. "Brother Avelon!" he called out.

The door opened and a thin man in a ragged brown robe motioned them in. Deirdre stepped shyly into the hut and looked around. It was so small and crude, she felt uneasy in her furs.

"Roman, thank you, son," he said, taking the basket. "I am grateful to God for your kind heart." His hand shook so that he almost dropped the basket until Roman guided it to the dirt floor for him.

"It is a small kindness, Brother Avelon. I want you to meet the Chataine Deirdre. Deirdre, this is the holy man who taught my mother."

"Oh!" she said. "I am honored to meet you! But—do you live here? In this?" In her concern she somehow lost her tact.

Brother Avelon smiled ruefully. "As of late, Chataine, yes. My health no longer allows me to travel my circuit preaching the Word."

"You must come live in the palace, then," she insisted. Roman flashed a quick smile at her, then a look that said "I told you" to Brother Avelon.

But the holy man declined, "I cannot, Chataine, though you are gracious to offer it. I have not endeared myself to the Surchatain." Deirdre then remembered he was the one who had posed as a minstrel and sung a song that angered her father.

"Well—what can we do to help you?" she asked.

"Roman does much, my child—too much, I fear. He has already come under criticism from the palace overseer for taking so much food out of the palace. Your silence on these matters spares him further censure," Avelon said, and Roman shifted uneasily.

"Certainly," she said, glancing at Roman. "But Father has always allowed charity to the villagers."

"Within limits—which seem to have become more stringent since your illness," Roman replied. Deirdre was offended at the suggestion that her father would blame them for her getting sick.

The holy man turned to Roman. "God is moving swiftly. I see so many of our prayers being answered, especially in you. As long as you are here, Roman, let us pray together for your father."

Roman startled. "Later, Brother. I must return Deirdre to the palace before she is missed. I'll be back—" he hustled her out to the sleigh. Avelon watched them dash away with a troubled face.

Deirdre turned to Roman beside her. "Does he know your father?"

"They have never met. Brother Avelon knows only that he needs prayer," Roman said.

"Do you pray for him?"

"Yes," he said defensively, looking away.

✥

It was spring, then, in a rush of green. When the Fair came, Deirdre and Roman spent a day shopping at their (rather, her) favorite booths. She picked up a jeweled bracelet. "May I buy something for Angelina?" she asked him.

He paused. "It isn't necessary on my account, Chataine. She has married another."

"Oh, Roman. I'm sorry," she breathed. He merely shrugged in seeming unconcern.

She, however, was awash in guilt. Looking over to a

nearby booth of woolens, she asked, "What do you need? Gloves? A hood?"

"I am well supplied for winters to come, thanks to my lady," he grinned.

"Oh, yes," she remembered. She looked hazily toward the weapons booth. "Well—your arms—"

"Your father raised enough in taxes to supply us, Chataine," he advised her.

"Special fare? You love Weinert's sausages," she reminded him.

"I eat at the Surchatain's table. How much better fare can you get?" he asked, a little bemused.

"Well, then—" she looked around somewhat desperately. "A finer medallion—"

"Deirdre." He took her by the hand. "What do I want with jewelry? It only gets in the way," he said softly.

At that painful reminder, subtle as it was, that soon he would be on a battlefield again, Deirdre turned her face away. "I must get you something. Let me get you something for all you've done," she insisted.

"Oh, Deirdre," he murmured, coming close as he dared. "You have given me dreams to last the rest of my life. I am content with that." She hung her head low and shed tears standing next to him while the crowds milled around them, heedless.

❖

Galapos returned from the border that spring. Both Deirdre and Roman were among those waiting to meet him at the palace gate. When he saw Deirdre, his face registered wondering admiration. "I left you a little girl and come back to find you a ravishing young woman! How old I must be getting!" But no—except for a trifle more grey at the temples, he was unchanged.

It was good to have him back and to hear his jocularity again. The three of them went riding together so that Deirdre and Roman could inform him privately of all the palace news. He had heard of her illness, and had waited anxiously to hear of her recovery. "To be frank, Chataine, I did not hold out much hope for you," he said. "That disease is most often deadly."

"Oh, I could not have died. Roman would not let the Reaper by!" she grinned. Galapos laughed; Roman shook his head, smiling. Deirdre loved seeing them together again. Galapos brought out such a light in Roman's eyes.

Later, Galapos and Roman stopped by the Counselor's chambers. They knocked, and the Counselor quickly opened the door. "Galapos." He grasped the Commander's hand warmly. "I heard you had returned."

"Yes, and I have some news for you, Counselor. May we come in?" The door opened wide, then was shut and bolted behind them.

Shortly thereafter, Caspar, Chatain of Calle Valley, arrived in Westford to visit Deirdre before her betrothal fest. She was irritated to see him given Roman's seat across from her at dinner. Roman was placed farther down the table.

"Well, Caspar, how do things fare in the valley?" Karel opened cordially.

"Quite well, Surchatain. We had a remarkable yield from the vineyards last year, thanks to careful planting and per-fect weather," Caspar replied knowledgeably. He shared his sister's curly black hair and green eyes, but his features spoke of greater seriousness underneath.

"The wine from your valley is always excellent," observed Karel.

Caspar inclined his head. "I am honored it pleases you, for I have brought twenty casks of our best vintage as a small gift." His eyes rested on Deirdre. "This fest has been long in coming, but I feel it will be worth the wait."

Deirdre raised her eyes. "Will Laska be there?"

"No, I regret that she will not. She married Gastin last year. She sends you her love, by the way."

"Please give her mine," Deirdre murmured.

After dinner, Caspar took her hand and they retreated to a private balcony overlooking the garden. For once, Roman was not standing in the shadows. He did not guard her in her own palace.

"Deirdre," Caspar began, "you know why I am here. I want you to marry me." She was about to say something sarcastic, such as "stand in line," but he stopped her. "I know I'm not as pretty as Artemeus nor as powerful as Rollet but, in time, you will see I am the best choice. I will love you, Deirdre."

She was silent a moment. "What will become of Lystra if I marry you?"

"Why, nothing evil. We will rule it together. Of course, we will pay taxes to Tremaine, and the troops at your outposts will be sent elsewhere, but Tremaine will let us be," Caspar said.

"Why?" she demanded. "Why does he need us, or anyone?"

Caspar began to explain, "He cannot rule the entire area himself. He needs governors—"

"Puppet rulers," she said contemptuously.

"I have heard a saying that it is better to be a live dog than a dead lion," Caspar observed softly.

Deirdre looked down at the espaliered pear trees, the branches of which resembled arms reaching up, pleading. "What then will become of Father? And Commander Galapos?"

"I'm very sorry, Deirdre. They must be put away," he whispered.

Her stomach churned. "Say it outright. Say that my father is to be killed," she demanded.

"It is Tremaine's order. The present leaders must be set aside. We have no choice about that, my love," he said.

"But, if Tremaine plans to do away with my father, why should he spare yours—or Savin?" she asked coldly.

He shrugged a little uneasily. "Tremaine spares those useful to him. All he wants of Karel is his sea trade—and you. It is no secret that he despises your father." He added, supposedly in kindness, "You are very fortunate Tremaine decided to use you instead of kill you."

Deirdre turned away from him. "What about the other officers in the army? Will they all be executed too?"

"Tremaine says that any heads that rise above the others must be cut off," he answered. She closed her eyes. "Will you marry me, Deirdre?"

"Ask me after the fest," she replied, wishing fervently that the day would never come.

❧ 12 ❧

Scant weeks after Caspar's visit, it was time for Nanna to make her usual bubbling preparations for the trip to Ooster. This time, however, the Chataine took little pleasure in the exquisite gowns laid out for her approval. She felt as if she were facing her own execution.

With relentless inevitability, the day arrived for the journey. Deirdre had requested that no soldiers accompany them this time, and her father agreed that Roman was sufficient. Departing at dawn, the two of them traveled in silence toward the watershed at Ooster.

With each mile they covered, the Chataine's burden grew heavier and heavier. Finally she reined to a stop. . . .

❖

"Roman, what am I going to do?" Deirdre cried. "If I marry one of Tremaine's allies, you will all die. If I don't, Tremaine will kill us all anyway!"

"Not necessarily," he quietly replied. "Chataine, we have not been sitting on our hands since Tremaine threatened you. Galapos has been gathering men and weapons into the greatest army this country has ever seen. We are now ready to fight. So follow your own judgment."

Deirdre knew then what she would do.

Arriving at Ooster, she saw that the splendor of Corneus's preparations was unmatched, as usual. But Deirdre eyed them with disdain. As she watched several pranksters drape flower garlands on the stone lions that stood guard at the palace gates, a voice at her side said, "You have grown since I last saw you." She turned to see Rollet.

"It happens, with time," she replied coldly, then nodded to Roman as he stepped up with her bags. She followed Corneus's servant through the crowd of chattering guests, aiming only to get to her room.

Artemeus stepped in front of her. "Hello, beautiful creature."

She paused long enough to say, "I am not the beast here," and lifted her skirts to start up the stairs. Artemeus looked dumbfounded.

On the stairs she encountered Caspar. He took her hand, saying sincerely, "Deirdre, seeing you makes me want to sing."

"Thank you," she said. It was harder to be rude to him.

He whispered, "How long will you keep me waiting?"

She looked down at her mud-covered riding boots. "A while. I must change now."

"Don't be long. The hall is empty without you." He squeezed her hand and continued down the stairs.

Looking after him, she whispered, "Wait forever, Caspar." She directed a deliberate glance at Roman on the step below. He was frowning slightly, peering at her, trying to read her mind. She smiled, aware of how anxious he was to know her marriage choice. Their whole defense hung on it. Turning, she resumed climbing the stairs.

Deirdre stayed in her room until dinner, dressing with determined slowness. Servants were sent several times to inquire after her, but she did not bestir herself until Corneus came up to plead for her presence. *When they look at me, all they see is river trade,* she thought caustically. Opening her door, she saw Roman waiting patiently outside, at his post, as always. *Everyone but him,* she amended.

It would have been utterly presumptuous for him to offer his arm as they descended the stairs; that was Corneus's privilege. Her uncle took her hand, saying something she never heard. Roman kept a few paces ahead of them to prevent her falling down the stairs should her foot slip. At the bottom of the stairs, he left her with a glance to assume his position against the wall with the other chaperons.

Jason met up with them as Corneus chatted on about how lovely Deirdre looked. "Doesn't she, Jason?"

"Yes, Deirdre. You will sit with me tonight," he said with carefully rehearsed cordiality. He took her arm, and she allowed herself to be escorted to the banquet hall between them.

The hall was already filled with waiting guests. Corneus took his seat at the head of the table, placing Jason to his right with Deirdre beside him. Roman took his place behind Deirdre's chair, and Corneus motioned for the serving to begin.

The platter of steaming mutton set before her almost made her gag. Jason was saying, "Deirdre, you are one fortunate girl. I turned Musa away to court you." Deirdre imagined the mutton plate upturned on his head and smiled. He returned the smile with a wink.

Artemeus, to her right, smiled genially as he said to Jason, "Your father's table is legendary at these fests." Then he leaned toward Deirdre to whisper, "But Jason is an idiot."

Not hearing the whisper, Jason raised his nose. "Certainly

no one living on a rock can match it." Artemeus's smile vanished.

Caspar paused beside Roman behind her to say, "The greenness of Calle Valley is both handsome and productive. It can grow anything—"

"Including greenhorns," smirked Artemeus.

Caspar quietly replied, "Innocuous appearances are intended so as not to alarm harmless morons." Jason laughed so suddenly he choked.

Deirdre stood abruptly. "Excuse me. I need fresh air." As Caspar and Jason began elbowing each other to accompany her, she added, "Alone! For a moment. Please."

Quickly, she turned and walked the breadth of the hall to the gates of Corneus's verdant garden. The reassuring footfalls of her guardian pursued her. She stopped to let Roman open the gate for her, then walked on down the pebble-lined path. For some minutes they stood silently enshrouded in the fragrances borne by the evening breeze. Here, in the garden, she felt eons away from malicious charades and murderous hearts.

She touched a rose petal. These things were real. This was entirely a rose, from its petals to its roots, and the generation it produced would be roses, and the generation after that roses. Long after Jason turned to dust and Artemeus grew old and feeble, roses would grow to grace someone's hedges and walls. These things were reliable, trustworthy, *eternal*—

"Did you speak to me?" she asked Roman with a start.

"Not aloud," he said quietly.

She was searching his eyes when Rollet approached the gates and called, "Deirdre?" Sighing, she returned to the fest.

The following day she remained detached throughout the amusements, hardly speaking and showing no interest in the men around her. Strangely, the more she withdrew, the more attention she drew. Perhaps it was because she was a challenge, or an enigma, that one young man after another joined the siege to break down her ennui. They irritated her with their fawning and chafed her spirit raw in their attempts to arouse her interest.

After the noon meal she slipped away, intending to sneak up to her room. She had made it beyond the great double doors when two bony fingers jabbed into her sides. She gasped and spun around. "Otto!"

A large-boned blond man laughed and demanded, "Where are you running off to, pretty thing?"

"I am going up to my room to rest," she said through gritted teeth.

"Not when I came across a continent to see you." He grasped her hand to drag her away from the stairs. At that, Roman began advancing with a predatory look.

But another fellow grabbed Otto. Roman hesitated. "Maybe she doesn't want to see *you!* Deirdre, I brought you some little silver bells for your mare's bridle," the other said.

"Take those bells and hang them on your ear, Morin!" growled Otto.

Morin shoved Otto. "That insult just earned you a pugil lesson!"

"To the courtyard, then!" agreed Otto. They stalked out together, expecting Deirdre to follow and watch them fight over her.

But with a breath of relief, she bounded up the stairs. Glancing back at Roman, she saw him watching her feet as he followed. Laughing.

Deirdre fought down a strong desire to feign illness and instead attended dinner that night. She said very little, allowing the conversation to flow around her. In between the onion soup and the roast duck, talk at the table turned to what women found interesting in men. Thoughts of Roman sprang to Deirdre's mind. As he stood behind her chair, she felt his presence like a warm fire at her back.

One girl said she liked a man with dark eyes. Someone said, "Oh-oh, that means you, Jason," and everyone laughed. Another girl said she preferred strong, muscular men. Another said she was attracted to men with beards.

Then someone asked, "Deirdre, what do you like in a man?" They fell silent, waiting.

She put her cloth napkin to her mouth. The fire burned warmly at her back. "It is good for a man to be strong," she said. "A strong man can do so many things. But a man who is both strong and gentle is wonderful. A man must be intelligent, of course, but if he is also humble, that makes him all the better . . . a man who is strong enough to live a disciplined life, but who is easy on the faults of others . . . a man who is honest above all, but kind . . . a man with courage, who will sacrifice his life for someone else, yet who also has the kind of courage to stay with the same task year in and year out, even if it's boring or tiring or painful, simply because it's his duty . . . a man with the courage of faithfulness. I love all these things about a man." There was a momentary silence.

"You sound as if you are describing someone you know, my dear," observed Corneus.

"I am."

"The man you love," a girl said.

"Yes," Deirdre answered.

"Who is it?" "Are you going to marry him?" several asked at once.

Deirdre swallowed. "I cannot say who it is—I won't force his hand. But if he asked me, I would marry him."

The conversation turned to other things, and Deirdre said no more. As she rose from the table she looked at Roman, and the expression of love in his eyes made her catch her breath.

But someone spoke in her ear and pulled her away. She had no chance to speak with him alone that evening. He was only her chaperon, one of many there. He did not share her suite nor eat with her at the banquet table. Now, when she desired his presence more than ever, he melted into the background.

The day after, the men continued to harass her, leaving her no moment alone until she locked herself in her room again. Before the evening meal Corneus came to her door and knocked. "Deirdre, my dear, are you well?" he asked with some impatience.

She opened the door slowly. "No, uncle, not really. I have been weak ever since my illness, you know." She tried not to look at Roman standing next to him.

"Well, we will get you some medicines so you will be able to come downstairs for the finale. You are coming down, are you not?" Corneus commanded.

"Yes, I will be down directly, Uncle," she murmured. He withdrew to let her get ready.

Looking over the vast hall from the top of the stairway, Deirdre felt an unsettling sense of déjà vu. Of course she had seen it before—two years ago at her coming out. Every year they all went through the same silly pantomime of falling in love.

She looked down on the couples dancing below her, then dismally gathered her skirts to descend the stairs. She did not want to dance. Why should she dance with anyone here? Roman trotted down ahead of her. Watching his back, she saw him as he was stretched between the whipping posts because of her childish disobedience. There was one person she would dance with.

As she came off the stairs someone approached, but she veered aside to circle in front of Roman, stopping him short. "Dance with me."

The eyebrow arched up. "But—Chataine—"

"Dance with me, Roman." She would hear no arguments. To her surprise, he took her hand and led her out onto

213

the floor. He placed his hand at her waist and paused to listen for the music. As he guided her around the floor in perfectly placed steps, Deirdre soared inside. When had he learned to dance? Had he learned for her? Wasn't that just like him, to learn on the outside chance that someday they would dance together?

"Roman," she whispered, gazing up at him, "let's leave here. Tonight."

"No, Chataine. It's too dangerous traveling the road to Westford at night," he objected.

"Not to Westford . . . somewhere else. Anywhere else!"

He looked at her for a long moment, then lowered his eyes. "I can't leave," he whispered. "There is too much at stake. . . ." Artemeus then cut in with a grin. Roman relinquished her hand and took up his position near the wall.

Artemeus was talking to her—"and wouldn't our children be beautiful?" he finished. Deirdre tore her gaze from Roman to look at him with a hopeless sigh.

"What's wrong with you?" he demanded.

"Nothing that won't soon be right," she avowed, drawing away from him. She left the fest without a backward glance and shut herself up in her room again.

She rose before the sun the next morning. Packing, she fretted about how to find Roman to leave early, but he was waiting as usual—albeit groggily—when she opened her door. Wordlessly, she handed him her bags and they made like ghosts down the echoing stairs. She even accompanied him to the stables to help saddle their horses. This way, they were able to slip out unmolested by anyone but the overseer of the fest, who ran out in his nightshirt to throw himself on Deirdre's saddle and beg her not to leave yet. He fell away when she dug her heels into Lady Grey's sides and departed at a gallop.

Mists rose down the road in the early dawn. At the speed they were traveling, the fog opened before them just a little at a time. Sudden curves or obstructions would have proved disastrous to someone who did not know the way well. But under Roman's guidance, she had learned the way. She had learned to watch for wolves and robbers; she had learned to read the stars. She had learned to look past obscuring mists for the truth.

"Roman!" She suddenly reined in her horse and he careened to a stop. "Don't you understand?" she shouted. "I love you! I love you!"

He trotted to her side, took her face in his hands, and kissed her with a yearning born in tears and blood. At length he said, "Deirdre, I have loved you ever."

"You understand, then, that I will not have anyone but you," she gasped.

"I understand." He drew away and inhaled deeply, setting his face like a flint toward Westford. She followed him in a euphoria of love.

❖

When they arrived at Westford, they were given only a moment to wash up before being summoned for the evening meal. When Deirdre came down the stairs, Roman was waiting for her. As they entered the great hall together, Galapos greeted them joyfully: "Chataine, sweetheart, you're home! Tell me, are you betrothed yet?" Deirdre inadvertently glanced toward Roman, then dropped her eyes and blushed. Galapos jumped to another topic, and they took their seats.

But then an unnerving chain of events began. A messenger arrived bearing a letter, which the Surchatain took and read silently. "Deirdre," he said, causing her stomach to wrench. "This is from Chatain Artemeus, son of Savin. He offers his country to you in marriage."

"No," she said quietly. Karel nodded and waved the messenger out again. Those at the table began to eat under the weight of expectation—or dread.

Moments later another messenger arrived. He carried a proposal from Caspar. "No," she said. Then, in sequence, came proposals from Morin, Carlin, and Otto. Deirdre turned them all down.

The table became uncommonly quiet. Roman sat staring at his plate, and Galapos calmly smoothed his moustache, keeping his eyes off the Captain. Deirdre sat with her hands folded in her lap, not even pretending to eat.

Another messenger arrived. Karel took his letter and then sat back, beaming. "Here it is, Deirdre—a proposal from Rollet. What do you say?"

She opened her mouth. "No," she choked out.

He startled. "No? No?" He began to boil. "What do you want? Six proposals—seven, including Gastin—whom will you have?"

Galapos laughed, "She's merely stacking them up to select from!" But he and the Counselor exchanged uneasy glances.

In the midst of that turmoil one more messenger arrived. Karel seized his letter and ripped it open. "Jason? Will you have Jason, Deirdre?"

"No," she said, but he did not react immediately. He seemed to be reading more.

He laid the letter aside and turned full toward her. "Who is it?"

She blanched. "What?"

"Corneus said he hoped the man you described—the one whom you love—is Jason. Obviously it is not. So who is it you *will* marry?" Karel demanded. Deirdre bit her lip and said nothing. "Answer me!" he shouted. Silence. Karel rose from his seat. "Deirdre, you will answer or I—"

"High Lord," interrupted Roman. "I am the one."

There was a shocked silence around the table. All eyes were fixed on Roman. Then Deirdre stammered, "Father—

he lies! He—"

"He never lies," the Surchatain said calmly, walking over to face Roman, who stood. "He does not know how to lie. Soldier, have you made love to my daughter?"

"No, High Lord."

"Have you touched her? Kissed her?"

"Yes," Roman answered. Galapos put his head in his hands.

"You know the penalty you have incurred," Karel said in a low voice.

"Yes, High Lord." Roman's face was stone.

"Guards," Karel turned, "take him—"

"No!" Deirdre shouted, bounding up. "No!" She kicked her chair over backwards and faced her father. "You will not do this again. You won't punish him on account of me again. You won't!"

"Take your seat, daughter," Karel warned.

"No! Father, I swear, if you execute him, I will kill myself! You will have no heir! I swear it!" Deirdre cried.

"Deirdre, no!" Roman uttered in dismay.

Karel ordered, "Guards! Take him to the prison. Escort her to her chambers and post a guard at her door. Counselor, to my chambers!"

There was swift movement on every side as his orders were carried out. Roman moved to walk between two guards who would not lay hands on him. As his eyes met hers over the table, she saw them pleading, commanding, *Don't— don't.*

Within his chambers, Karel slumped into a chair. "What do I do *now*?" he spat.

The Counselor stroked his beard nervously. "Well, High Lord, you yourself decreed the punishment for such an offense: death by torture."

"But what if Deirdre makes good her threat?" Karel worried.

Eudymon waved his concern aside. "An impetuous outcry from an angry child. He has been at her side constantly for eight years, so she simply rebelled at the idea of losing so faithful a servant. We must entertain no thought of mercy for her sake. Roman must be punished to the full extent of your commands."

Karel shook his head slowly, musing, "But he has saved her many times. He has been so reliable—why did he have to do this, now, when she was so close to marrying?"

Eudymon opened his mouth but Karel straightened with authority. "No, Counselor, I will be merciful, for both their sakes." Eudymon relaxed visibly. "He will only be hanged," decreed the Surchatain. "In the morning. And send a messenger to Rollet accepting his proposal. Ask him to come immediately for the wedding. You are dismissed, Counselor."

❖

Deirdre sat in her darkened room, waiting for some word as to Roman's fate. She had begged the guard at the door to allow her to go to him in prison. He had refused, though kindly. So she sat. And waited.

Nanna quietly entered. Deirdre looked up expectantly. "Dear," Nanna began, "you must not—"

"Just tell me what will happen to him," Deirdre said in a whisper.

"I don't know, dear. No one will tell me anything. Just rest for now, Chataine. I'm sure your father will be lenient with him," Nanna said, lying.

"Leave me alone now," Deirdre said, turning back to the darkness.

"Dear, your father has ordered me—"

"Leave me alone," Deirdre repeated. Acquiescing as usual, Nanna slipped into her own room.

Deirdre closed her eyes and prayed to the God she had

never known, begging for the life of her beloved guardian. "He believes in you, and look what you've brought on him," she whispered. "Why do you treat your faithful this way?" So musing, she watched the shadows slip by into the night until she fell asleep.

At dawn she awoke with a start. The guard was banging at her door. "Chataine! The Surchatain summons you to an open audience!" She dressed and stumbled fearfully out of the room. An open audience could only bode ill.

The audience hall was crowded, even this early. As soon as Deirdre had taken her place before the dais, the Counselor stepped up and announced, "The High Lord and reigning Superiority of the independent state of Lystra, the gracious and beneficent Surchatain Karel." *Liar*, Deirdre seethed. The audience bowed on their knees while Karel entered and took his seat.

He glanced at Deirdre and waved at the guards: "Bring out the prisoner." Roman, his hands bound behind his back, was led out between two guards to stand in judgment before the dais. Her heart broke at this humiliation of him who was blameless. But he raised his tired, unshaven face to look Karel in the eye.

The Surchatain read a statement: "You, Roman, for the crime of indecency with the Chataine Deirdre, are sentenced to hang by the neck until you are dead. Have you anything to say in your defense?"

"No, Surchatain," he replied. Deirdre felt nauseated.

"Guards—to the courtyard." Karel stood, and the people kneeled. Roman was led out of the hall.

Karel, Galapos, and Eudymon escorted Deirdre to a balcony overlooking the courtyard. Deirdre grasped the railing to steady herself when she saw a monstrous scaffold standing in the center of the grounds. A noose hung swaying in the wind above the trap door in the platform. Close around the structure stood many soldiers, rigid. The crowd from the audience hall milled in behind the soldiers to watch the execution.

"Father," Deirdre turned, beseeching, "please, please, he is not to blame. Please—I'll do anything you say—marry Rollet, anything—if you will let him live."

Karel only lifted his chin. She turned to Galapos, who looked down on her with moist blue eyes and shook his head. Eudymon—she did not even began an appeal to him. It was useless.

Roman appeared between the guards on the grounds below the balcony. When he looked up, Galapos put a firm hand around Deirdre's arm. She was unaware how far she was trying to lean over the railing.

Karel said, "Have you any last requests?"

"Yes, High Lord. I wish the Chataine not to view my face while I hang—only after I am dead; and that she receive my bequest to her," Roman said. Deirdre sank to her knees under the weight of horror.

"It shall be done," said the Surchatain. "Bring the hood," he motioned. A soldier stepped up and covered Roman's head with a black hood. He was then led to the back of the scaffold by the soldier. Disappearing momentarily behind it, they ascended the steps and reappeared on the platform.

The noose was fitted around the condemned's neck. Deirdre opened her mouth to cry his name but no sound came. The soldier left the platform. The Surchatain raised his hand, and dropped it.

The trap door sprang open with a terrible creak and bang. His body twisted and jerked for several moments, then swung lifelessly. Deirdre gazed in shock. Some people in the audience applauded the show before wandering away, but the soldiers were still.

Finally, the Surchatain gave a signal and the body was taken down. A soldier began to lead her from the balcony. "No!" she pleaded, coming to herself. "Oh, no, no." She collapsed in tears and would not move.

Galapos leaned down to her. "Deirdre, go with him," he urged. When she sobbed refusals he said in her ear, "A soldier's beloved would not refuse his last request." Shakily, she rose to follow the soldier.

He took her through the courtyard to the back of the platform, where he lifted the curtain that shut off the little room within. The body lay on the ground, covered with a blanket. Soldiers were preparing to place it in a wooden casket and nail down the lid.

One of them uncovered his face, but she could not look. She could not bear to see him dead. "Chataine, look!" the soldier hissed. She shook her head. He forced her to look down on the body.

It was not Roman. In her confusion and grief, she would have cried out but the soldier clapped a hand over her mouth. "He wanted you to know so you would not harm yourself," he whispered. Other soldiers were watching out the back to allow no one near the body until they had it packed away.

Then he gave her Roman's gold medallion. "And he wanted you to hold this until he returned for it."

"Where—how—?" she stammered.

"He has gone into hiding for now," he whispered, adding, "You are not the only one who cares for him."

"Who is that poor man?" she asked, turning to the dead man again. His form was quite similar to Roman's.

"A condemned prisoner. He had confessed to the murder of a kitchen maid, Hana, years ago."

The soldiers put the body in the coffin, and were lifting the lid to cover it when the Counselor could be heard just outside: "I will view the body for you, High Lord."

"Stop him!" gasped Deirdre, but it was too late—he had already stepped inside. He looked down on the dead man, then backed out through the flap and said loudly, "He is quite dead, High Lord."

When he came inside again, Deirdre gaped at him in bewilderment. Was there something familiar in his face . . . ? "In spite of what you may think, Chataine, I would wish Roman no harm," he said quietly. "He is my son."

Deirdre's head began spinning. "Come," said the Counselor, "we must allow these men to dispose of the body quickly. We will talk in my chambers."

As they approached the balcony, the Counselor looked up and said, "High Lord, I will put the Chataine under a protective watch so that no harm comes to her before the wedding." High above them, the Surchatain nodded.

Deirdre held back a thousand questions until they were safely in the Counselor's chambers. "This is yours, then," she said as she held out the medallion to him.

"Yes, I gave it to him; but no, he gave it to you—as rightly he should. He told me many times of his love for you, and how he feared it would only betray him to his death." Eudymon bolted his door as he spoke, then checked behind the curtain dividing his chambers.

A cautious man, Deirdre observed, even while her heart ached to realize that Roman loved her long before she had awakened to him. "Did you plan the switch, then?"

"I and others, obviously, but I will bear the responsibility if it is found out. No matter. I believe I have finally redeemed myself in the eyes of my son," Eudymon said.

"The counsel I have heard you give Father has always been against Roman," Deirdre observed carefully.

"I must tell you how that came about," he said quickly. "When I first became your father's Counselor, I discovered he is one of those men who believe themselves too wise to need a counselor. However, it is good form for a ruler to have one. So every counsel I gave him, he would consider and then take another course. I believe he has never really trusted me. I soon found that if I played the devil's advocate—if I suggested extreme or hasty moves, he would consider and then choose the wiser route. Your father has made some wise decisions with my help."

"You mean you deliberately gave false counsel?" Deirdre asked, alarmed.

"No. I merely encouraged him to think along certain lines. It is a tricky business, and sometimes ricochets. But when I ascertained there was a plot against your life, that is essentially how I persuaded him to assign you a guardian," Eudymon related.

"You suggested Roman?"

"Oh, no, then he surely would have rejected him. I merely pointed out all the qualifications a guardian must have, then I made certain he saw Roman display each of those characteristics. Your father selected him himself." Eudymon watched the slim shaft of light from the crack under the door, looking for telltale shadows of someone listening outside.

"Why did you want Roman selected?" Deirdre asked, caressing the medallion.

"An advancement for my son—you understand. And also because he truly is the best," Eudymon said with some pride.

"But becoming my guardian prevented his advancement under Galapos," Deirdre protested. "Or—is that what you wanted?"

He shrugged. "A tradeoff, Chataine. He could not have it both ways."

She considered this silently, knowing what Roman had really wanted. "Does Roman know how you give backward counsel? Does he understand what you are trying to do?"

"Yes, of course. But he does not appreciate it. He says it is deceptive at best, and may actually weigh against him more than help him. He claims your father does not trust me because of that practice. I maintain I began it because he did not ever heed my counsel. But that never prevented

Roman from seeking my counsel regarding you, Chataine," he added dryly.

Deirdre blushed, clutching the medallion. "And what did you advise him?" she asked shyly.

"That he should be ready to die the day he let slip his love for you. It was a marvelous lesson in self-control," he observed with that same dry humor.

Before deciding that she had been wrong about Eudymon all her life, she had to know more. "Why did you desert him?"

"What?" he asked. "When?"

"Why did you stop sending money when his mother died?" she demanded.

"He told you that as well? Oh, my. I did send money, Chataine, even for months afterward, not knowing she had died. It was much later I discovered that the rogue I had employed as messenger not only kept the money after she died, but had been skimming from what I sent them while she lived. Once I discovered this, I made certain he never stole again," Eudymon noted chillingly, playing with a dagger.

"Did you love her?" Deirdre asked.

"Of course I did," he said defensively.

"Then why didn't you marry her?" She was relentless.

The Counselor sighed. "Roman has never forgiven me for that, either. My dear, a man in my position, to marry a prostitute—it would have ruined me. I did the best I could for them. I just never could be—the father to Roman I wanted to be."

"Is that why you dislike Galapos? Because Roman loves him as a father?"

"Your blade is very sharp, Chataine," he said ruefully, then admitted, "Perhaps. When I discovered her to be dead, I searched the whole province for Roman, but found no trace of him. I thought he was dead as well. Then I came to the palace, and lo and behold, he was in Galapos's care. Roman saw me, too, and hated me. It was years before he would even speak to me. Even so he has never acknowledged me as his father, though I have done what I could for him here."

"You killed the assassin," she said, suddenly remembering. "But why did you lie about it?"

"How would I explain to the Surchatain that I killed the man he most wanted to get his hands on? Should I have said, 'High Lord, he was about to kill my son'? Roman's life was not in the least important to him. He cared only to know who was trying to kill his heir and take his throne!" Eudymon asserted.

"I was beginning to think you were in alliance with Tremaine," she said thoughtfully.

"No, Chataine. I know who Tremaine's spies are in the palace, and keep them filled with what information I want them to have. Speaking of whom—your father has sent for Rollet to come marry you, posthaste. He should be here within three days."

Deirdre closed her eyes, clutching the medallion. "I won't marry Rollet, not as long as Roman lives," she said through gritted teeth. "Counselor, help me!" she pleaded.

He raised a finely arched brow. "Well, Chataine, perhaps I might suggest that your uncle may prove a sympathetic haven? Though of course, it would be extremely foolish for you to attempt to run away in the middle of the night to Ooster."

Their eyes met in understanding, and Deirdre smiled gratefully. "Thank you for your wise advice, Counselor. I will certainly heed it."

He regarded her with the mere hint of a smile. "May your guardian find you safe, Chataine," he whispered.

Deirdre was escorted back to her chambers by a palace guard. She listened at the door long enough to discover there were two guards stationed outside it. No matter—she would never get through the palace unseen anyway. Deirdre slipped Roman's medallion around her neck, then waited quietly through long hours until nightfall.

As always, Nanna attended her at bedtime. The nurse-maid, having witnessed the execution, was pale and subdued as she hovered at the foot of Deirdre's bed. "There, dear, is that all right? More covers? No? Very well."

She sat on the bed, patting the velvet quilts with a trembling hand. "You know, dear, I remember the night you were born, in this very bed . . . yes, the joy on your mother's face to see you . . . how lovingly she held you and nursed you that night. . . ." The memory clouded the elderly woman's eyes with tears.

But Deirdre stared at her. "Nanna, you always told me my mother died in bearing me—that she closed her eyes before she ever could see me—remember?"

The woman startled and blanched. "Oh yes, of course—silly old me—"

Deirdre sat up. "How did my mother really die?" she demanded.

Nanna had the appearance of a trapped animal. "She—she fell down the stairs when you were but weeks old."

"If that's true, why didn't you tell me that? Why did you tell me she died in childbirth?" Deirdre asked, perplexed.

"Oh, Chataine!" Nanna cried. "May you never know the burden I have borne for you!" She fled the room.

For some minutes Deirdre sat upright in bed, breathing hard. Then she shook it off and got up. No time to pump Nanna now. Some day, perhaps, if she ever returned.

She selected some old, dark riding clothes and dressed with shaky hands. Fastening her cloak, she opened the window. The ground was at least forty feet below, but there was an ivy-covered trellis that ran from the ground to her window and beyond. No one had ever bothered to cut it because it could not hold the weight of a man. But she was much smaller.

She reached for the trellis, thinking, *If Roman could see me doing this, he would be furious.* The thought of him caused a sudden ache, but she repressed it and swung out of the window onto the trellis. *Careful, now.* Step by step she found footholds and descended closer to the ground.

At one point the trellis ripped partially away from the wall, but she held steady until she finally dropped the last few feet to the ground, breathless. Softly she ran to the stables, where Lady Grey whinnied at seeing her. Deirdre saddled and bridled her quickly, remembering ironically how Roman had insisted that one day she might need to know how to do just this.

She led the mare toward the rear gate. Hiding in the shadows, she watched for the guard. He was nowhere that she could see—hiding himself with a bottle, probably. She took a deep breath and made for the gate.

"Halt! and be recognized!" A heavy hand forcefully spun her around to stare up into the stern face of a soldier. "Chataine Deirdre!" He released her and fell back a step.

"Please, please let me go!" she begged. "I am betrothed only to Roman!" *He won't understand that,* she thought.

But he blinked once, then deliberately turned his back. Deirdre scrambled up on her horse and rode out of the gate at a run. She found the familiar market road in the moonlight and, contrary to the good Counselor's sage advice, struck out for Ooster.

13

Impelled by panic, Deirdre rode all through the night. Before the distance was half covered she was trembling with exhaustion. But she feared the sinister shadows too much to sleep in the forest. Fortunately, Lady Grey was a steady, sure-footed mount who knew the way to Ooster. Even when the limp hands on the reins failed to give clear directions, the reliable horse galloped on.

But how awful the trip was without Roman! And how empty the air to Deirdre's right, where the Bay Hunter should have been. As she dismounted to rest Lady Grey, she nearly persuaded herself that any moment he would come galloping around the bend to her. But no—he was her guardian no longer. It was up to her to mount again and push on.

With the wearing of the hours, she slipped into a daze and began to see things not there. At one point she was alarmed to spot troops approaching her from ahead. But it was only a clump of trees. Later, she thought she descried Roman riding beyond her in the forest. But it was only a stag.

At length, shaken and weary, she arrived at her uncle's before daybreak. The guards let her in, and Corneus came down to see her. . . .

❖

"Deirdre, my dear, whatever has happened?" he cried, catching her in his arms.

"Oh, Uncle, help me! I have refused Rollet, and Tremaine is going to attack us!" she pleaded.

"There, my dear, you're safe here. No need for alarm. I have already conferred with Galapos, and we will fight with him against Tremaine. For now, you must rest." He summoned servants who took her to guest chambers, where she collapsed immediately.

After watching her go upstairs, Corneus turned to his wife, Bedelia, to instruct her, "Have your servants unpack your wedding gown. And summon Jason. She will marry him tomorrow." Bedelia pursed her lips, looking in disapproval up the stairs.

Deirdre slept clear through until the following morning. After she had been served breakfast in the sleeping room, a maid brought up clothes to her—specifically, a spectacular wedding gown and veil, heavy with lace and pearls. The Chataine was informed that Surchatain Corneus wished her to wear it. She refused. Shortly, Corneus himself came up to see her.

"My dear," he said, "you can't be married without a proper gown."

"I'm not getting married, Uncle," she said uneasily.

"Yes you are, dear. To Jason, of course. Or shall I simply send you back home?" he proposed.

"You wouldn't!" Deirdre gasped.

"I would hate to, of course—Jason wants you very much. And the marriage would solidify our two small provinces

230

into one large one. I don't wish to force you, Deirdre, but if you choose to be stubborn, I will." He turned to leave. "Don't delay us, Chataine."

Alone, Deirdre sat thinking, then rushed to the window. No escape that way—there was sixty feet of smooth wall from ground to window. She moved away from it to the washbasin, sighing hopelessly.

Those in the hall below turned to look as she descended the stairs in the magnificent gown. "It's too tight on her," muttered Bedelia.

"My dear, you are a vision!" Corneus praised, lifting one hand to her and the other to his son. "Jason?" he prompted.

He stepped forward to take her hand off the stair railing. "Thank you for accepting me, Deirdre. We will be the greatest rulers the Continent has ever known!" he said, as rehearsed. Deirdre looked at Corneus and bit her lip.

"Our carriage awaits!" Corneus said heartily, but Deirdre planted her feet like a mule.

"No. I never ride in carriages. They make me ill. You must let me ride my mare, or I will not go at all," she said stubbornly. All she knew was that riding Lady Grey offered her the best chance to escape.

Bedelia uttered, "You are not riding a horse in that dress!"

"There, Bedelia, we will allow her this. We do not want her becoming ill on the way, do we?" Corneus said consolingly, with a warning look at Deirdre. He addressed a guard: "Have our horses and the Chataine's mare dressed out in the finest regalia and sent to the front straightway—with an outfit of soldiers. We want the Chataine well protected." The guard departed in haste.

In minutes Deirdre, Jason, Corneus, Bedelia, and Colin were all mounted and riding up the thoroughfare toward the cathedral of Ooster. On the road, they passed groups of citizens who had heard of the Chatain's wedding to a mystery bride and turned out to watch. Although Deirdre's face was covered by the veil, a number of people still tried to get close enough to see who she was. The soldiers surrounding her kicked them away.

There was one old man they had difficulty with, however—a filthy beggar who was reeling drunkenly in the middle of the road. As the wedding party approached, he brazenly greeted them with fragments of a drunken song: "A man an' 'is luv 'ad a *turrible* spat—"

They were upon him now, and the soldiers pushed him aside, but he just seemed to bounce from one place to another until he was somehow beside the Chataine's horse. Then instantly he sprang up behind her on Lady Grey and kicked in his heels with a shout.

The horse bolted, crashing through the soldiers ahead, trailing fragments of ribbons and bells. The soldiers sprang after them, but were hampered in their pursuit by the cheering crowds who poured into the street to watch the escape. Deirdre's horse disappeared down a side road that led out of Ooster and the race was on.

They came upon a stretch of road that fell away at the shoulders in a steep, grassy embankment. "Get ready to jump," her abductor said in her ear, and she gasped, "Jump?" The grass passing them was a blur.

They rounded a curve and he said, "Now!" They half leaped, half fell down the embankment as the horse continued on. A layer of lace from Deirdre's dress caught on the saddle and ripped clean away. The man's shock of white hair flew off as they rolled to the bottom of the hill, then they scrambled for cover in a nearby grove.

Deirdre threw her arms around his neck. "Not yet," he grunted, hustling her to a horse tied nearby. They mounted again and plunged into the forest.

Riding in front of him, she hugged his arms around herself with joy. "How did you know where to find me?"

"The soldiers got word to me of your escape," Roman

said. "Then Corneus announced to all and sundry of Jason's marriage. I knew it had to be you."

They galloped steadily until they reached the little town of Sittle, where Roman guided the horse straight up to a dingy inn. A weathered sign fixed to the doorpost read "Notary Within." The couple dismounted and hurried past staring faces to a back room. There, an elderly man was sleeping behind a portly desk.

Roman gently shook him awake. "Old man—we want to be married. Quick."

"Eh? What? Married?" Rousing, the notary squinted in disbelief at Deirdre, disheveled in her magnificent gown, and Roman, disheveled in his beggar's rags. "Are you certain, Lady?" he asked her.

"Yes, yes, and please hurry!" she cried.

"Well!" he harumphed, then began searching around for his ledger, and his quill and ink, muttering, "These young people today, in such a hurry. No sense of decency."

"We don't have much time, old man," Roman reminded him tersely.

"Everything is here, sonny. Names?"

"Roman of Westford and Deirdre, Chataine of Lystra," answered Roman. The old man looked askance at them but wrote the names in his book.

"Now, Roman of Westford, do you swear to take this woman as your only wife, to provide for her needs and protect her from harm until the day you die?" asked the notary.

"Yes."

"And, Deirdre, Chataine of Lystra, do you swear to accept this man as your husband, to be faithful to him alone until the day you die?"

"Yes!"

He wrote it all down, then handed them a paper. "That will be two silver pieces," he said. Deirdre and Roman stared at each other. Neither had any money.

"Do you still have the medallion?" Roman asked.

"Yes, but I'm not giving that up. Will you take payment in pearls?" she asked, callously ripping off a handful.

The notary took them eagerly, then began, "Now, would you two be interested in our best bridal suite . . . ?" but they were already out the door.

"Where are we going now?" she sang as he lifted her onto the horse.

"To Outpost One. Galapos is there."

They arrived within a few hours. The soldiers greeted them cheering and whistling, and Galapos himself opened the gate for them. "Chataïne!" He hoisted her down from the saddle, twirling her in the air, while the men piled hearty congratulations on Roman. Acknowledging them distractedly, he tossed off the reins and grabbed Deirdre's hand to lead her into the fortress. She exulted to the Commander following them: "We did it, Galapos! We're married!" and pulled the paper from her bodice as proof.

Roman guided her into a small room and paused as Galapos looked at the paper, exclaiming, "So you did! So you did! A celebration, then—" he was just warming up when he caught Roman's eye: "—a little later tonight." He excused himself from the room with a wink.

Deirdre frowned and turned to Roman, but the question died when she saw the look on his face. "Deirdre," he whispered, holding her hands. He faltered, kissing her fingertips as he searched for the right words. "Deirdre . . . you'll never know how I longed for this day—how I suffered believing it would never happen. I swear to you, Deirdre, I'll never again allow you to be separated from me! But you, now that it's done—are there no regrets? Do you really want me as your husband?"

"Roman! Yes—no—how could I love anyone but you?" she cried.

Tears welled up in his eyes. "Come then, my love." He opened his arms and she fell into his strong embrace.

❖

"Tremaine, I assure you we will find her right away," Karel said anxiously. "She can't have gone far, and we have soldiers combing the forests and towns for her." They were speaking in Karel's chambers, with a glowering Rollet and somber Counselor standing by.

Tremaine appeared unconvinced. "Two days have passed since she escaped you—time enough to get much farther than you think. Especially with that guardian of hers."

"Roman is dead. He was executed," Karel said.

"What kind of a game are you playing with me, Karel? One of my own scouts spotted him on the border with Galapos on our way here!"

Karel whirled on his Counselor. "You said he was dead!"

"He is," Eudymon replied calmly. "Obviously, good Tremaine's soldier was mistaken."

Tremaine narrowed his eyes at them both. "I do not like deceptions, Karel. Your Chataine has disappeared and your Commander has been gathering his army. Rollet and I are returning to Corona. If you do not send Deirdre to me within three days, you will see me in a very bad humor. Goodbye, Karel. Counselor." Tremaine and his son stalked out, and the Surchatain angrily turned on his Counselor.

"What is Galapos doing?" Karel demanded.

"High Lord, I gave Galapos the same report I gave you—that Tremaine promised to lay waste our province if Deirdre did not marry into his alliance. Galapos's actions after receiving that information are his own. But do you not see, High Lord, that Tremaine—?"

"I see you are the one playing games, Counselor. Tremaine wants to unite with us, not attack us. You will find

Deirdre *at once* and send her to Tremaine, or face a charge
of treason. You are dismissed." The Surchatain turned his
back, then wheeled: "And Roman had better be dead!
Dismissed!"

✣

Deirdre and Roman lay very close on the narrow cot. She
caressed his chest as she listened to his rhythmic breathing,
then kissed the scars of hoofs. With his eyes still closed, he
barely moved his lips in response. "Roman," she whispered.

"Umm." He stirred and put his other arm around her,
which had been under his head.

"I spoke with your father, at some length," she said softly.

His eyes opened. "Oh, he told you," he said mildly.

"Yes, he told me many things. He really loves you,
Roman."

"He wasn't around when I needed him," he said.

"But surely he told you that he didn't know she had
died—"

"He would have known had he married her," he said
tightly.

She paused, then pleaded quietly, "If it weren't for him,
we would not be together right now. He wants your for-
giveness. He wants you to forgive him, Roman." He did not
reply.

Then came a pounding on the door. Galapos's voice
boomed from outside, "Fall out, soldier! To the dining hall!
And bring the hussy you have hidden in that room!"

Deirdre giggled and Roman sat up, reaching for a uniform folded neatly nearby. The beggar's rags he had been
wearing were scattered on the floor. "I suspect we're in for
the celebration he promised," he said grimly.

She leaned over to pick up the gown. "Then I am so glad
this lovely dress was not wasted." She smiled up at him as

he dressed.

He glanced at her over his shoulder. "Don't look at me like that, or I will have to disobey my Commander," he murmured.

Deirdre laughed gleefully, falling back on the cot. Then she sat up again, seeing him don the leather shortcoat. "Oh, Roman—you brought it!"

"It was the one thing I asked them to take from my room," he said.

"Not even your medal?" she exclaimed.

"Not even the medal."

"Then you must take this." She began to remove the medallion from around her neck.

"No," he said quickly, raising a hand. "Please leave it on. I—like the way it looks on you."

When they finally arrived at the dining hall, the soldiers crowding it stood, clapping and cheering. Galapos, at a head table, pretended to wake from a deep slumber and motioned them forward. Then he raised his hands for quiet from the soldiers, who sat expectantly.

"Now lads," Galapos began pompously, "I have invited you all here for a double celebration. You already know this man is an outlaw, having escaped the Surchatain's gallows by cunning and deceit—*whose,* I won't say," and a ripple passed through the soldiers. "Now, I wish to formally announce that since he was not good enough to be hanged, I have selected him as my Second-in-command." The soldiers stood again, laughing and applauding, and Deirdre threw her arms around Roman.

But Galapos motioned again for silence. "Wait—there is more. It seems that this rogue repented of the heinous crime for which he was sentenced, and determined to make amends by marrying the lady. Now fellows—what do you think of a Chataine who would marry a common soldier?" The response of the men was thunderous as they stomped and clapped and shouted. Deirdre hid her blushing face in Roman's shortcoat, and the men laughed harder. Roman hugged her, tears of laughter streaming down his face.

Galapos raised his goblet, prompting a multitude of goblets to come up. "A toast," he declared. "Deirdre and Roman, may your lives be full and joyful together. May you reign over Lystra in peace and prosperity. May you set your first-born on the throne and know the love of your children's children."

"To the Chataine! To the Second!" the soldiers shouted and drank the goblets down. Deirdre wept openly, and Roman drew in shaky breaths. She left him briefly to embrace the Commander. "I love you, Galapos!"

"Fie! You fickle woman!" he chastened amid deafening laughter. She saw his bright blue eyes were very wet.

They feasted on cabbage, beans, bread, and ale from the modest store of the outpost's supplies, receiving toasts and congratulations far into the night. When they finally returned to bed, she did not know it. Roman carried her in his arms.

When she awakened the following morning, he was gone. She found a note on the small table: "My love. I am with Galapos drawing battle plans. There is a soldier outside your door who will bring you breakfast or whatever you need. Also, when you are ready, he will bring you to me."

She smiled. How like him. Stretching, she reached for the dress, then made a face. This was Bedelia's, and she did not want to wear it anymore. Her eyes widened in inspiration, and she sprang to the door, opening it a crack. "Soldier?"

"Chataine." He faced her and saluted.

"Will you kindly bring me a uniform?"

"Chataine, the Second is already dressed and with the Commander—"

"Not for him. For me," Deirdre clarified.

He sputtered, "Chataine—I do not believe we have one

that would fit you!"

"Then bring the smallest you can find."

"As you wish, Chataine." He hurried away.

When he returned, he shoved clothes in through the crack of the door to her. She thanked him and shut the door to try them on. She pulled on the brown deerskin trousers and tied them with a rope. The deerskin coat was hopelessly large, but the unbleached cotton shirt she could wear. She rolled up the sleeves and trouser legs and slipped on her little embroidered shoes to complete the ensemble.

When she opened the door the soldier contorted his face so as not to smile disrespectfully. Deirdre handed him Bedelia's dress. "You may find enough pearls in this to pay for several dozen uniforms." He took the dress with gratitude and she said, "Now, please take me to Roman."

In the Commander's room, Roman and Galapos were drawing their plans over a large map. "Our scouts have reported no movement of troops as yet," Galapos was saying, "but it can only be a matter of days. And when Tremaine comes, I expect it will be through Falcon Pass. Going around the Fastnesses would take too much time, and he is an impatient man. Besides which, he does not need stealth. So you and I, my boy, will bear the brunt of the attack. It is likely, however, that Outposts Two and Three will be hit simultaneously by a combination of Tremaine's and Savin's forces. Therefore, we have pulled men from Hycliff to fight there. Now, Corneus's troops should assist Outpost Four in keeping Merce busy—" At that point there was a knock and Deirdre entered.

Roman raised his face eagerly, then coughed to cover a laugh at her outfit. He kissed her while Galapos concealed a grin behind his hand. "I had expected you to sleep later," Roman murmured, smoothing a tangled blonde lock over her shoulder.

"How could I?" she demanded. "I had to be with you.

Good morning, Commander."

"Chataine," he nodded, his eyes twinkling. "Would you like to see our plans for the gaudy?"

"Yes." She moved toward the map, but detoured when she saw a plate of rolls on another table. After taking a roll and pouring herself a cup of water from the clay pitcher, she came to stand between Galapos and Roman.

The Commander smiled again. "As I was saying, Corneus's troops will be divided between our outpost, his border defense, and Outpost Four. Now—"

There was another knock on the door, and a messenger appeared with a letter in his hand. Deirdre recognized Corneus's crest on his tabard and melted back behind Roman. Taking the letter, Galapos said, "It is from Corneus." He read it silently, then bowed his head.

"What is it?" Roman asked uneasily.

Galapos said heavily, "He knows Deirdre is here, and he very much resents your taking her. He says that if you do not send her back straightway, he will withdraw his troops from our defense."

"That's madness!" Roman exploded. "If we are defeated, his province is next. He must know that!"

"Nonetheless, that is his threat. If Deirdre is not sent back to Jason today, he will withhold his soldiers at his own borders. Roman," Galapos said soberly, "we do not have a prayer without his troops. Tremaine will surround and garrote us."

Roman turned to the window and bowed his head. In the seconds that he was silent, Deirdre stood immobile. "Return her to Jason," he whispered.

"Roman!" she cried in pain and disbelief.

He wheeled to face her. "I will come get you again, Deirdre. I swear it!" But he had just sworn never to leave her at all. The memory of that rash vow closed his eyes.

Deirdre, shaking in bitter tears, was led from the room by Corneus's messenger. Galapos came over and put his hand on Roman's shoulder. "She'll be much safer there for now, my boy," the Commander said softly. "And when we're done here, we'll both go and get her."

Roman pressed his face to the stone and let the tears come.

❖

Deirdre arrived once again at Corneus's gates, this time towed by the messenger. She shuffled up the steps to face a hostile family. Bedelia bristled, "Where is my dress?"

"Torn in shreds, by now," Deirdre answered listlessly.

Corneus took her arm in an iron grip. "We will send another up to your room. Go wash for the ceremony."

"You are too late," she asserted defiantly. "I am already Roman's wife."

Jason croaked, "Your guardian?"

"Yes. Only now he is Galapos's Second," she said proudly.

Jason began cursing, but Colin gave a little smile of admiration. Corneus slapped Jason's face with his open hand. "Control yourself!" To Deirdre, he spat, "You are your mother's daughter, wench. Where did you marry?"

She refused to tell him, lest he find the notary and destroy his record book. Corneus said, "Regardless, as Surchatain of Seir, I invalidate your marriage on the grounds that you were already betrothed to Jason." Deirdre opened her mouth to contradict him, but he commanded, "To your room and ready yourself! We will ride in the carriage to the cathedral. Guard—escort her upstairs!"

The wedding ceremony was private, with only Corneus, Bedelia, and Colin observing as the priest gave Jason and Deirdre their vows. Deirdre refused to repeat them, and when asked if she would take Jason as her husband, she firmly replied, "No." The priest continued the ceremony as if nothing were amiss. The wedding party exited to the cheers of the townspeople gathered outside and returned to the palace.

As soon as she and Jason were alone, Deirdre turned on him and said, "You will not touch me. I am Roman's wife."

"He gave you up to me," Jason replied. "He sent you away. Why should you be faithful to him?"

"Because I love him—and I have sworn to," she said.

"He broke his vow to you," Jason observed.

Deirdre's eyes watered. "No. He has never been false. He will make it good; I know it." Jason uttered a satirical laugh, but let her be.

Deirdre refused to touch the dinner set before her that evening. She could think only of how she might escape back to Roman. Jason was sullen and withdrawn, and Bedelia glared at her with undisguised hatred. Corneus must have divined Deirdre's thoughts, for from that point on she was guarded by two soldiers every moment she was out of her room. Once or twice Jason attempted to gain her favor, but she spurned him so vehemently he soon gave up and left her alone altogether.

❖

The day after Deirdre's departure from the outpost, Galapos received a communiqué from Surchatain Karel. His brows knitted as he read it. "He wants to know why I believe Tremaine is going to attack us. And he asks if it is true that you are here," he told Roman. "I wonder if someone has exposed our little ruse—in which case I fear for the Counselor. Well. I will refer the Surchatain to his good Counselor for information on Tremaine, and express a surprised denial concerning you. Is there any message you wish to send to the Counselor?"

Roman slowly shook his head. Galapos wrote several lines, then sealed the paper shut with wax and handed it to the messenger. "Here is my reply. And you never saw this man here, soldier!"

The messenger saluted. "Yes, Commander!"

For days the defenders at the outposts sat waiting for word of Tremaine's advance. Each day the scouts returned with no sighting of movement. Corneus's scouts also reported no sign of Merce's troops. Corneus's troops, still stationed at his borders, would be sent to the outposts once the assault began.

The days stretched into weeks. The tension of waiting in readiness began to tell on the soldiers. Quarrels became common and fights erupted repeatedly. Roman was doubly affected by the waiting, for he had no way of knowing Deirdre's state. Corneus absolutely prohibited messages between them. Supplies, too, had to be constantly renewed, for the outposts never knew when their supply lines would be shut off by the attack.

At the palace in Westford, each day that passed with no hint of a threat from Tremaine helped to confirm the Surchatain's suspicions that Eudymon was working against him. At that time, Karel sent orders for Roman's body to be exhumed so he could see for himself that it was indeed Roman. After much inquiring, the guards reported that it could not be located. Each soldier they questioned gave a different explanation of what had been done with it.

With heightened suspicions, Karel assigned a spy to monitor the Counselor's movements and intercept his messages. The Surchatain even began to suspect Eudymon of assisting in Deirdre's disappearance, as there had been not a word of her anywhere.

And how Nanna suffered because of it! She had cried for days after the Chataine's escape. She had accosted every returning soldier for news of her whereabouts. As weeks passed with no word, she slipped into the meaningless compulsion of continually straightening Deirdre's rooms and brushing out her clothes. "She'll want to wear this when she returns," Nanna would say to herself. Or, "How she loves that doll! I will dress it up and put in on her bed for her."

And Nanna cursed herself for failing to tell the Chataine what Regina had made her promise to tell. She had told Roman—but he was dead. Then the old nurse began to reason, "She loved him. She loved Roman. But her father had him killed, and that is why she ran away. The Surchatain killed the man my little girl loved. . . ." And she began to brood over other knowledge she had never made known . . . dark memories that haunted her each day the Chataine was gone.

❖

The weeks of waiting stretched into months. Deirdre remained a prisoner in Corneus's palace. Corneus and Colin had ridden out to the border to watch for Tremaine, but Jason stayed behind to run the affairs of state and act as Deirdre's husband.

She, meanwhile, roamed the palace, always accompanied by soldiers. Looking over the empty halls, she remembered her betrothal fest, just months before . . . how she and Roman had danced . . . the memories of him kept her steady.

She still had his medallion, and for the first time she studied it closely. It was engraved only on one side. There were words she did not understand—*ecce homo.* And there was a drawing of a man wearing a spiked wreath. This was the Christ, she assumed. *Christ, can you help him now?* she pleaded. Roman had sworn to return for her. He was always as good as his word. He *would* come for her—if he could.

At this point another thought presented itself to her. Roman had once said something about how he believed he had a heavenly guardian who protected him. Could that be true? Could such a guardian defend him from Tremaine and all his army? Roman had even hinted that she, too, had a guardian . . . but that was impossible. She was not a believer as he was. Deirdre despairingly rejected the whole line of thought.

Wandering into the library, she looked over rows and rows of pompous leather volumes. They were mostly books on philosophy, on the nature of the universe and the nature of man. Books on trade and atlases of trade routes. Books with detailed drawings of great buildings on the Continent. Books that taught geometry and language and law. "Are there no books that will teach me to endure being a prisoner?" she moaned. "God, if you are there, give me some help. Give me a reason to live through this."

She turned from the shelves and looked through the window at a piece of purple sky. She crossed the room to stand at the window. The setting sun streaked the sky with colored fire. How she loved the sky. How she wished to soar into that beckoning expanse. . . .

Her eye was attracted by movement, and she looked down on servants working below. A farrier was beating out a horseshoe on an anvil. The clang, clang of his hammer rang up to her window. A goatherd led his flock toward their pen for the night, rapping the feed bucket and calling their names. Two girls hurried in with bushels from the early harvest. Watching, she felt something stir within. *So close to life, how can I give up?*

There was a rustle at her back and the guard with her said, "Chataine, you are summoned downstairs for dinner." Straightening, she silently followed him out.

Over time, Deirdre began to suspect, then to be certain, of a change in herself. She was pregnant. But this knowledge, which should have made her sing for joy, only brought her dread. Jason would know it was not his child, and how he would react she could not guess. So she kept it to herself as long as she could.

❖

At the outpost, the months of waiting finally wore the men's fighting edge to bluntness. Roman sat in the dining hall, watching without seeing as a group of soldiers rolled the dice. He was thinking of Deirdre—always thinking of Deirdre. He relived every moment of their one night together. Those eyes looking to him . . . the feel of her lips, her skin. . . .

He inhaled and sat back. He must not allow those memories. It would madden him to think of her, not having her now, not knowing if he would ever see her again. He set himself to cleaning his sword, which already shone brightly. The soldiers nearby roared at a lucky toss.

Another soldier passed by with parchment and charcoal in hand. Noting Roman's sword and buckler, he made a notation on his paper. "What are you doing?" asked Roman.

"Taking stock of our weapons for the Commander, sir," he replied.

"Pilar has already done that," Roman said testily. "Besides, these are my personal arms. They do not go in the armory."

"Only doing what the Commander ordered."

"It's a waste of time," Roman grumbled.

"Well, sir, how do you suggest I spend all this time?" the soldier asked sarcastically.

Aggravated, Roman stood, but one of the men playing dice suddenly shouted, "Cheat! These are shaved!" He grabbed a fellow by the throat and began shaking him. Several others fell on him.

Roman threw himself in their midst, tearing them apart and ordering, "Stop! Now!" They desisted, glaring, and Roman demanded, "Will you kill each other before Tremaine has the chance?"

The first cursed and spat, "Where is this ghost Tremaine? What makes you so sure he's going to attack us? I say somebody should tell him we're holed up waiting for him so he'll know to come!"

There was a moment of tense silence, then Galapos's voice behind them all said, "Good thought, Dero. Will you carry the invitation to him?"

Dero reddened and mumbled something. Galapos continued, "Have faith, my boy. I promise he'll not disappoint us. Meanwhile, you and your fellows go check to see that all the horses have been reshod. We won't have time for it later."

"Commander." Dero saluted, and the soldiers filed out submissively, each saluting him.

"To my chambers, Roman," Galapos nodded.

As they walked the narrow corridors, Roman asked in exasperation, "Galapos, what is he waiting for?"

"Well, he is either playing the waiting game with us, or— heaven forbid—building up his troops. Either way, each day that passes wears us down further," Galapos replied, opening the door to his small rooms.

"Then why shouldn't we attack first?" Roman pressed.

"We cannot, my boy, not yet. Our troops are too spread out and we don't know where his concentration is. We have to wait until our scouts can locate his troops, or until he shows his hand." Galapos stroked his moustache, closing the door behind them.

"Do you still believe he'll come through Falcon Pass?" Roman asked.

"Yes. When he does move, he'll waste no time." The Commander stood over the map that he had already memorized in minute detail. "Roman, I am a realist. I believe in facing the truth. The odds are against us . . . you realize we may not finish out our days as old men dreaming by the fire," he said drily. Roman stared into the empty grate.

At that moment a messenger came from the Surchatain

247

with a routine inquiry as to conditions at the border. Galapos wrote out a standard reply, then asked, "Roman, do you have any message for the Counselor?" Roman still stood gazing at the fireplace. "Roman?"

"Tell him . . . all is forgiven," Roman said.

The message was written. Galapos handed two letters to the messenger. "This is for the Surchatain. And this one is for the Counselor's eyes only. Understood?"

"Yes, Commander." The messenger saluted and departed, letters in hand.

Roman turned. "Galapos, I have something to tell you. About Deirdre." The Commander cocked his head, listening. Roman took a deep breath. "She is not the Surchatain's daughter. She is yours."

Galapos straightened. "You are sure of this?"

"Yes," Roman sighed. "Her nursemaid told me that Regina confessed it on her deathbed."

"But—how could she know for certain?" Galapos asked in a low voice.

"It seems that Karel knew you two had been lovers, but married her anyway to establish the alliance with Corneus. He held off lying with her to satisfy himself that she was not pregnant . . . but she *was* . . . and Deirdre was the child. He could not make an issue of it without insulting Corneus, so carried on the pretense that Deirdre was his, even after Regina died," Roman related miserably.

Galapos covered his face with one hand. "All these years, he knew and I did not. All these years, what was Deirdre to him?" He suddenly raised his face. "Does she know?"

"No," Roman said, drooping.

"She will, my boy, when we go after her. Call your units together, Roman; we're going to drill. These men are getting fat and lazy."

That hour scouts returned with the word: Tremaine's troops were moving through Falcon Pass.

¾14¾

With definite word that Tremaine was on the move, Galapos agreed to attack. Informed by scouts that the Selecans had made camp for the night on the south side of the Pass, he planned for his men to ride out before daybreak and strike while Tremaine's soldiers slept. Galapos sent a messenger to Corneus advising him of Tremaine's advance and requesting troops to aid them in the assault. Then they waited for the hour to leave the outpost. . . .

❖

A scout roused Roman from uneasy sleep. "The Commander summons," he whispered. Roman, already dressed, sat up to reach for his gear. He strapped on a stiff leather jerkin and belted his sword on his hip. He fastened on leather shin guards and arm guards, then pulled a helmet down over his forehead. Taking up a buckler, he said inwardly, *Lord, I am going to be very busy today. If I forget you, please don't you forget me.* From there, he hastened out to meet Galapos.

The Commander was overseeing the organization of the troops in the deep blue of a night half gone. Seeing Roman, he stopped in mid-sentence to address him: "No armor, my boy?" He himself was dressed in mail.

"No, Galapos. I can't fight with all that weight," Roman said, looking over the men closest to him by torchlight.

"You had better do it well, then," Galapos said, continuing his instructions. Roman watched as two thousand men gathered silently into units. When all was ready, Galapos gave the command to move.

After only a short ride north they could see the watchfires of the invading Selecan army burning in the distance. Now came a critical phase of the attack. Roman and five other soldiers dismounted; they had to dispose of the sentry guards quietly to ensure surprise—the only element they had in their favor. The six soldiers split up and crept silently across the plain, watching for the guards.

Roman spotted his target shortly. He inched up closer and closer, freezing when the man turned his way. Then he sprang from the darkness and silenced the guard with a blow.

He continued on—there would be more sentries. But as he crept ever nearer to the campfires, no more guards came into sight. This was unusual. Finally Roman was almost on top of their camp—still no more guards. Bemused, he made his way back to his troops and reported to Galapos. As the other scouts returned, they gave the same report of few or no sentries. Galapos nodded grimly. He spread his troops to form a half moon facing the enemy's encampment, and there awaited the arrival of Corneus's troops.

And waited. The time to attack came upon them while there was no sign of Corneus. "What do we do?" whispered Roman. "Return and wait for him?"

"No," Galapos replied. "One way or another, the waiting has ended." With that, and without Corneus, Galapos gave the signal and his men attacked in a thunderous rush.

It was a total surprise. Hundreds of the Selecans were slain before they could even roll out of their blankets. Galapos's soldiers took full advantage of the surprise, tossing the enemy's weapons in watchfires and scattering their horses. Roman and Galapos spearheaded the attack together, driving their horses straight into a sleeping company. Galapos charged toward the officers' tents while Roman scattered the campfires onto blanketed forms. An alarm sounded, and Tremaine's army pulled themselves together to respond to the attack.

At first it appeared that Galapos might drive Tremaine's army back to the Fastnesses. Disjointed and uncoordinated, they were cut down as they fumbled to form ranks and find their weapons. Galapos's men responded eagerly to the easy kill. Soon, they were deeply advanced in the midst of the camp, fighting with flaming intensity.

Roman fought from his horse as long as he could, but when he was pulled down he held on to his sword and fought on foot. He cut into one man and then felt a stinging slash at his back. Wheeling, he answered it and dodged an attack from his side. He had not a second to pause in the battle. The instant he struck down one man, two appeared in his place—they seemed to spring up from the earth.

The battle intensified as the sun rose. Roman leaped on a soldier about to spear Galapos. They rolled in the dust until Roman gained the advantage and plunged down his sword. At that moment he felt a crashing pain on the back of his head and he collapsed in the dirt.

He came to only a few minutes later. Mercifully, he had been left for dead and the fighting had roared beyond him. He lay still for a moment to let the dizziness pass, then rose unsteadily to his knees and looked around. His stomach knotted at what he saw. Instead of his troops pushing the enemy back to the Pass, they were being absorbed into the middle of the Selecan ranks. They were fighting enemy troops at their front *and* rear. Roman steeled himself and seized a nearby sword to rejoin the battle.

But then he saw something else that froze his heart. Through the Pass appeared a regiment on horseback—more of Tremaine's troops. Roman watched in mounting horror as they came and came and still came out of the Pass—thousands more men riding furiously toward the battle. He shouted hoarsely, gesturing wildly toward the advancing troops.

Galapos spun to see the approaching legion and shouted retreat. Those of his men who were still mounted wheeled and spurred toward the rear. Others on foot sprang for riderless horses or doubled up with their fellow soldiers.

At once they found their retreat blocked by lines of Tremaine's soldiers. The Lystrans faltered in confusion and panic. Galapos shouted, "Drive! Drive!" and the men spurred fiercely, crashing right into the lines. This maneuver opened holes for their escape, but lost them many men.

Behind on foot, Roman yanked a Selecan from his saddle and swung up, then pulled a wounded Lystran up behind him. He charged through a fast-closing hole just as Tremaine's fresh troops joined the lines.

The men rode back to the outpost as if the devil himself were giving chase. They slowed only to pick up their fellows on foot. As the last man slid safely into the fortress, the heavy gates crashed shut behind them.

❖

That morning as Deirdre dressed, she found she could no longer fasten her bodice. So she left it open and covered herself with a shawl. Studying her reflection in the looking glass, she knew there was no hiding it any longer.

At breakfast Surchataine Bedelia observed, "My, you dress very sloppily as of late, Deirdre. Why would that be?" Her eyes were like knives. When Deirdre did not reply, the Surchataine commanded, "Open your shawl, and let us see what you are hiding." Deirdre did not move, so Bedelia motioned to the guard.

"That's not necessary," Deirdre said hastily. "I am . . . with child."

"Not by me," Jason said coolly.

"No. By my husband," Deirdre shot back.

The Surchataine gestured vigorously. "Your presence is an affront to me," she hissed at Deirdre. "You will remain in your room from now on. Out of my sight! Guards!"

Deirdre was escorted back to her room, where she collapsed in a chair. It was so difficult to endure this imprisonment and hatred—and now she was further confined. But at least in confinement she would not have to face Bedelia day after day.

Moments later Bedelia entered the room, her hands behind her back. Deirdre looked up in surprise. "Jason has finally given up on you, now that you are pregnant," Bedelia informed her with a thin smile. "He has agreed that a Chataine who sleeps with her servants is not worthy of him. So you see, you are no longer required here at all."

Deirdre started to assure Bedelia that she was not interested in being here, but the Surchataine cut her off. "It may interest you to know of a little agreement Corneus has made with Tremaine as of late. My husband has agreed to fight with him instead, and he in turn will leave our province alone— even give us Lystra. We need only pay him taxes."

"You are a fool if you think Tremaine will stop with gathering taxes," Deirdre replied. She had learned much from Caspar.

253

"You!" Bedelia hissed. "What have you done but spit on my son?"

Deirdre eyed her with interest. "Let me go, then. Let me go die with my husband."

Bedelia smiled, her eyes glittering strangely. "Yes, I will do that. I will release you from the agony of waiting for Tremaine to come cut your heart out. I will do that!" And Bedelia raised the dagger she had been holding behind her back.

The Chataine leaped aside with a cry as the Surchataine rushed toward her. Bedelia hacked at the air, then spun on Deirdre, who grabbed her hand and wrenched the knife from her fingers. It clattered to the floor.

Bedelia fell on her knees to retrieve it with both hands. Deirdre kicked her to the ground from behind, and waited breathlessly for her to rise and attack again.

She did not. She lay still on the floor. Cautiously, Deirdre rolled her over and saw the dagger plunged to the hilt in Bedelia's midriff. Gasping, Deirdre drew back in horror as Jason, alerted by the guards, entered with them. He saw his mother on the floor and turned his dark eyes on Deirdre. "You murdered her."

"No!" she gasped. "She attacked me—and we struggled— she fell on the knife—"

"I am not interested in how it happened," he said. "Nor do I care enough to kill you for it. Father will, though. It will be interesting to see what he does with you when he returns." He motioned to the guards, who lifted Bedelia's body to carry it out. Jason stopped them long enough to retrieve the dagger and throw it to Deirdre's feet, taunting her with her own powerlessness. Then he left.

Deirdre fell across the bed, holding her stomach. "Roman, can you really come for me? Are you even alive now? Or will it be Tremaine after all? I can't bear the waiting, not knowing, not knowing . . ." she moaned. Then she remembered the curse the witch had placed on him—that of death being all around him—and she gave herself up to sobbing despair.

❖

Roman surveyed his battered troops. Of the two thousand who had marched out that morning, seven hundred had returned. Of those, only six hundred could still stand and hold a sword. Roman himself had suffered injury enough to warrant withdrawal from the fighting, but he knew he would have no choice but to fight again. He looked over the wall toward the enemy. They had encircled the fortress two hundred yards out, and just sat. Waiting, it seemed.

A soldier called him to Galapos. Roman found him standing over the large map, but not looking at it. His arm was wrapped in bandages and he limped as he moved toward Roman. "I am afraid, my boy, I have seriously underestimated Tremaine. I understand now why he kept us waiting so long and then posted so few guards at the camp. He was baiting us to come out and fight, so he would not have to waste time sieging the outpost. And like a fool, I rushed to his waiting arms. He has men to waste—thousands more than I had guessed. I have let you all down rather badly."

"What happened to Corneus?" Roman asked, his head burning.

"I don't know. I suspect we have been betrayed."

Shortly afterward, a soldier arrived at the outpost, wounded and exhausted. He was taken to Galapos right away. "Soldier! Where are you from?" Galapos cried, seeing that he wore the insignia of Lystra.

"Outpost Two, Commander," the man panted.

Roman poured him a cup of water, asking, "How did you get through Tremaine's lines?"

"They did not hinder me. They let me come straight through," he gasped, then quaffed the water down.

The Commander asked quietly, "What news do you have?"

"Outpost Two has fallen, Commander," the soldier choked out. "We were attacked at daybreak and held them off a good long while, but they brought in ramming equipment and fresh soldiers every hour—thousands, Commander! We were surrounded and overcome."

"How did you escape?" Galapos asked.

"I did not," he replied bitterly. "They spared me alone to come tell you of our defeat."

Galapos sighed and dismissed the soldier to rest. "It seems that Tremaine is not content merely to kill us. He wishes to play with us first. You best go get what rest you can, Roman. The days ahead promise sufficient activity."

Roman turned to the door. He opened it to another Lystran messenger outside, poised to knock. This one carried a letter. Roman waited as Galapos read it, then sat down. "It is worse than I feared," Galapos muttered. "This is an urgent summons for reinforcements from Outpost Four. Captain Basner reports that they were attacked at daybreak by a combination of Merce's—and Corneus's—troops." Roman sucked in his breath at the treachery of Corneus.

Galapos calmly stood to roll up the large map on the table. "We are finished, Roman. We will make our last stand at Tremaine's convenience. Go rest now, my son, and pray if you have anything left in you."

Roman numbly turned again to leave. "Roman." Galapos had one more thought. "You have been a good and faithful soldier. I have been proud to fight with you."

Roman stumbled from the room and found his way to his quarters. He put his hands on the rough bed. He and Deirdre had slept here together—was it years ago? *Deirdre! Chataine!*

He sank to his knees beside the bed, and the words came rushing out: "Oh, God! You have been with me all my life—

protecting me, I know, enabling me, guarding me—why have you left me to die like this?" He steadied himself and went on: "I've done my best all my life to serve you—not perfectly, I know—my faults are too clearly before me. But what purpose could you have in allowing Tremaine to slay us all and rule the Continent? He does not regard you, Lord—he cares only for his power. Christ Jesus! If I have found any favor with you, or if only out of mercy, save us from Tremaine! And oh, my God," he moaned, "protect my Chataine, as I have failed her in my vow." Then, racked with pain and exhaustion, he fell on his bed and slept.

❖

The Surchatain Karel summoned the Counselor to his chambers. "Well, Counselor, any word from the border? Still no sign of Tremaine's supposed attack, eh?"

The Counselor bowed. "Not yet, High Lord. But it is coming."

"So you say," Karel noted with alarming cheerfulness. "But there seems to be a message that you missed. Shall I read it to you?" The Counselor was silent. "It says, 'All is forgiven. R.' Now, Counselor, what do you make of that? Who could this 'R' be? Not Roman, surely, Counselor?" Karel was smiling fiercely.

"Of course not, High Lord," smiled Eudymon. "It is a soldier under Galapos—Rollo—from whom I mistakenly withheld pay. I sent it to him recently with my apologies. He was merely acknowledging my note."

"You are a clever liar, Counselor," Karel said through gritted teeth. "But when I saw this, I did some inquiring of my own." He whirled. "Guard!"

A nervous-looking Arin appeared from behind a curtain. "Tell the good Counselor what you have told me," Karel ordered.

"Well, High Lord, at Roman's execution . . . I saw that when they took him to the scaffold, they—they switched him with another man, and the soldiers crowded in and hid him. Someone else was hanged in his place," Arin confessed.

"Well, Counselor?" Karel cried triumphantly.

"You had better thank the powers that be that he is on the border with Galapos, because you are going to need every man alive when Tremaine strikes," answered Eudymon.

"You have deceived me and betrayed me!"

"Deceived you, yes, but not betrayed you, High Lord. Your daughter is alive today because of my son," Eudymon answered.

"Your son?"

"Yes, my son. Roman is my son," Eudymon said.

"Then you did help her! Where is she?" The Surchatain was white with fury.

Eudymon smiled, finding a liberation in the truth that he had never known before. "I do not know, High Lord, but I earnestly hope they are together."

"Where is she?" Karel screamed. Beyond control, he grabbed the Counselor's throat and shook him. "Where is she? Where is she?"

The Counselor could not have answered if he tried. Karel squeezed tighter and tighter, until Eudymon stopped struggling and dropped lifeless to the floor.

Shaking, the Surchatain stepped back and wiped his brow, then turned on paralyzed Arin. "Why are you standing there? Take him out."

Numbly, Arin hoisted the body under the arms and began dragging it out. Karel paused to seal up the death warrants he had written for Roman and Galapos, then took them out into the corridor to deliver them personally into the hand of the messenger waiting at the palace gate. Karel caught up with Arin at the head of the stairs.

Nanna, wandering the palace, came upon them there.

"What—?" she gasped as she saw the Counselor's body. Then her eyes filled with rage, and she turned on the Surchatain. "You! You murderer! You were a murderer from the beginning! First Regina, and then Roman, and now your own Counselor!"

Karel stopped dead and gazed at her. Arin looked sick, desperate to slink away. "Oh, yes," Nanna laughed. "You thought no one knew. Well I knew! I saw you push her in anger—I saw her scream and fall. You are a murderer!" With a scream she fell on him, and they tumbled down the long stone stairway together.

❖

The following morning at the outpost, Galapos evaluated their situation and called his soldiers together. "Men, Outposts Two and Four have fallen, and we've had no word from Outpost Three. It seems our backs are to the wall, and I see no escape for us. But if you'll lend me your swords one last time, we'll give Tremaine nightmares of his last battle with Lystra. Are you with me?"

The soldiers shouted at once and raised their weapons. "Very well, then," he continued, "attend to your wounds and rest up. We'll answer when he charges."

So the men readied themselves and waited, but the charge did not come that day. The Selecan encampment could be clearly seen day and night just out of bowshot, but they merely held themselves there and waited.

A messenger arrived at the outpost on the following day, grey-faced and trembling. He fell breathless before Galapos and said, "Commander, Westford has fallen. The Surchatain is dead." Having given that message, he died.

Galapos hung his head in grief. Roman stood like stone. At that instant they heard a trumpet blast outside. They hurried to a high window in the tower to see what was happening. The Lystran defenders were gathering all along the wall to look.

Tremaine himself had ridden up close to the gates. He wore the robe woven of strands of gold, and the sunlight reflecting off it made him appear more dazzling than the sun itself. Everyone had to shade his eyes to look at him.

"Men of Lystra," Tremaine shouted, "you have heard by now that your Surchatain has fallen. I am your new ruler, and I am willing to give you your lives in exchange for a small present. Send out to me the heads of your Commander and his Second, and I will allow the rest of you to live in peace under my rule. I await your response!" He spurred back to his lines.

Galapos and Roman looked out over their ranks. The men seemed stunned at first. Then one by one their raised their faces toward the Commander's tower and shouted, "Hail, Commander! Hail, Second!" Roman breathed out in relief.

Then the waiting began once again. More of Tremaine's troops arrived continually at the lines, presumably fresh from victories at the other outposts and Westford. Corneus's troops also appeared. Corneus himself rode up before the gates and shouted, "Galapos, my boy, how are you doing? Tell Roman his Chataine was safely married to Jason before she could waste herself grieving as a widow!"

On hearing, Roman pounded his fists on the stone, then leaned on it and closed his eyes. "I had her once," he murmured. "It was enough. I pray that Tremaine spares her."

One day followed on another, and the defenders at the outpost numbly waited. Each day Tremaine, wearing his fiery golden robe, rode out and shouted, "Men of Lystra, have you an answer for me?" Each day the soldiers were quiet. Little by little, however, rumblings began among them.

"Why shouldn't we live?" one said.

"Have we pledged them our lives?" another asked. Others hushed them up, but soon more and more began to grumble.

One week passed, and then two. The outpost had plenty of rations stored for just such a siege, but the prospect of awaiting certain death from either starvation or the sword was more than some of the men could face. Several who began screaming, weeping, or trying to run from the outpost were locked up. And Tremaine continued to taunt the rest of them with offers of freedom in exchange for treachery.

Then one dawn Roman found Galapos staring in puzzlement out the tower window at the sea of soldiers surrounding them. "What are they doing?" Roman asked.

Galapos knit his brows. "I don't know. Giving some soldiers a rest, I suppose. He has drawn many of them away from the siege lines."

Roman nodded absently. "Why have twenty thousand do what five thousand could? . . . How long can we hold out, Galapos?"

"Longer than Tremaine's patience, my boy. When he tires of this game, he will devise another creative way to end us," Galapos said with certainty.

Shortly thereafter Tremaine rode up to again demand an answer. But today he shouted, "Men of Lystra, I am getting impatient. If you do not answer me today, we will attack on the morrow and spare no one!" Some of the Lystrans looked around. A few even began shouting. But no one laid hands on Roman or Galapos.

At dusk, Roman said, "We should ride out to him. The men won't betray us. If we can spare their lives, we should."

Galapos shook his head. "It would gain us nothing. I know Tremaine's treachery—he will kill them all regardless, for the sport of it."

That evening, sitting on his cot with his back against the wall, Roman contemplated death. It would be easier if he knew for certain that he would die in battle, and not be spared for Tremaine's leisure amusement. Some soldiers within these walls would not last through the night, he knew—facing death, they choose to meet it falling on their own swords. But that was the death of a coward, and Roman could not bear to think of Galapos fighting for the last time without him by his side.

He thought back over his years warding Deirdre and smiled. Not one moment of it was wasted time, for it earned him her love. Whatever the Almighty chose to allow on this little field of conflict would never erase that, and he was content.

None of the men slept that night, waiting for the morning. With the first weak light of dawn, the survivors gave mute farewells to each other and readied themselves for the last battle.

A heavy fog that had rolled in during the night obscured the enemy lines around the outpost. But as Roman peered into the dense whiteness, he saw a shape slowly emerge from the mist. His last vestige of stubborn hope trickled away as he watched a battering ram being positioned in front of the gates. The defenders rained down arrows on the operators, but they were shielded by the armor of the ram.

It crashed once, twice, then on the third blow the gates buckled and men swarmed in. "To the front!" cried Galapos. And the small band of defenders rose to the charge.

But something was unaccountably odd. Tremaine's soldiers seemed to be moving too slowly in their attack. Roman rushed on an invader to fight, but the man stared at him blankly, then fell in a dead faint.

Bewildered, Roman rushed to the next man. He collapsed before Roman could lift his sword. Incredulous, he spun around. Once they had penetrated the gates, the attackers seemed utterly spent. Galapos's men cut them down effortlessly, then looked to the shattered gates for the next onslaught.

It did not come. The men looked uncertainly to Galapos. "Another ruse to draw us out," he muttered.

"If it is, what of it?" cried Roman. "Won't they kill us eventually? Charge out!" he shouted. The defenders poured from the broken gates behind Roman and halted in astonishment at the scene.

The fog was blowing away in wisps to reveal a deserted plain. Horses were standing idle, and the ground was littered with the prostrate bodies of a thousand or so men. "What the—?" muttered Galapos.

Roman raised his eyes and saw makeshift tents far off. He ran to a horse, calling the men after him. They leaped on horses and pounded to attack the encampment.

Reaching the lines, they leaped from their horses, braced to fight. But not a soul answered. Roman stared across rows and rows of soldiers, thousands of them, lying on the ground. Some were in tents, but most by far were unsheltered. Most were dead; the remainder on the threshold. "This place looks like a damn infirmary," whispered a soldier at Roman's side.

Roman began shuffling through the rows while his men stood rooted in bewilderment. As far as could be seen, the bodies were laid out in death throes. Tremaine's whole army, reduced to nothing. The battle was won before they ever had a chance to make their last stand. He shook his head. It was impossible. It was inexplicable. Then he saw a water pot.

Not by might, nor by power, but by my Spirit, says the Lord. Roman gasped in the sudden realization of what had happened and fell to his knees, clutching the water pot. "God, you have done this! You heard my prayer and fought for us! Lord God, my strength and my redeemer!" He was shouting and crying at once.

That seemed to awaken the Lystrans, who leaped on each other, whooping and laughing. Galapos seized Roman's shoulders and shook him in joy. Then the Commander cried, "But what *happened* to them?"

"This," said Roman, handing him the water pot.

"It is a water pot," Galapos said mildly.

"It is one of the villager's water pots," Roman corrected. "Tremaine's men must have been drawing water from the Village Branch ever since the fall of Westford." Galapos looked blank. "The disease, the villagers' disease that almost killed Deirdre!" Roman reminded him. "God used it to answer my prayer."

Galapos stared. "What did you pray?"

"For God to save us from Tremaine!" Roman exclaimed. Galapos stood pondering the unthinkable. "Did your cunning save us, Galapos? Did my skill, or the courage of our men?"

The others gathered around them, listening. "God heard my prayer and sent this plague in answer. You may choose to ignore Him—Tremaine did—but I will acknowledge this as deliverance!" Roman declared.

Studying him, Galapos's eyes suddenly twinkled. "Your God is a mighty warrior, my boy." Roman smiled. His heart was still pounding with the thrill of the gift given him.

Word of Roman's prayer and the water pot spread like a blaze through the troops, and the soldiers who knew hymns began singing as they picked through the battlefield. Some others sang slightly altered versions of drinking songs.

Then someone shouted, "Hail, Surchatain Galapos! Long live the Surchatain!" The chant picked up strength through the ranks.

But Galapos raised his hands for silence. "That means nothing till we find Tremaine! Him and Corneus." So everyone began searching through the bodies, but only Galapos or Roman knew both enemy leaders by sight.

Roman, scanning the myriad of dead and dying, murmured, "Galapos . . . I will never again call another mortal High Lord—not even you. That title belongs to Another."

"Nor would I allow anyone to call me that," Galapos answered. "Dare I parade myself as a lord before such a God as yours?"

Then Roman startled in remembrance. "Deirdre! Galapos, we must go get her!"

"We will as soon as we are able. Send a messenger to her right away," Galapos said. He bent to pick up a good-luck charm from the body of a Selecan, shaking his head.

Roman grabbed the nearest Lystran. "Ride to Ooster— find the Chataine Deirdre—tell her God has given us victory, and Galapos is the new Surchatain. Tell her we are coming for her very soon, and ward her till we arrive! Go!"

The messenger bounded on a horse and galloped off. However, when he arrived at the border of Seir, he was intercepted by two of Corneus's border sentries. They heard his message, then murdered him. They repeated his news to Jason at the palace in Ooster.

At first he refused to believe it. But one of the soldiers said, "Chatain, it must be true. The last message we had from the Surchatain was of a terrible plague in the camp. That was two days ago, and we've heard nothing since."

"Then Father too is dead!" Jason seethed, strangling on impotent fury. Then he calmed, resolving, "There is one last thing I can do for her."

He went to Deirdre's room and found her sitting by the window. She turned to face him. "I have news of the battle that may interest you," he said. "Your husband and his Commander are dead. Tremaine is the victor and he is coming to kill you." Then Jason left her alone. Unseen by her, he went to the pinnacle of the palace and leaped to his death.

Deirdre sat gazing out the window. "It's over," she whispered to the sky. "He is dead, and I am soon to join him." She looked up with a certain irony to the clouds. "Will *you* permit in death what you did not allow us in life?"

With a hand on her swollen belly, she rose from the window and crossed the room to pick up Bedelia's dagger. In her mind, there was absolutely no reason to wait for Tremaine to come perform the inevitable. In her condition, he could make it exquisitely horrible.

She lifted the dagger, pondering where to place it. She could not bring herself to plunge it in her belly, so placed it at her throat instead.

❖

When I determined that her mind was set to carry out her own destruction, I intervened according to your instructions. It was then that I opened her eyes to see me and know that she was not alone. She blanched and fell to the floor.

❖

Roman searched feverishly through the dead soldiers, anxious to ride to Deirdre. He and Galapos looked through the tents first, assuming that the leaders' rank would assure Tremaine and Corneus the most protection. But they were not there. Galapos searched the front lines, but they were not there. Roman faced the sea of dead in exasperation. "Where are they?" Then a sickening thought struck him: "Oh, Lord—has Tremaine escaped?"

Then he heard a soldier shout from the very rear of the ranks, "Commander! Second! We may have found something here!" Roman ran over to meet up with Galapos over a group of bodies.

Roman turned one face up. "It is Corneus. But look— he has been run through!" The Surchatain's coat was split and bloodied.

Galapos turned up another. "Why, this is Savin—and he also has been slain by the sword."

Roman rolled over the third body. "This one also. But I don't know him."

"That is Merce," Galapos said. They searched each other's eyes, trying to formulate an explanation. At the same time, they concluded, "Tremaine."

Galapos growled, "He must have gathered all the troops here for his grand finale—he always had a weakness for overkill. But these three did not reckon the finale he had planned for them."

"Commander!" another soldier shouted. He pointed to where other soldiers were waving and calling.

Roman and Galapos sprinted far behind the lines to a grassy depression where a group of Lystrans were clustered. Here was set up a fine silk awning over a gold and velvet couch. A small table stood nearby, still bearing fresh vegetables and a large golden goblet of water. Stretched out on the couch with a cold cloth on his forehead was Tremaine, dressed in the splendid golden robe that dazzled the eyes in the sunlight. He was dead.

Roman slowly picked up the golden goblet and poured out the deadly water onto the ground. "So powerful a man, done in by such a little thing," Galapos mused, shaken.

"While we mere mortals survive," Roman said ironically, looking around for the nearest horse.

"Mortal, humble, and grateful," Galapos affirmed, saluting skyward. He turned to a soldier nearby. "Kam, you head up the salvage and pyre. Roman, shall we be going . . . ?" But his Second was already riding west. Galapos commandeered a horse to catch him on the road, and together they pounded to Ooster.

Arriving at the palace, they found it deserted and still. "Deirdre! Deirdre!" Roman called, running from the audience hall to the banquet hall. But there were no answering echoes.

"I don't like this," he said fearfully to Galapos. "Where is the messenger?" They split up and began a room-to-room search. While Galapos combed the lower halls, Roman shot up the stairs, praying feverishly as he pounced from one empty room to the next: *Oh, my God, after all this—would you take her from me now? Have mercy, Lord, she is yet unredeemed!*

He threw open the door to her room, and his heart stopped to see her sitting very still on the floor, facing the window. "Deirdre!"

"Roman." She dropped the dagger and held his neck tightly.

"Are you well, Chataine?" he asked tenderly, then his hand rested on her thick midsection and his eyes took on a gleam. "Are you . . . ?" Hardened soldier that he was, he could not even say the word.

"Yes," she whispered. "I have kept my vow to you, also." She suddenly searched his face. "Jason told me you were dead, and that Tremaine was coming to kill me! I—I was going to take my life . . . but he prevented me."

"Jason?" he frowned. "Where is he?"

"No, not Jason . . . someone else. I don't know who he was, but he just appeared, in a shining white robe . . . very white . . ." she trailed off and he studied her anxiously. "Roman, I believe you now," she said, stronger. "All that you said about the Christ—I believe you, and I want you to tell me more." As he gazed at her she added, "I love you so."

He kissed her deeply because he could not speak. As the tears ran down his rough face he whispered, "I love you, Deirdre."

They just held each other tightly for a few moments. Then he wiped his face and coughed. "I've been weeping like a woman ever since we got married."

"Oh," she said through her tears, "I have something of yours." She took off the medallion and hung it around his neck. "What do the words mean?"

He inhaled, looking at the engraving on it. Thoughts of the one who gave it to him crossed his mind. "They say, 'Behold the Man.'"

"The Christ?" she asked.

"Yes . . . the One who forgives," he murmured.

For a moment she took in every line on Roman's precious face—the scar, the beard, the deep brown eyes. "I have been seeing Him for years, and never knew it—His face in your face, His voice in your words. . . . It is true that He is living in you, isn't it?" she asked. He nodded. "I want to be like that, Roman. I want to be like you." He smiled, trembling a little.

She looked off, disturbed. "I cannot stay the same and survive. Oh, Roman, I glimpsed a war raging that I only wanted to avoid, but I could not—not any more than I could avoid a war with Tremaine. I would either be victor or captive. . . . But tell me what happened at the outpost! How did you defeat Tremaine? And—" her voice lowered, "is there word of my father?"

"I am well, my dear," Galapos said as he entered the room. "And look here!" He drew up in joyful surprise. "My first grandchild will arrive soon! What more could I ask?" Deirdre frowned and smiled at the same time.

"Chataine," said Roman, grinning, "meet your father the Surchatain."

✢

They continued at length with many questions and explanations and many embraces and tears, but for my purposes, this report on the charge you gave me is concluded. I am Penuel, guardian angel of Deirdre of Lystra, and I close for now, O Lord of Hosts.

✢

(The story continues in *Stone of Help*.)